To my family and friends
who support me no end
*And to Nellie and Emm*a
who inspire me no end

Diversion Books
A Division of Diversion Publishing Corp.
443 Park Avenue South, Suite 1004
New York, New York 10016
www.DiversionBooks.com

For more information, email info@diversionbooks.com

First Diversion Books edition March 2014.

Print ISBN: 978-1-62681-279-6
eBook ISBN: 978-1-62681-265-9

THE NEW
COLOSSUS

A NOVEL

Marshall Goldberg

DIVERSIONBOOKS

AUTHOR'S NOTE

This is a work of historical fiction.

The term has always seemed oxymoronic to me: "historical" suggests grounded in verifiable reality, "fiction" suggests a flight of fancy. Readers of historical fiction are comfortable with this contradiction and even embrace it. Others often need to know what "really happened" and what was made up.

I was quite taken with Emma Lazarus and Nellie Bly, and wanted to learn more about them, but I kept running into blanks, even after reading dozens of books. As a fiction writer, I decided to fill in those blanks with what might have been.

Nothing in *The New Colossus* is a deliberate lie. I worked with the facts and honored them as if under penalty of perjury. I simply completed the story in a plausible way. Please feel free to write me at *Facebook.com/MarshallGoldbergAuthor* and I will tell you what is in the history books and what is not.

PROLOGUE

The little girl couldn't sleep.

She hadn't slept through the night since her father died four months before. She would imagine him walking in with a big smile and a present and then sitting on her bed, telling her all about his train ride to Philadelphia or Harrisburg and promising he would never leave the house again. Then she would realize it was all in her mind and start crying and hide under the blankets so no one would hear the sobs.

Her father had adored her. She was his favorite, more than her younger sisters, certainly more than her stepbrothers and stepsisters from his first marriage. She hadn't even met any of them. They were all grown-up and had moved away. When her father remarried, none of them came to his wedding, or so she'd been told. Then when he moved his new family into the biggest house in town, one that he built from the ground up, they stopped writing him altogether.

Now, though, it wasn't heartache that kept the little girl awake but the sound of loud voices downstairs. Her mother was crying, and some men with heavy feet were walking around the living room giving orders. The little girl got out of bed, went out to the landing, and peered below. Half the furniture was gone. Her mother was sitting on the couch crying, her face in her hands, while a man with a badge and long coat directed two men to remove her father's favorite desk.

"Momma. What's going on?"

Her mother looked up with the most pained face the daughter had ever seen. The same way she looked at the funeral.

"Pink," said her mother, her voice cracking. "You need to get dressed."

"Where are we going?"

Her mother closed her eyes tight and shook her head. "Momma? Where are we going?"

"Just get dressed, Pink."

It was not so much an order as the only thing her mother seemed able to say. "Should I pack a bag?"

Her mother closed her eyes even tighter and nodded. Tears streamed down her face. The little girl watched as the man with the badge and long coat tapped her mother on the shoulder and motioned for her to move away from the couch.

CHAPTER ONE

BELLEVUE ASYLUM

The elegant young woman in the emerald bustle dress shivered as the police steamer made its way up the East River toward Blackwell's Island. The temperature hovered around freezing, and a soupy mist made the winter air feel even colder, but the real source of her trembling lay in their destination: the Bellevue Asylum, New York's only hospital for the insane. The other nine women aboard shared her fears. One with raspberry blotches all over her face and a grayish-yellow fungus on her scalp babbled incessantly and pulled out tufts of her hair near the roots. Another with a high fever ranted incoherently. A third seemed perfectly normal and pleaded to be returned to shore, but spoke only French. The young woman tried to engage several of the women in conversation, but the policeman who kept eyeing her told her to be quiet, patting his billy club to show he meant it.

Hours earlier, at the Essex Market Court on the Lower East Side, the young woman had been unable to recall her name or anything of her past. Presiding Judge Duffy had ordered her committed to Bellevue, drawing gasps from the courtroom, and then summoned reporters from all seven of New York's major newspapers to ask for their help in locating the young woman's family. When the male reporters saw her rich auburn hair, mournful green eyes, and beige freckles sprinkled on a lovely face, they had wanted to comfort her and make her world right. But male stirrings and judicial entreaties aside, they also knew a good story when they saw one. And New Yorkers needed a good story. The city was still recovering from the February 1888 blizzard that had dumped forty to fifty inches of snow on the streets and produced drifts fifty feet high that still lined the Manhattan shore. People had been confined to their homes for weeks. They would be more than ready to grab on to the tale of a halting young woman with a hard-to-place accent who had no idea who she was.

But the gentlemen of the press seemed far away right now. The young woman was no longer in the relative safety of a New York courtroom. She was in a filthy police boat with at least six babbling lunatics and two sadistic policemen steaming up the East River to an insane asylum.

The boat docked in front of an enormous white concrete warehouse more than two hundred yards wide and four stories tall, surrounded by a wrought iron fence with jutting spears. This was the Bellevue Hospital Asylum, and upon visiting it forty years earlier, Charles Dickens had described his reaction as "deep disgust and measureless contempt." A half-dozen female guards, steel-eyed and gruff-looking, stood by idly and made no effort to help with the landing or unloading. One of the policemen muttered that they were inmates from the women's prison up the road—convicted prostitutes, thieves, even a murderer. The chief female guard—tall, broad-shouldered, and mannish-looking in her late thirties—signed the receiving papers and bantered with a police guard. None of the other female guards bothered to make conversation or smile hello.

The chief female guard signed the last document and handed it to the policeman, who hopped back on board. The steamer shoved off. The young woman watched it head downriver toward Battery Park, taking with it her last connection to the outside world.

The chief guard turned to the new arrivals. Her smile disappeared.

"My name is Grady. *Miss* Grady. You are now on Blackwell's Island. I hope you plan on staying here awhile because you will not be leaving anytime soon. Do as I say, and we will get along nicely. Question me or disobey me, and your life here will be unpleasant. That I promise. Now follow me inside."

She walked toward the main entrance to the building. The other guards surrounded the women like cowboys herding cattle and prodded them along. The young woman looked around to get her bearings.

"Move along," snapped a guard and gave her a firm push.

The young woman clenched a fist and shot her an angry look but nevertheless trudged inside with the others to a large, brick room. It was damp and cold, with a dirt floor and high windows that shed little light. In the center of the room was a cast iron bathtub that resembled a horse trough, a wooden barrel of water, and some oaken buckets.

"Take off all your clothes," Miss Grady ordered the group. The women balked.

"Do it now or we will do it for you," snapped Miss Grady.

The guards held out their hands for the clothes. The women reluctantly began undressing, but the young woman wanted no part of this. She didn't like the idea of taking off her clothes in front of strangers, and certainly not when she was shivering from cold.

"It's freezing!" she protested.

"And it's going to get colder," snorted Miss Grady. She motioned for one of the guards to start undressing the young woman.

"I'll do it," said the young woman, and she took off her

shawl, bodice, and skirt.

"Underskirts, too," said Miss Grady.

The young woman recognized the inevitable and reluctantly took off her underskirts. She stood there in only a slip, covering up against the damp chill.

Miss Grady smiled approvingly. "Now your slips," she ordered.

The women didn't move. None of them had ever been naked in front of another woman.

"Now!"

The guards took a menacing step forward, and the women compliantly took off their slips, each of them now standing naked, pointlessly trying to cover up in the freezing cold.

"You!" Miss Grady motioned to the woman with the terrible skin disease, who had pulled out clumps of her hair. "Get in the tub!"

The woman submissively stepped into the empty tub and slowly sank down. One of the guards filled a bucket with water from the barrel and poured it on her. The woman gasped.

"It's cold!"

"Of course it's cold," said Miss Grady. "Now be still."

They poured two more buckets on her. The woman cried out from the cold. One of the guards grabbed her by the hair and scrubbed her with some soap and a brush that made deep, red scratches on her head and back.

"Stop! Please!" screamed the woman.

"Quiet!" barked Miss Grady. "It's just a bath!"

The guard kept scrubbing, drawing blood on the woman's back and scalp while she cried and whimpered and begged her to stop.

"No more! Please, no more!"

Finally, mercifully, the guard lost patience.

"All right. Done!" said the guard and stood up. Two other guards filled buckets from the water barrel and flung the contents at the woman, rinsing her off. The woman sputtered and fought for air.

"You're clean. Get out!" shouted Miss Grady.

Dripping wet with cold water and crying from the shock and humiliation, the woman stepped out onto the dirt floor. One of the guards handed her a towel. The woman dried herself furiously, trying to warm up and yanking tufts of hair from her scalp onto the towel. One of the guards tossed her a ratty slip, motioned for her to put it on, and grabbed the towel back. The woman stood there in the moth-eaten slip, her hair still wet, rubbing her body to try and get warm.

"You!" said Miss Grady to the woman who spoke no English, pointing to the tub.

The woman hesitated. "Pardon?"

"Get in!"

The woman waited for the guards to drain the tub. But nobody moved.

"Now!" Miss Grady shoved her forward.

The woman looked at the dirty water with revulsion, but as the guards menacingly stepped toward her, she got in the tub, cringing and trembling with fear.

"Sit down!" Miss Grady motioned for her to sit, and the woman willed herself to sit in the cold, dirty water. The woman shut her eyes, hoping to block out all sensation. The same guard as before began scrubbing her with the same harsh brush and soap. The Frenchwoman tried to maintain her dignity and suffer in silence, but she sobbed from the pain and humiliation, her shoulders heaving with shame.

Finally the scrubbing guard stood up. "Done."

"Up!" snapped Miss Grady.

The Frenchwoman stood up. The two guards once again filled their buckets from the barrel and tossed cold water on her. She gasped as if lashed by a whip.

One of the guards handed her the same towel the woman with the skin disease had used, the tufts of hair and fungus still on it. The Frenchwoman shook her head adamantly.

"Use it, or stand there and freeze!" said Miss Grady. But the Frenchwoman just shook her head.

"Suit yourself."

She motioned for the guards to remove her from the tub.

Two of them grabbed her and pulled her out, her leg smacking hard against the side, and deposited her on the dirt floor. The woman sat there in the freezing air, soaked, shivering, and dirty. A guard tossed her a ragged slip. She put it on. It became wet immediately, but at least she had covered herself. The guards lifted her again and moved her away from the tub.

Miss Grady pointed at the elegant young woman.

"No, thank you," said the young woman. "I don't need a bath."

"A funny one, eh?" Miss Grady nodded, and two guards grabbed the young woman by the arms. She tried to resist, but the guards were stronger and lifted her harshly into the tub. The water was brown from the two other baths.

"Sit down!" snapped Miss Grady. "Now!"

The young woman looked at Miss Grady with pure hatred and sat. The water was so cold that it burned, but the young woman masked any reaction except loathing and didn't say a word. As the scrub guard grabbed her arm, however, the young woman made a request.

"Please don't touch my hair." She loved her hair. As a child, she had always brushed her hair a hundred times on each side before going to sleep.

"I won't," said the guard quietly. The two guards poured the buckets of cold water on the young woman.

The young woman had gone swimming in cold water as a child but never in something like this. She bit her lip, hoping that would help the pain pass.

Suddenly the guard grabbed her hair and started scrubbing.

"I said not my hair!"

"Yes. You did, didn't you?" said the guard and laughed. She scrubbed the hair with the same brush she had used on the other two women, but with even more intensity. The young woman tried to break free, but the guard had her by the hair and yanked it to get her under control.

"Stop!" cried the young woman. She despised them. She wished they were all dead. But the guard seemed to savor the humiliation and scrubbed the hair extra slowly.

"Do her back!" barked Miss Grady.

The guard, still holding on to the hair like the mane of a horse, began scrubbing the young woman's back, who felt wire tearing at her skin. She tried to block out the pain and humiliation with thoughts of revenge, a vow to remember every single moment of the suffering and make these people pay.

Finally the scrubber backed away. "Done!"

The young woman opened her eyes. A moment later, she was drenched in two buckets of cold water that took her breath away.

"Get out!" said Miss Grady.

The young woman stood up. As the water fell off her, she saw the guards appraising her lustily. She grabbed the used towel and covered up her breasts and genitals, but she thought of the blotches on the first woman's face and saw the clumps of hair still on the towel, and could not bring herself to use it. One of the guards tossed her a ragged slip, and she put it on before she bothered to dry herself. She stood there shivering, her teeth chattering. It was the coldest she had ever been in her life. But the cold did not temper her fury.

And so it went with the rest of the women: a scrub bath in the freezing, filthy water; drying off with the same damp, contaminated towel; then putting on a ragged slip and standing on the dirt floor in the bitter cold while waiting for the others.

After the baths, the women were herded to a large hall for their first Bellevue Hospital Asylum meal: spoiled, fatty meat and molded toast, with tea that was essentially undrinkable. The young woman cried silently in frustration. She had not eaten in two days, yet she could not bring herself to eat the putrid meat or molded bread. She wondered how long she could survive this ordeal. And she was one of the stronger ones. Most of the other women, she realized, would not last a month.

Following the meal, the women were ordered to sit on stiff-backed chairs outside the dining hall in complete silence. After four hours, the women were taken to a dark room with thirty beds, no windows, and no heat. The mattresses were wafer-thin and lumpy, resting on uneven planks, and the pillows were stuffed with straw. The women were each assigned a bed. There were no lockers, of course; the clothes the women wore upon their arrival had been confiscated. The new arrivals sat on their beds, trying desperately to get warm with the thin cotton blankets. But even with comfortable bedding and thick blankets, extended sleep at Bellevue would be impossible—a half-dozen women in the room screamed continuously from delusion or fever.

The young woman felt completely alone and abandoned as she lay in bed that night, but she was wrong about one thing: the outside world had not forgotten about her.

The *Sun* had placed the story in the lead right-hand column, under the banner headline, "WHO IS THIS INSANE GIRL?" The more cerebral *New York Herald* approached it as a medical mystery: "WHAT AILS THE POOR DARLING?" To *The Evening Telegram*, she was "undoubtedly, hopelessly, sadly insane." The *Times* wrote movingly of the "mysterious waif" with the "wild, hunted look in her eyes and despairing cry, 'I can't remember! I can't remember!'"

The public became obsessed with the story, as they had been with Jay Gould cornering the Gold Market twenty years before, with Reverend Henry Ward Beecher facing adultery charges a decade ago, and with the bachelor President Grover Cleveland siring a child out of wedlock three years past. Who was this pitiful young woman, and what would become of her? Her plight was the talk of supper clubs, train stations, streetcars, hansom stables, and afternoon teas. Yet none of the stories mentioned the abominable conditions at New York's main asylum for women because none of the reporters had ever been inside Bellevue Hospital Asylum nor interviewed former patients. None of them, in point of fact, ever thought to question the assurance from Bellevue's warden, which they repeated verbatim in their papers, that New York's mentally ill were being cared for in a "most humane and generous way, for which the city fathers should be exceedingly proud."

The young woman, of course, never read any of the press reports on Blackwell's Island. Her days consisted of sitting on the stiff-backed benches from morning until night, save for the meals in the dining hall, during which she could only avert her eyes from the inedible food. Her nights consisted of lying on her bed, staring at the rafters, listening to patients wailing, occasionally trying to comfort one of the women pleading for their daughters or husbands or mothers. By the third day, she was half-crazed from not eating or sleeping. Two of the guards made it clear that for sexual favors she could have warmth and food choices other than putrid meat or molded toast, but she wanted no part of that either. If delusion and a blinding headache were her lot, so be it.

Over the next week, the young woman saw more things that shocked her. An elderly woman who cried uncontrollably was beaten and then tossed on a bed unconscious. The next morning, she was dead. The doctors attributed her demise to "convulsions," and that was the end of it. Patients injected freely with morphine or chloral would beg for water when the drugs made them thirsty, and the nurses would deny them even a drop. Nurses would take raisins and grapes and nuts left over from the doctors' meals and eat them slowly in front of the patients to torment them. Women who upset the nurses, whatever the reason, were put on the "rope gang," where they were dragged around by the hair, kicked, and choked, while one of the nurses stood guard in case a doctor approached. One victim of the rope gang did tell a doctor what had happened, but he dismissed her complaints as the ravings of a madwoman and never bothered to investigate further.

And then, ten days after the young woman had been taken away from the Essex Market Court to Bellevue State Hospital, the public's prayers were answered. Attorney Peter A. Hendricks, a prominent member of the New York bar, came forward and arranged for the young woman's release to the custody of anonymous clients. All seven newspapers trumpeted this development on their front pages. The *Sun* attributed it to the vigilance of the *Sun's* loyal readers. The *Times* credited the medical staff at Bellevue, concluding that it had achieved "gratifying results," and with further care, "the poor waif might have a complete recovery." Two days after the release, however, the *World* gave a fuller account of exactly what had happened:

INSIDE THE MADHOUSE

Nellie Bly's Experience in the Blackwell's Island Asylum
Ten Days with Lunatics
How the City's Unfortunate Wards Are Fed and Treated
Attendants Who Harass and Abuse Patients and Laugh at Their Miseries

The young woman in the Essex Market courtroom had not been insane at all, but a 24-year-old reporter named Nellie Bly, out to reveal the horrors of Bellevue. And she held back nothing, setting out in detail everything she had experienced and witnessed.

Her powerful account swept the country. Newspapers all over North America carried the story, extolling Nellie Bly's daring and courage and castigating Bellevue State Hospital and the city of New York. The embarrassed *New York Times* dropped all mention of the story it had placed on page one every day for two weeks, but the *Sun* unabashedly interviewed medical personnel and ran a story on Nellie Bly's stay in the asylum, with a rare headline praising a rival's reporter:

PLAYING MAD WOMAN

Nellie Bly Too Sharp for the Island Doctors
The Sun Finishes Up Its Story of the "Pretty Crazy Girl"

Sitting at the writing desk in her tiny Harlem bedroom, her mother asleep on their bed, Nellie felt unabashed pride. The New York City Council had toured the hospital with her and appropriated an additional $1 million to the Department of Public Charities and Corrections to improve conditions at Bellevue. The entire nursing staff was either fired or placed under arrest, and the mayor took personal responsibility for installing a new administration. Journalistically, her feat was unprecedented. No reporter had ever become a victim in order to write a major story. Reporters would routinely identify themselves and even give their subjects a chance to comment before a story was published, but Nellie had seen people get away with murder that way. The rules of journalism, she smiled to herself, were about to change.

Just as revolutionary, and an even greater source of pride, was the fact that the person so dramatically changing the practice of American journalism was a woman. No woman had ever had a front-page story before, certainly not like this.

But the ten days had been hell. Their memory would not go away soon. Her limbs ached, her lungs felt singed, and her stomach could still not tolerate solid food. She wrote about it every day in her journal, sometimes twice a day. Yet it had all been worth it.

Nellie reread again and again the telegram she had received only minutes ago. Colonel John Cockerill, the editor in chief at the *New York World*, wanted to see her immediately. Of New York's seven major newspapers, six—including *The Sun*, the most sophisticated, and the *Herald*, the wealthiest—were owned by well-heeled Republicans and spouted the pro-capitalist, anti-labor, and anti-immigrant polemics of their publishers. The seventh, the *World*, was owned by Joseph Pulitzer, a Hungarian-born immigrant of reputedly Jewish ancestry, and directed toward the middle class, the poor, and the scandalmongers. That the *World* had catapulted into first place in both circulation and revenues in only four years under Pulitzer's ownership stuck in the craws of established newspapermen, who considered their papers far better written, far better edited, and infinitely more American. The *World* was where she belonged.

To be invited back to the *World* by Cockerill was a remarkable accomplishment—one more reason her story had been worth it. She had taken quite a chance leaving the *Pittsburg Dispatch* a year before. Her editors had reassigned her to gardening and fashion stories after advertisers complained about her investigative pieces. She quit on the spot, even though she had several family members to support. She had moved to New York City with her frail mother and for eight months tried to find newspaper work, but literally could not even get through a front door, as company after company along Newspaper Row stationed bodyguards to keep out unwanted job seekers and irate readers. Several sentries offered to provide assistance in return for an afternoon of fornication, but Nellie would have none of that and told them so in most indelicate terms. Though she tried everything from polite conversation to amusing chitchat to righteous indignation, the guards unfailingly shooed her away, laying hands and billy clubs wherever and whenever they liked.

Finally, fighting exhaustion and despair and destitution, she managed to convince Flaherty, the goon at the *World* who had given her the hardest time, to pass her clippings from the *Pittsburg Dispatch* to management, along with word that she had an "irresistible story to tell, and the editors would look like fools if it were published elsewhere." Eventually she was informed that Colonel Cockerill, the managing editor, would see her, and was shown into a cluttered cloakroom by the main door, away from the regular traffic.

Two hours later Colonel Cockerill, an imposing figure with a thick mustache and military bearing, had walked into the cloakroom and listened to the idea—she would travel to Europe and return in steerage class to report on the immigrant experience—then summarily dismissed it as too ambitious for an inexperienced reporter, especially a woman.

"What if something were to happen to you on the journey?" he had said. "What if you become ill or even die? How would it look for the *World* to put a woman in such a vulnerable position for the sake of a story?"

"I will write out a document before I go, absolving you of all responsibility."

"No." He was adamant, and handed her back her clippings.

"Good day, sir," she had said tartly, making no attempt to hide her disappointment. She had expected more from the editor of the *World*. He was as small-minded as the others.

"I may have a counterproposal," he had said as she opened the door.

He had then mentioned the asylum story idea, clearly not expecting her to accept the assignment. In fact, she wasn't even sure if he meant it. But the *World* was pushing the edges of American journalism, and as soon as Nellie realized Cockerill was serious, she accepted on the spot. What Cockerill didn't know, of course, was that Nellie would have gone through far worse to work for the *World*. This was her first moment of hope in eight months.

"When do I start?" she had said without hesitation.

"Right now. But we need to keep this story a secret until you finish."

With a hint of summer in the fresh May air and the remnants of the Great Blizzard finally beginning to melt, Nellie walked briskly past the complex web of streetcar lines on Newspaper Row—five blocks from Wall Street and two blocks from City Hall—and up the concrete steps of the *World*'s eight-story headquarters. Her mood matched the sunny day, for the first time since moving to New York. No doubt Cockerill knew that the publishers of the *Sun* and the *Tribune* had invited her in for interviews—"no doubt" because she'd made sure he learned of it. But in truth, she preferred to work for the *World*. As the biggest and boldest paper in New York, it suited her style perfectly.

She wasn't sure what Cockerill had in mind. He would probably offer her another assignment, but she wanted something more: a permanent position, at a good salary, to deliver stories that would set New York journalism on fire.

"Not so fast."

It was Flaherty, the oversized guard who had turned her away every day for eight months. She hadn't seen him since Cockerill had assigned her the asylum story; to maintain secrecy, Nellie had stayed away from the *World*, and a runner had delivered her copy to the editors.

"Good morning, Mr. Flaherty," she said with a chill, no

longer needing to make nice.

But Flaherty moved to block her way, his face right up to hers. "And where do you think you're going?" It was the same expression, said with the same brogue and disdain, he had used with her every day for eight months.

"I believe this should gain my admission." She produced the telegram from Cockerill, with the assurance of a checkmate.

"That is of no concern to me," he said.

"It is from Colonel Cockerill himself—"

"I have my instructions." He towered over her. He also had a mean streak.

Flaherty had been a street cop for ten years in the lower Bronx, reputedly banging the heads of Italian street thugs on every corner, and if he didn't want someone getting into a building, that person wasn't getting in. He also didn't like being turned down for sex, even if he was married with four children. But Nellie Bly had a temper of her own and didn't care one whit that Flaherty was a foot taller and fifty pounds heavier or even that he carried a gun.

"Listen to me, you foul-smelling imbecile. If you could read, you would know I had a front-page story in the *World* with my name in the headline. *Two* stories, in fact. And the editor in charge has summoned me here—"

"That may be, but Mr. Pulitzer would like to see you."

Invoking the name of the *World*'s publisher quieted her abruptly, something that rarely occurred with Nellie Bly.

"Right away. In his office. Mr. Cockerill is with him."

She saw a faint smile at the corners of Flaherty's mouth. He enjoyed letting this uppity woman know he could still keep her out at any time, he didn't care how many front-page stories she had. Pleased with himself, he stepped aside to let her pass. But she hesitated.

"Mr. Flaherty. May I ask you a question?"

"What is it?"

"You remember when I told you I had a story and asked to see Mr. Cockerill, and you didn't turn me away?"

"I remember."

"You were the only guard on this entire street who let me in."

"I know that," he said, his chest swelling with pride.

"You do?"

"Yes. All of the guards tell one another what goes on. It makes our jobs easier."

"Then why did you pass along my request when no one else would?"

"You're Irish, Miss Bly," he said with a lilt. "We need to stick together. If you'd been a guinea or a kike, I'd have thrown you out on your ear."

"And if I had been a guinea or a kike, Mr. Flaherty, I would thank God Almighty not to be of the same race as the likes of you." She spit on his shoes with total contempt and strode past him through the doors.

CHAPTER TWO

JOSEPH PULITZER

She should have known Pulitzer would want to see her, she said to herself, as the Otis Company elevator lifted her through the eight-story rotunda, past the marble steps, majestic tapestries, and electric chandeliers. The *World* had not gotten to the top of the newspaper heap by being conventional. Pulitzer was known for aggressively going after whatever he wanted. He had arrived in America as a teenager during the Civil War, penniless and speaking no English, and within twenty years owned two of the country's largest papers, *The St. Louis Post-Dispatch* and *The New York World*. He was a self-promoter on the scale of P.T. Barnum. Nellie particularly remembered his reaction when the asylum story broke. He had been in St. Louis and was quoted in the *Post-Dispatch* as saying that "Nellie Bly is our very bright and very talented new staff member, and I will reward her with a handsome check. With our help, she thoroughly understands the profession which she has chosen. She has a great future before her."

As she walked down the marble floor, past the massive Ionic columns toward the twelve-foot-high oak doors and the two male secretaries seated at large desks beside them, Nellie told herself not to be intimidated; she had interviewed two of the richest men in America, Andrew Carnegie and Henry Clay Frick, for the *Dispatch*. Then again, as rich and powerful as they were, they didn't own *The New York World* and have her dreams in their hands.

One of the secretaries rose from his chair. "Miss Bly?"

"Yes."

"Wait here." No warmth, no friendliness, no offering her a chair. The secretary, like most men at the time, wasn't keen on having a woman at his place of work. He went inside, making sure to close the door behind him. The secretary at the other desk continued with his work as if she weren't there.

"Good morning," she said.

"Yes, thank you, it is," he replied curtly.

Ignored, she stood there awkwardly and waited for the other secretary to return.

Finally, after she'd mentally run through a dozen barbs, the first secretary came out. "Mr. Pulitzer will see you."

With no assistance from either man, she opened the heavy wooden door to behold the largest office she had ever seen. At least, as far as she could tell it was the largest.

Pulitzer, who had notoriously bad eyesight, kept the lights dim in his office. His oak desk was fully eight feet wide, and the ceilings appeared to be fifteen feet high. Several overhead gas lamps with green shades provided what light there was, while sunlight peeked through curtains that sheltered archway-shaped windows ten feet tall. Oriental rugs on the dark wood floor set off leather couches, Gustav Stickley sitting chairs, and a long wooden table with piles of papers on it. Bookcases stuffed with newspapers and books lined the walls. For a moment, Nellie thought she had entered a library.

Both men rose to greet her, although Pulitzer was so short he wasn't much taller standing than sitting. He had wild, unkempt hair, a dark goatee, pince-nez glasses, and a gray wool suit and vest befitting his station as the nation's premier publisher. Most striking were his eyes, of unbounded energy and intensity and perhaps even a touch of insanity. He walked over to her and extended his hand.

"Mizbly. Dis iz a playzure."

Nellie had heard that Pulitzer, an immigrant, spoke with a thick Hungarian accent, but she hadn't expected one quite *this* thick. She could barely understand him. Yet he plunged into animated conversation, seemingly oblivious to his impenetrable pronunciation. She strained to listen, hoping to get the gist of his words.

"Congratulations on your story," he said, pumping her hand. "Wonderful! Just wonderful!"

"Thank you, Mr. Pulitzer. And thank you and Colonel Cockerill for the opportunity."

"Ah, you were right, Cockerill. She is a charmer. Please, Miss Bly. Sit down."

He indicated the leather couch. Nellie hesitated to sit on something so luxurious—furniture like that was for admiring, not using—but she implored herself not to think small-town, and obliged her host.

"Cockerill and I want to express appreciation." She wasn't sure what he said.

"Excuse me?"

Irritation flashed across Pulitzer's face. Cockerill jumped right in. "Mr. Pulitzer believes in rewarding performance, Miss Bly."

Suddenly she understood the roles. Pulitzer hated when someone asked him to repeat himself; it ruined his image as the people's publisher. Cockerill was there for cover, to fill in the holes whenever someone couldn't understand him.

"We would like for you to work for the *World*, on the permanent staff."

"I would like that very much, Mr. Pulitzer. Very much." She tried to hide her excitement.

"And you will have your own byline."

"Usually a reporter must work eight or ten years for that," chimed in Cockerill.

"That is true, Cockerill," said Pulitzer, "but Miss Bly showed us more than promise; she showed courage and intelligence. There is no reason to wait."

"That's generous of you, Mr. Pulitzer," said Cockerill, making sure Nellie got the message.

"Very generous," said Nellie.

"You will be paid twenty dollars a week. I trust that will suffice?" he asked.

Nellie's heart sank. Twenty dollars a week was not even what she'd made writing gardening stories in Pittsburg. And rent in New York was much higher.

"I was hoping for more, sir." In fact, she had been hoping for forty but could feel her nerve leaving her.

"We are offering you a permanent position!" said Pulitzer with irritation. "Your own byline! At the largest newspaper in New York!" Cockerill didn't bother to translate. The gist was clear.

Nellie went flush with anger. She started to deliver a sharp retort when suddenly she wondered if Pulitzer, like Cockerill before him, wasn't testing her.

"Is that what most of the permanent staff make, sir? Twenty dollars a week?"

"What other reporters make is a private matter," said Cockerill.

"You're right. There's no need to tell me. Any reporter fit to work at the *World* should be able to find out employee wages easily enough."

A dark look came over Pulitzer's face again. He was a man of many moods—she could see that—and he wasn't good at hiding any of them.

"I have rent to pay," Nellie said, "just like your other reporters. And family members to support. You wouldn't be offering me less money because I'm a woman, would you, Mr. Pulitzer?"

"Of course not. I am offering less money because I hope you will take it." He smiled. And, with great relief, so did she.

"I will pay you what everyone else in your position is making: thirty dollars a week. Begrudgingly."

"In that case I will accept thirty dollars a week. Begrudgingly."

"Good."

"You won't be disappointed, Mr. Pulitzer. I promise." She could barely contain herself.

"No need to promise, my dear. Pulitzer does not make

mistakes. Now, for your next story—"

"Actually, I have an idea in mind." She had been waiting for this moment and had rehearsed it to herself dozens of times. "Are you familiar with Jules Verne?"

Pulitzer glanced at Cockerill. "What about him?"

"Do you know his book, *Around the World in 80 Days*?"

"Yes, yes," said Pulitzer impatiently. "What about it?"

"I want to track the journey of Phileas Fogg and write about it as a journalist. What it would *really* be like to go around the world in eighty days. I could telegraph dispatches from Italy, Ceylon, India, China."

Verne's book had ignited her imagination. She was sure that newspaper readers would be equally captivated by a running account and had planned out the entire itinerary. It was a story she had wanted to write all her life.

"It won't do," snapped Pulitzer.

"Why not?" She was disappointed. She had her heart set on this story.

"Because I have something else in mind for you."

He slowed down his speech, to make sure he would be understood. "Have you seen Liberty Enlightening the World, Miss Bly?"

"Of course. Almost every weekend."

Anyone wanting to work at the *World* was expected to know the story of Pulitzer's obsession with what had become the most famous sculpture in America. A gift from the people of France to the people of the United States to celebrate the centennial of American independence, it had arrived only a year before, ten years late, on June 18, 1886, in 214 wooden packing crates. Once assembled, it was 310 feet high, taller than any building in New York. Its copper patina could be seen from each of the five boroughs, and Nellie was not exaggerating when she said she visited it almost every weekend.

The idea for the statue was conceived by the French sculptor Frederic Bartholdi as a way of expressing disapproval for the rule of Emperor Napoleon III, and the French Parliament had commissioned it. Congress authorized the land for the site (Bedloe's Island in New York harbor), but determined that payment for the $150,000 pedestal should rest entirely with the people of New York since the statue would be exhibited there. The politicians of New York City, however, refused to allocate the necessary funds, deeming it a waste of money. The situation became a national embarrassment—the massive statue, a gift from the people of France, broken up into crates, awaiting shipment in the French ports because the United States would not supply an appropriate pedestal—until Joseph Pulitzer took it upon himself to spearhead the fundraising drive. First he contacted people of wealth all over New York City, but funds only trickled in.

Undaunted, he took his case to the public and promised to publish the name of every contributor, no matter how large or small the donation, on the front page of the *World*. In a remarkably short time, the drive raised the $150,000, nearly all of it coming from 120,000 working class men, women, and children—including Nellie and her mother—while the wealthy, wrote Pulitzer, "looked on with an apathy that amounted to contempt." The 27,000-ton base, its construction overseen by Pulitzer himself, was the largest concrete structure ever built. The statue was dedicated on October 28, 1886, in a ceremony that made the entire country proud.

Pulitzer was pleased that Nellie had visited the statue repeatedly, but she was not simply humoring him. Her admiration was genuine. Without Pulitzer, there would have been no statue. In fact, at the opening ceremony two spikes had been driven into the statue's toes, one with the name of the sculptor, Bartholdi, the other with "Pulitzer" etched on it.

"Now," he went on, "do you know the name Emma Lazarus?"

Nellie had to think a moment. "The poet?"

"Yes."

Nellie was not one for poetry. She preferred newspapers and serials in magazines. But part of her job at the *Dispatch* had been to proofread copy, and occasionally the paper would print poetry, as did most newspapers of the day. A few of Emma

Lazarus's poems appeared in the *Dispatch*, though at the moment Nellie couldn't remember them.

"What does Miss Lazarus have to do with the statue?" asked Nellie.

"Emma Lazarus is the only reason the statue is standing today," said Pulitzer. "Without her, I would not have been involved, and no one else would have raised the money."

He went to his desk and picked up a sheet of paper. "When I first heard this poem, I was moved to tears. It captures America for all who come here. My ambition is to have a plaque of it affixed to the base so that every visitor to the statue will read it. Sadly, that requires approval from several people, and we have been unable to obtain it."

He handed Nellie the poem.

"I don't know how long it will take or how much it will cost, Miss Bly," he said emphatically, "but before I die, I will see this poem on the base of Lady Liberty."

He had circled a stanza of the poem:
Not like the brazen giant of Greek fame,
With conquering limbs astride from land to land;
Here at our sea-washed, sunset gates shall stand
A mighty woman with a torch, whose flame
Is the imprisoned lightning, and her name
Mother of Exiles. From her beacon-hand
Glows world-wide welcome; her mild eyes command
The air-bridged harbor that twin cities frame.
"Keep ancient lands, your storied pomp!" cries she
With silent lips. "Give me your tired, your poor,
Your huddled masses yearning to breathe free,
The wretched refuse of your teeming shore.
Send these, the homeless, tempest-tost to me,
I lift my lamp beside the golden door!"

Nellie read it quietly to herself. It was indeed stirring, expressing remarkably the dreams of those who came to this country in search of a better life. But Nellie was thinking about a job, not words for the heart, and she had no idea what Pulitzer wanted. She handed him the poem.

"I'm sure Miss Lazarus will be pleased when that happens, sir."

Pulitzer frowned. "Miss Lazarus is dead, Miss Bly."

"Oh, I'm sorry. I had no idea."

"She died six months ago. At the age of 38."

"How?"

He looked at her with those steely eyes. "That's what I want you to find out."

"Me? Mr. Pulitzer, I know nothing about medicine."

"I'm not sure that matters in this case."

She caught the darkness in his voice. "What do the doctors say?" she asked.

"The doctors," he said with unconcealed contempt, "believe it was a cancer."

"But you suspect malice?"

"I suspect murder. She was much too young, much too vibrant, to die."

"Many people die too young, sir. My own father was one of them."

"I understand that. But my wife and I had seen Miss Lazarus often over the past several years. She was in excellent health. Then she made a trip abroad and came back in terrible health. We did not recognize her. She was bedridden, had stopped writing, could hardly speak. Within two months she was dead."

"Have you spoken to the police?"

"The police barely investigated," he said dismissively. "They simply went along with the doctors and ruled out foul play."

"What makes you think they are mistaken?"

"Too many people have reason to be pleased with her death. For at least one of them, I am convinced it was more than a happy coincidence."

" 'Pleased?' How? Who?"

"That you will come to learn." He stared at her with those intense eyes. "Mrs. Pulitzer and I feel it is our duty to learn what happened to Miss Lazarus. I admired the way you went about the asylum story. I need that same determination here."

She saw how much this meant to him and was flattered he trusted her with such a personal assignment. But she knew that disappointing him would have unfortunate consequences, and that sobered her quickly.

"I am not a police detective, Mr. Pulitzer. I'm a journalist."

"I told you, the police have been useless."

"But they have certain powers a journalist does not."

Again that dismissive wave. "They said that everything is fine, just as the warden at Bellevue said everything was fine."

Nellie's stomach tightened. She wouldn't know where to begin on such a story. And yet if she said no to Pulitzer, her time at the *World* would be finished.

He stood up. The meeting was over.

"Mr. Pulitzer, I'm still not sure I'm the right person for this story."

"I told you: Pulitzer does not make mistakes. Cockerill will give you more details of Miss Lazarus."

He walked over to his desk.

"After you finish, you can pursue Mr. Verne and Mr. Phileas Fogg." He began poring over some papers.

"Uh, Mr. Pulitzer," she said.

"Yes? What is it?"

"You mentioned something in the papers about a check, for doing such a good job."

He looked at her, flabbergasted. "Miss Bly. You should know better than to believe what you read in the papers."

CHAPTER THREE

NEW YORK CANCER HOSPITAL

Nellie lifted her skirt hem several inches as she followed Cockerill through the newspaper room, past the reporters and spittoons. The floor of the *World*, like the floor of her old paper, the *Dispatch*, was half an inch deep with expectorated tobacco juice. The male reporters, not the least bit embarrassed at the slovenly state of their workplace, eyed Nellie with defiance and hostility. If she was put off by the spit on the floor or anything else, it was her problem, not theirs.

She and Cockerill reached his desk in the far corner of the room, where he could gain some privacy but still keep an eye on his reporters. Nellie had done her research on Cockerill when he assigned her the Bellevue story. Just over 40 years old, with leathery skin and a disposition to match, he was a lifelong newspaperman and had the complete trust of Pulitzer, along with the respect and fear of his staff. He once shot and killed an irate reader who pulled a gun on him in a newsroom, which left no doubt to his reporters who was in charge.

Cockerill motioned for Nellie to sit. "Congratulations."

"Thank you, Colonel." It was finally hitting her that she had a permanent position, at an acceptable salary, at the biggest and most forward-thinking paper in New York.

"I'll be frank, Miss Bly. You proved me wrong on the asylum story. I didn't think you had it in you."

"I don't know whether to say thank you or apologize."

"Do neither. Simply continue to prove me wrong."

"I shall look forward to that," she said sweetly. Cockerill had taken a chance in hiring her for the Bellevue story, but he had also been the editor in New York most resistant to women working in journalism.

He picked up the top sheet from a stack of documents in front of him.

"Miss Lazarus's family is one of the oldest in New York, in fact in America. Her ancestors came over from Portugal in the 1600s and settled in Newport, Rhode Island, where they built the first synagogue in the United States."

"Miss Lazarus was a Jew?" asked Nellie, surprised.

"Yes," Cockerill responded with mild distaste. Nellie's enthusiasm for the story, already low, sank even further. Only an hour before, she had imagined herself traveling around the world to fulfill a dream. Now she was investigating the death of a Jewish poet.

"Why did they settle in Newport and not New York?" she asked, trying to muster some interest.

"New York was not always so friendly to Israelites. Massachusetts was even less welcoming. Only Rhode Island, among the northern colonies, let them be. Eventually, as the religious and commercial climate changed, the family did move to New York, though they maintained a presence in Newport. Emma's father became a sugar merchant and managed to ship to customers in the Rebel states during the war. It almost cost him his membership in the Union Club."

"What's the Union Club?"

He looked at her. "You *are* new to New York, aren't you?"

"My family has been barred from clubs for centuries, Mr. Cockerill. I was simply wondering if the Union Club was any different from the rest of them."

"The Union Club is the oldest private club in New York. Membership is based entirely on social standing. Mr. Vanderbilt, Mr. Gould, even Mr. Morgan have yet to be admitted."

"And yet a Jew was a member?"

"A *charter* member. The Lazaruses are on Mrs. Astor's list as well."

Even Nellie knew that "Mrs. Astor's list" designated the 400 most exclusive families in New York City.

"And all these connections ... is that what opened doors for her poetry?"

"No, Miss Lazarus was a prodigy. Emerson himself read her when she was a teenager and insisted on mentoring her. By the age of 20, she had been published in the leading literary magazines in America and had a following in Europe as well. Browning, James, all the literary types showered praise upon her."

Nellie was impressed but not about to say so to Cockerill. She didn't like this assignment and was going along with it only because Pulitzer had insisted on it.

"She was a first-rate talent with great promise," he continued, "and then something happened. We aren't sure what exactly, but Miss Lazarus suddenly became a champion of social causes, first in her writings, then in her activities. It was during that time that she wrote 'The New Colossus,' the poem Mr. Pulitzer showed you."

"What sorts of causes?"

"The plight of immigrants, especially from Russia. She went to the docks and greeted them as they came off the boats, and started organizations to house and clothe them and find them work. She became quite the hero to them, though apparently her family wasn't keen on it. They threatened to disown her. But she had an independent streak and told them she wasn't going to stop, no matter what they did."

For the first time since Pulitzer had assigned her the story, Emma perked up. "I thought you would like that," remarked Cockerill.

Nellie let it pass. For all she knew, Emma may have been a spoiled girl rebelling against her family rather than an independent woman. "She was unmarried?"

"Yes."

"Any engagements?"

"None that we know of. But she was often seen with the brother-in-law of her editor at Harper's. A Charles DeKay."

"And what do you know about Mr. DeKay?"

"Attended Yale. A fencer with social connections but not much money. Something of a failed poet. Writes art and drama critiques for the *Times*."

"Not a Jew, I take it?"

"No. Most definitely not a Jew."

A rich Jewess who dabbled in poetry and social causes and fencers from Yale wasn't Nellie's favorite subject for a story, but more than that, she still wondered if a story was even there.

"May I ask you a question, Mr. Cockerill?"

"Go ahead."

"Do you think foul play was involved? A thirty-eight-year-old woman dying of a cancer is hardly unheard of."

"I don't know what to think, Miss Bly. The doctor and the police were firm in their opinions. But when Mr. Pulitzer has a strong feeling, I have learned to respect it."

"What if your doubts are correct and Miss Lazarus did indeed die of natural causes?"

"Let's just see what you learn."

He pushed the pile of documents toward her. "He is testing me, isn't he?" she said.

"No, I don't think he is testing you. I think he is using every resource at his disposal to obtain justice for a friend. And he can hardly be blamed for that, can he?"

Nellie took the Sixth Avenue Elevated train back to the room she shared with her mother in Harlem. It was an arduous ninety-minute trip: a four-car train, pulled by a coal-powered locomotive twenty rickety feet above the street, connecting with the newer Ninth Avenue Elevated at Fifty-Third Street, then making the dramatic "suicide curve" 150 feet above the street at 110th Street and Morningside Heights, where Nellie closed her eyes and prayed like a schoolgirl that the tracks would not collapse. On this trip, she carried two carpetbags filled with *World* clippings on Emma Lazarus. At first she had kept the bags closed, as Cockerill warned her that reporters on Park Row were notorious for stealing stories, but then curiosity got the best of her. She was also eager to get moving on the story—the sooner she could finish with Emma Lazarus, the sooner she could get to work on her Jules Verne story. By the time she arrived in Harlem, she had formed a plan, or at least her next step.

When she walked inside the shabby Harlem brownstone, her mother was in the downstairs sitting room, staring out the window. Life had been fickle and cruel to Mary Jane Cochran. All the heartache since her husband died had destroyed most of her spirit, and she was incapable of taking care of herself. Despite two other children and ten older stepchildren, the burden of caring for Mary Jane had fallen solely on Nellie.

"I have a job, Mother. I think," said Nellie.

"Well, do you or don't you?"

Nellie explained the meeting with Pulitzer and her fear that if she didn't deliver the story he wanted, he would fire her.

"I don't believe that," said her mother. "You're a wonderful writer."

"He doesn't know that."

"Now, Pink." Nellie's mother had always dressed her in pink, from the time she was an infant, and had given her the color for a nickname. "They were smart enough to hire you in the first place. They know what they're doing. What about pay, dear?"

"Thirty dollars a week."

"Well, that's good, isn't it?"

"It's less than I was making at the *Dispatch*."

"Yes, but you're in New York now."

Nellie didn't respond. Sometimes her mother didn't make sense these days. She wished her father were alive so that she could tell him all about the new job. He would be so proud and want to hear every detail. But her mother had shown great resilience, she had to acknowledge that. Though the accommodations were less than ideal, Mary Jane had been uncomplaining about moving to New York, albeit a little daft from the idleness.

"Mother, we need to put on your coat."

"Where are we going, dear?"

"To see the doctor."

"Are you feeling ill?"

"No, Mother. You are."

The New York Cancer Hospital on Central Park West between 105th and 106th Streets, the newest and largest hospital in New York, was a favorite target of Joseph Pulitzer and the *World*. In the summer of 1884, while living in Manhattan, former President Grant had developed throat cancer. Out of loyalty to the man who had shielded their fortunes from the rapacious masses, some of the country's wealthiest men—John Jacob Astor, Joseph Drexel, J.P. Morgan, and Henry Clay Frick—laid the cornerstone for a cancer hospital that same year. It opened three years later, in March 1887—for a sum, as Pulitzer liked to point out, that would have paid for twenty-five bases for Lady Liberty.

Nellie and her mother made their way through the rancid butter smell of carbolic acid and up three flights of steps, through what looked to Nellie like a French chateau, to the office of Doctor Nathaniel T. Barker. The two women from western Pennsylvania had never been inside a hospital before. After a two-hour wait in a reception area decorated with Rococo furnishings, they were taken to an interior room for another hour of waiting. Finally, three hours after they arrived, the doctor walked in.

Barker was younger than Nellie expected, in his late thirties. He wore a business suit with a long cutaway coat and had wavy brown hair parted down the middle, a thick handlebar mustache, dull eyes, and a surprisingly unimpressive mien. Nellie had anticipated more gray matter from one in his position.

"Good afternoon," he said, extending his hand. "I'm Dr. Barker."

Barker momentarily dropped his professional air when he beheld Nellie and held on to her hand longer than was the custom. She didn't mind. She hoped his leering would make him more cooperative.

"Hello, doctor. I'm Elizabeth Cochran and this is my mother." It felt strange to use her given name working on a story. She had taken the pen name "Nellie Bly" after a character in her father's favorite Stephen Foster song.

"How may I be of help, Miss Cochran?"

"We moved here recently, doctor. My mother has been feeling tired and weak, and it's gone on much too long."

"How long is 'too long,' exactly?"

"Three weeks."

He frowned and turned to Mary Jane. "Let's have a look at you, Mrs. Cochran."

"I don't think she has a cancer—" said Nellie.

"That's all right. Cancer is only a part of my practice."

"See?" said Mary Jane. "I told you."

"We were afraid you would send us away," said Nellie. "My mother was insistent we see you and only you."

"And why is that?"

"We are both admirers of Emma Lazarus."

Barker smiled at the mention of Emma's name. He enjoyed being linked with the rich and famous.

"Yes. Very sad. A marvelous woman."

"Had you treated her for a long time?"

"The past few years."

"Since she developed the cancer?"

"Well, actually, she became my patient a year prior. I was recommended to her by a former classmate at Yale."

"Mr. DeKay?" asked Nellie.

"Why, yes. How did you know?"

"I told you, doctor. Mother and I are devoted admirers. We read everything we can about Miss Lazarus."

"Yale," nodded Mary Jane with approval. "I told Elizabeth I was in good hands." Mary Jane almost overacted the part, but Barker was too vain to notice.

"Lean forward, Mrs. Cochran."

Mary Jane leaned forward. Barker crouched, placed his right ear against the back of her ribs, and stole a glance at Nellie. He saw her staring at him and looked away, though he smiled with vanity.

"Breathe deeply."

She did so. Barker listened intently with his ear. Then he stood erect and impassively took Mary's wrist in his hand and pulled out a gold pocket watch. He counted her pulse rate while checking his watch.

"Nothing irregular," he pronounced and returned the watch to his vest pocket. "Do you ever get colds, Mrs. Cochran?"

"Not very often."

"Any fevers?"

"No."

"And yet you feel tired."

"Yes. Almost all the time." She looked to Nellie for confirmation that she was playing her part right. Nellie nodded reassuringly.

"What about your breasts?"

Mary Jane blushed. "Excuse me?"

"Do you feel pain or discomfort in the breasts? Irregular pain in the breasts, coupled with fatigue, can indicate something serious. Have you experienced any of that?"

Mary Jane was so tongue-tied, she didn't know what to say.

"I'm sorry," interjected Nellie. "Mother has never seen a male doctor before."

"Or even discussed such matters with a man," added Mary Jane in a huff.

"I am here to help you, Mrs. Cochran," Barker said soothingly.

"I suppose next you'll want to look at me there."

"As a matter of fact, yes."

"No!" said Mary Jane firmly. "Absolutely not!"

"We need to explain the fatigue. It could be related to hormonal imbalance or something else, and it would affect the breasts—"

"No!!"

Nellie saw her opportunity to question Barker slipping away. Unless she acted quickly, it was about to come to an end.

"Mother, I'll let Dr. Barker examine me. You'll see that it's not so bad."

"I don't want you examined either. Or whatever it is he wants to call it."

"Just watch, Mother."

"Thank you, Miss Cochran," said Barker, struggling to contain his eagerness. "Remove your waistcoat, please."

"I don't believe this—"

"Mother! Stop it."

Nellie removed her coat and placed it on a chair.

"And now your blouse."

She unbuttoned her blouse, revealing a satin undergarment with thin straps and a shallow neckline that barely covered her breasts. Barker tried to remain professional, but his eyes and an involuntary gasp betrayed him. Nellie was a beautiful woman, and he could not help admiring her. He motioned for her to place her blouse on the chair.

"Sit on the examining table, please. Facing me."

Nellie did so. Her stomach tightened. Flirtation to get a story was one thing; baring her breasts was something else altogether. But she willed herself to sit on the table in her satin undershirt and uncovered shoulders.

"Stop this! Right now!" snapped Mary Jane.

Nellie, too, wanted it to stop—she knew where it was headed—but if she didn't find out the medical specifics of Emma's death, there was no story to tell, and she would probably find herself back on the street scrounging for work, trying to talk her way past foul-mouthed sentries for another eight months. Who knew how Pulitzer would respond if she came up empty so early on?

"Mother. Please."

"Remove your undergarment, Miss Cochran."

Nellie took a deep breath and did so. Barker's eyes widened at the sight of her pointed breasts and tender, cream-colored skin.

"Is it all right if we talk about Miss Lazarus?" Nellie asked. "It will relax me."

"Of course." He would have talked about recipes for maggot pie at this point. He reached out to touch her left breast as if it were a sacred jewel.

"What was the nature of her cancer exactly?" she asked.

"I surmised it was a cancer of her lymph nodes." He touched it. The experience was even more wondrous than he expected.

" 'Surmised'? " she said. "You weren't sure?"

"Not entirely."

She sat up tall and thrust out her chest so he could touch even more, since it seemed to have the effect of truth serum. He caressed the breast, affecting an examination.

"But you told the authorities she died of cancer."

"That was my best assessment. Miss Lazarus was abroad during most of the period when she was ill. I only saw her for the three months after her return."

"Did she receive treatment in Europe?"

"Medications and rest. No surgery."

He reached for the other breast, cupped the front of it in his hand and stroked the nipples with his thumb. She flinched.

"Problem?" asked Barker.

"No. Sorry."

His touch was rough, and she was feeling violated. Not only did she find Barker unappealing in every way, but he was enjoying himself far too much. She fought to take her mind off his fondling and focus on the story.

"How can you be so certain it was cancer?" asked Nellie.

"I examined her blood on the microscope. I saw many more white cells than there should have been. She also had weight loss, exhaustion, and pain in her abdomen and joints. All consistent with lymphatic cancer."

He probed both breasts for irregularities—or for pleasure, it was hard to say which. She could feel his quickened breaths against her cheek.

"And what is the standard treatment for lymphatic cancer?"

"Arsenic."

"I thought arsenic was a poison," she said, surprised.

"It can be, yes. But arsenic has had profound medicinal properties for thousands of years, dating back to the Greeks."

She couldn't bear it any longer. He was hurting her now,

his fingers pressing and squeezing without any regard for her dignity or, she suspected, medical information.

"Doctor."

The term seemed to bring him back to professionalism. His touch became more detached, more clinical.

"Yes?"

"Did you prescribe arsenic for Miss Lazarus?"

"No, no. It was too late. The cancer was not reversible." He pulled his hand back. "Nothing untoward or amiss, Miss Cochran. You can put your blouse on now."

Nellie walked over to the chair and began putting on her clothes. Barker did not turn away or make any effort to give her privacy, though she did notice he had an erection. Instead he turned his attention to Mary Jane.

"Not on your life," she snapped.

"What about your fatigue? And pain?" he asked.

"I'll endure them."

"Perhaps you can prescribe some medicine?" asked Nellie tactfully. She didn't even bother to button her blouse. She simply put on her coat and buttoned it up.

He handed Mary Jane a piece of paper with his scribbling on it.

"Get this from the apothecary on the first floor. Take one spoonful every night. If the problem persists, I want you back here promptly. Along with your daughter."

A dozen insults flashed through Nellie's mind, but she held her tongue.

"I promise I will bring her, doctor," she said politely. "No matter how much she resists. Thank you for your time."

"My pleasure."

CHAPTER FOUR

NELLIE BLY

Nellie was not always so restrained with men. After being thrown out of their home when she was eight and then growing up in a tenement, she had declared war against her half brothers, the bank, and all other exploiters of women, children, and the poor. She would get into fights with bullies at school and almost took one's eye out with a shovel. As a teenager, her contempt expanded to authority figures in general, and she was arrested a dozen times. It was about that time that men like Barker began looking at her in uncomfortable ways and making unnerving comments. At first she would throw punches or scratch their faces, but she came to realize that her good looks could work for her as well as against her. She saw how boys would blush and be sweet if she seemed to take a shine to them but would say nasty things and get rough if she didn't. Her insight didn't mute the anger, of course, not in the slightest; it just showed her how someone weaker and poorer could gain an advantage if she kept her wits about her.

She grew into a striking young woman, which only led to more problems—more wounds, more anger, more arrests. She joined the labor movement, thankful to find like-minded people who shared her sense of injustice, and for the first time since her father's death and living hand-to-mouth, she felt something akin to happiness. She laughed and sang and chronicled accounts of brave strikers setting up picket lines and goons bashing their skulls. Her love affair with writing blossomed, and she became a compelling storyteller, a talent nurtured by spellbinding union men out to organize local mills and mines. But those fellows couldn't keep their hands off her either, and she had to quit the movement after slicing off one organizer's ear when he forced himself upon her.

She had felt the same destructive urges when Barker was taking liberties in his office, but she had held back with a greater purpose in mind. She wasn't sure if that was a sign of progress or weakness. Or maybe she would just give Barker his just desserts when the time came.

Unlike Barker, Francis A. Ingram took a noble approach to medicine. Perhaps it was the idealism of youth—Ingram was only 32—or his apprenticeship as an Army surgeon during the Indian wars, but in addition to maintaining a regular practice near Union Square and founding the New Jersey Medical Society, he was the assistant superintendent at Bellevue Women's Asylum. All this despite a constitution left weak by his mother's rubella when he was still in her womb. The Bellevue position was nowhere near as lucrative as private practice, but Ingram was caught up with the wave of mental illness theories sweeping Europe and the U.S. He had read everything by Brucke in Germany and Charcot in France that he could get his hands on, and he engaged them both in a regular correspondence based on his detailed observations at Bellevue.

Nellie had been taken to Ingram during her undercover work at Bellevue for complaining about cold baths in the middle of winter. He had discerned immediately that she was faking her illness, but after confronting her, he played along because he, too, found the conditions appalling and hoped she might change them. Ingram became a valuable resource, and she mentioned him favorably in her stories. He had also been one of the few men in New York not to undress her with his eyes, and she appreciated that as well. When she had questions about Barker's diagnosis and care of Emma Lazarus, it was only natural she would turn to Frank Ingram for answers.

Ingram's private office was in the basement of a three-story brownstone on Twenty-First Street. His receptionist, Edith Fairley, the middle-aged, pear-shaped widow of a former colleague, did not care much for Nellie. On her desk she kept a clipping from the *Boston Transcript* that warned, "Homes will be ruined, children neglected, all because woman is straying from her sphere." For Edith Fairley, Nellie represented all that was becoming wrong with America.

The reception area was devoid of patients, as Nellie knew it would be, when she walked in with Mary Jane. Ingram tended to see patients in the morning and early afternoon and caught up on correspondence and research late in the day.

"Good afternoon, Mrs. Fairley."

"Good afternoon," replied Mrs. Fairley frostily.

"This is my mother. Mrs. Cochran."

"How do you do, Mrs. Fairley?" said Mary Jane politely.

"How do you do?" replied Mrs. Fairley with no warmth whatsoever.

"Is something wrong?" asked Mary Jane.

"No. Should there be?"

"When you can't even give a proper hello, I'd say there is. You sick or something? Someone die in your family?"

Nellie let the words linger. She had no desire to lessen Edith Fairley's discomfort.

"Is Dr. Ingram in?" asked Nellie.

"Is he expecting you?"

"No. But I need to see him. Please tell him it's important."

It was a directive, not a request. Mrs. Fairley knew enough not to defy Nellie and went to the rear hallway, but her horselike snort made her feelings known nonetheless. Nellie didn't care. She was used to it. Women like Mrs. Fairley were as resistant to change as the men she encountered. Maybe even more.

"Who does she think she is?" asked a perturbed Mary

Jane. "Back home she wouldn't last ten minutes with a manner like that."

"Her husband was a friend of Doctor Ingram's."

"I bet he's happy to be dead."

Mrs. Fairley came out of the interior office, the picture of disappointment. "The doctor will see you. He is finishing a letter and will meet you in the examining room."

"I can show myself in. Mother, wait here please. I won't be long. Mrs. Fairley will keep you company."

"Well, that should be fun."

Nellie went down a corridor and entered a room on the left. It was dark, with gas lanterns and azure blue shades, furnished with a burgundy Oriental rug, an examining table, a mauve couch with tassels, an oak French Empire sitting chair, and a wooden desk with medical instruments and an ink well. Nellie, still worked up from her meeting with Barker, paced about the room.

The door opened, and an earnest man of medium height, tired but gentle eyes, thick glasses, taut skin, and a professional air, with a tie and woolen suit that made him look considerably older than early thirties, walked in.

"Miss Bly. Good afternoon."

"Hello, Dr. Ingram."

He closed the door behind him, and they rushed to embrace in a deep, passionate kiss. She clutched his lapels and pulled him to her while his hands slipped under her skirt and inside her undergarments. She moaned at his touch but pulled back.

"We can't," she whispered. "Mother is outside."

"In the reception area?"

"Yes."

His hands still on her buttocks and moving to the inside of her thighs, he tried to pull her toward him, but she resisted.

"I'm sorry," she said. "Next time. I promise."

"I can make it quick."

"I don't want it to be quick." She kissed him hard, making clear her hunger for him.

It was during the latter stages of the Bellevue story that

Nellie's relationship with Ingram went beyond the platonic. She would meet him in his office nearly every afternoon to obtain information and go over records. His indignation with Bellevue had matched hers, and for a journalist, he was a gold mine. She was drawn to his heart, his mind, and his spirit, and to his vulnerability—his mother's rubella had left him with poor eyesight and shortness of breath. To Nellie's constant surprise, he never made a single advance toward her. Only later did she learn that he ached for her constantly, but he sensed the deep pain and anger inside her and had concluded that any step toward intimacy would have to come first from her or she would become mistrustful and hurt, and he could not bear the thought of that. He told her that he admired her so much, he was prepared to restrain himself even if nothing sexual ever happened between them. But Nellie did develop a trust, pushed along by desire, and one afternoon she simply held his face in her hands, kissed him tenderly, removed his clothes, and made love to him. At nearly every session after that, they made passionate love and then continued on with the work. Ingram never asked anything of her, never demanded or ordered or insisted. He left it up to her to set the boundaries, and she came to trust him as she had never trusted another man.

Yet that trust had its limits. Nellie had been too betrayed, too mistreated by the world to trust Ingram completely. Though she was falling in love with him, she always held something back. It was imbued deeply inside her, and as a result they never discussed their feelings for one another. Nellie wanted to tell him she trusted him so much it frightened her, that she yearned to be with him constantly and wanted to share her innermost thoughts with him, but she could not say such things, at least not yet, not even to herself. Ingram, for his part, felt just as reticent, but Nellie knew his hesitation was due only in part to protectiveness toward her. He was also driven by his work and was struggling to grasp where his emotions for her fit in with his ambitions. And so he, like her, would enjoy what they had and hope it did not vanish too soon.

"What explains this visit, or are you simply here to frustrate me?" asked Ingram as Nellie managed to pry herself away.

"Sit down and I'll tell you."

She led him over to the couch, clasped his hand, and told him about the events of the day, including the office visit with Barker. Even though she euphemized the most personal details, Ingram's fists tightened at hearing a physician abuse a patient like that, especially Nellie.

"What do you know about Barker?" she asked.

"I think he should be horsewhipped."

"I meant as a doctor."

The New York City medical community was small; fewer than 500 men called themselves physicians. Ingram, she knew, as one who approached medicine as a science and believed strongly in the importance of exchanging information with colleagues, made a point of knowing as many doctors in New York and New Jersey as he could.

"What is it you want to know?" he asked.

"Is he a good doctor?"

"No."

Nellie smiled. She liked Ingram's candor.

"I don't think he knows what he's doing," she said.

"He doesn't."

She didn't bother asking how Barker, a Yale man, managed an appointment at the new Cancer Hospital. That question answered itself. She had more important matters in mind.

"Why would Emma Lazarus see him?" she asked. "She was an intelligent woman. She must have known he was mediocre."

"Most likely she did not want her family to know about her medical matter."

Nellie looked at him with surprise.

"You think she was pregnant?"

"Not necessarily. She could have seen him for other reasons."

"Such as?"

"Are you aware of the Comstock Act?"

"I believe so. It makes pornography a crime."

"Yes. But its definition of 'pornography' includes any

discussion of contraception."

"You mean it makes contraception illegal?"

"It makes even *discussing* contraception illegal."

He did not need to elaborate. More than emancipation of the slaves, more than women getting the vote, contraception—the possibility of sex without risk of pregnancy—was the most threatening prospect in America. Sex without risk would mean the liberation of women and unbounded pleasure, i.e., the end of the American character and the very foundation of the country. Charles Goodyear had patented the first rubber condom in 1844, and by the 1870s, there was such widespread use of intrauterine devices and diaphragms that the number of women dying in childbirth had dropped by 30 percent in twenty-five years. Nevertheless, the prospect of sex without fear of pregnancy—and the emancipation of women—so appalled morals keepers of the time that thirty-four (out of thirty-eight) states passed laws outlawing dissemination or discussion of *any* contraception materials. Nor were these laws merely harmless platitudes. Anthony Comstock, the author of the federal law that bore his name, boasted that he was responsible for four thousand arrests and fifteen suicides.

"Miss Lazarus may have simply wanted someone discreet to protect her from becoming pregnant," said Ingram. "How did she find out about Barker?"

"From a college friend of his. Mr. Charles DeKay."

"The critic at the *Times*?"

"Yes."

"Was she intimate with DeKay?"

"I don't know. Possibly."

"Well, that might explain why she saw Barker."

Of course. Why else would she see an oaf like Barker? "Ingram, you are brilliant."

"No. *You* are brilliant."

"You're right. I am brilliant," she said, making him smile and clasping his hand even tighter. She felt so at ease, even girlish with him. She leaned against him as he put his arm around her.

"But you still have a problem," he said. "The doctors she

saw in England were superb. If they concluded she had cancer, she almost certainly did."

"And her symptoms were all consistent with cancer. Even if her doctor here was a fool."

"Then what is your story for Mr. Pulitzer?"

"I don't know," she said glumly.

She sat there quietly, nestled in his arms, quietly running her fingers over his hand. She remembered something else about her conversation with Barker.

"Would you ever give arsenic to someone in Emma's condition?" she asked him.

"Never."

"Barker did."

"He couldn't have. Arsenic *increases* pain."

"He denied giving it, but I know he was lying."

"Then he is an even worse physician than I thought. If she was in the advanced stages of lymphatic cancer, his sole concern should have been making her comfortable. Once a patient is certain to die, you stop prescribing arsenic. It only accelerates death and makes the last days extremely unpleasant. Even a fool like Barker knows that."

"And yet he ordered it for her." And then it hit her.

"What are the symptoms of arsenic poisoning?" she asked.

"Fatigue. Weight loss. Exhaustion."

"The same as cancer." It was becoming clearer to her.

"To the layperson, yes."

"So it's possible she was dying of cancer but was still poisoned, and the poison is what actually killed her."

"Yes. Of course. Very possible."

She sat upright. "How would I prove it was poisoning?"

"You would compare her blood samples in England with blood samples here just before her death. If the arsenic levels here were as high or higher, she was poisoned."

"Wouldn't the blood samples be destroyed?"

"No, the Cancer Hospital keeps vials for future research. As do the doctors in England. We should be able to obtain samples from both places."

"Ingram, you are fantastic."

She kissed him on the lips and jumped to her feet.

"But even if you can show she was poisoned," said Ingram, "you still don't know who administered it to her. Or why. Barker simply prescribed it."

"I have a good idea where to start."

For the first time since Pulitzer gave her the assignment, she was excited. She might have a story after all. She started to open the door but stopped and looked at him. She felt such love and warmth in her heart for him, and there was love and warmth on his face, but she could not bring herself to tell him she adored him.

"Thank you, Dr. Ingram."

"My pleasure, Miss Bly."

CHAPTER FIVE

CASTLE GARDEN

Nellie was afraid of no man. She had interviewed the most powerful manufacturers in the country and held her ground. Yet she had a knot in her stomach as she approached the desk of Alan Dale.

Just as Nellie was revolutionizing journalism, Alan Dale was revolutionizing criticism. She was a huge fan of his and never missed a column. In the 1860s and 1870s, theater critics had written in a genteel, formal style and decreed the dramatist's paramount responsibility to be the upholding of conventional morality. But beginning in the late 1870s, with the rise of a middle class eager for entertainment and with translations of contemporary European plays, American theater was forced to change.

Repertory companies were replaced by long-running productions, traditional authors were replaced by Strindberg and Ibsen, classical themes gave way to modern ones. Any critic who could help confused readers sift through the maze of theater offerings could sell newspapers all by himself. And no critic's opinions sold more newspapers than Alan Dale's.

He was feared by all of Broadway. The *Dramatic Mirror* said of Dale, "When he takes pen in hand, the playhouses throughout the land tremble upon their foundations and the faces of actors burn white with fear." But no one ever missed a column because Dale's way with words was simply unmatched. He once dismissed a George Bernard Shaw play as "a thick, glutinous, and imponderable four-act tract." Of another playwright he wrote: "Nothing comes through the oleaginous, permeating fog, and there's nothing worth coming through anyway. Better to have presented the fog without either author or character."

A coterie of producers repeatedly tried to have him fired, but Cockerill and Pulitzer knew they had a star on their hands, one that was eclipsing all the competition. And among that competition was Charles DeKay, the arts critic at *The New York Times*.

Nellie had read all she could about Charles DeKay, and by any meaningful measure DeKay and Dale were polar opposites: DeKay was Yale-educated, moved in New York's upper-tier social circles, enjoyed a reputation as a philanderer, and defended literary convention in a condescending, formal style. Dale was educated at public schools in England, Jewish (his real name was Allan Cohen), homosexual (his *A Marriage Below Zero* was one of the earliest novels of homosexual life in Victorian America), and breezily contemptuous of the old literary order. DeKay represented all that Dale loathed, and Dale represented all that DeKay despised. If Nellie wanted a frank assessment of Charles DeKay, Alan Dale was the person to ask.

So, despite the feeling of walking into a shooting range, she made her way through the *World* newsroom, lifting her skirts a few inches above the slimy floor, and approached a foppish man in his early thirties, who was wearing shirtsleeves and glasses, had a deeply receding hairline, and was toiling away at his desk.

"Mr. Dale?"

He looked up and frowned.

"How did you talk your way into the newsroom, madam?"

It irritated her that he had no idea who she was or had no place there. "I work here. My name is Nellie Bly."

"Ah. Well, I can't help you with theater tickets, Miss Bly. Sorry." He returned to his work.

"I don't want theater tickets. I am working on a story, and Mr. Cockerill thought you might be of assistance."

"Cockerill is wrong about most things," he said without looking up. "I'm sure this one is no exception."

Nellie was not surprised. At the *Dispatch*, the arts critics looked down on news reporters—just as news reporters looked down on arts critics.

"May I at least ask?"

"If you must."

Dale continued writing.

"I was instructed by Mr. Pulitzer to investigate the death of Emma Lazarus."

Dale abruptly stopped what he was doing and looked up at her.

"What exactly about her death does he want you to investigate?"

"He is convinced her demise was … not due to her cancer."

Dale measured her closely.

"And what does this have to do with me?"

"Her companion for several years until her death was Charles DeKay. I would like to know more about him."

Dale sighed. He had seen enough. "This story is beyond you, Miss Bly."

"Why do you say that?" she asked, stung.

"Sneaking into the women's asylum and writing about conditions there was quite a feat, and I salute you for it. But this undertaking is attempting to climb Masada, with Romans at the top ready to heave boiling oil down upon you."

"I've encountered goons before, Mr. Dale," Nellie said defiantly.

"But that's all they were: goons. Hired thugs. These are forbidding forces from a half-dozen different directions who allow nothing to stand in their way."

"I think you're exaggerating."

"Am I? Tell me, why did you accept this assignment?"

"Because Mr. Pulitzer asked me," she said.

"That was it? Because Pulitzer asked?"

"Isn't that enough?"

Dale shook his head and went back to his writing.

"So you won't help me?"

"I am a busy man, Miss Bly. I have no interest in wasting my time."

"And why are you convinced it would be such a waste of your time?"

"You lack motivation. You will put in a token effort, encounter resistance, tell Mr. Pulitzer you've done all you can, and hope he will accept your meager offerings so you can get on to a story that you really wish to write."

"Mr. Dale, you have no idea how far I will go for a story."

"That's the point. This is not a regular story. This involves the murder of the finest human being I ever knew. The finest anyone in this city, I daresay, ever knew. If I believed you were intent on getting to the basis of her demise, I would share with you all I know about Charles DeKay or anyone else. Gladly. But I fear it will more likely result in a disappointment for me that I have no wish to bear right now."

She was surprised at the depth of his passion.

"Can you at least tell me why you feel so strongly about Miss Lazarus since this may well mean the end of my story?" she asked.

"I shouldn't have to," he snapped. "You are investigating a possible murder, yet you don't even know the first thing about the extraordinary victim."

"Then educate me, Mr. Dale. Please. Because if I tell Mr.

Pulitzer I was unable to learn anything, the truth about her death may never be known. Is that what you want?"

Dale's eyes bored through her as he measured her fortitude. Perhaps he saw the anger she kept hidden most of the time, or maybe it was the resolve that allowed her to spend ten days in a medieval asylum, or maybe it was simply that Alan Dale was a wounded idealist and wanted to believe in justice even though his mind and experience told him there was no such thing. But he decided to take a chance.

"Come with me." He grabbed his coat.

"Where are we going?"

"Castle Garden."

Castle Garden, in Battery Park, was the main port of entry for all European immigrants to America. Nellie had heard all about Castle Garden as a girl—some of her father's relatives had landed there after the potato famine and land shark laws. Originally erected as Fort Clinton to protect the harbor back in the 1600s, Castle Garden became the arrival point for 250,000 immigrants a year from 1855 on. No federal immigration authority existed—immigration was considered entirely a state matter—and the immigrants who arrived at Castle Garden were free to walk off the boat and into the New World without permission from anyone. Throughout the country's first hundred years, nearly all the immigrants arriving at Castle Garden were Irish, Germans, and Scandinavians from Northern and Western Europe, following people like themselves to America. But in the early 1880s, with the pogroms after the assassination of liberal Tsar Alexander II in Russia, the earthquakes in Italy, and the wars in Poland and Hungary, the demographic profile of immigrants to America shifted to people from Southern and Eastern Europe—Italians, Slavs, Poles, and Jews, people very different in appearance and manner and aspiration from their Western and Northern European predecessors. Since 1880, the number of Italian immigrants to America each year had jumped tenfold, from 40,000 to 400,000. For Jews, the numbers were even more unprecedented: three million Jews lived in Russia and Poland in 1880, and one million of them took flight to the West following Alexander II's death. Though many went to France or England or Germany, hundreds of thousands made their way to America.

This enormous wave of strange people did not sit well with those already living in the United States. A nationwide hysteria arose against all new immigrants, leading to beatings and burnings and the Immigration Act of 1882, which removed all responsibility for immigration from the states and placed it in the hands of the federal government.

During the Congressional debates, Castle Garden was cited as the best example of the need for a federal authority, New York obviously not discerning enough in its choice of newcomers. A new federal immigration facility to impose strict controls upon entry was under construction at Ellis Island, not far from Liberty Enlightening the World.

The new Immigration Act did not go into effect until 1892, however, so the State of New York still oversaw the busiest entry point into America. Nellie had no idea why Dale was taking her there now, nor would he tell her. When they finally arrived, he pointed out a boat moored alongside a steamship, about two hundred yards from shore and just past the giant copper statue of Lady Liberty, bearing the insignia of the newly established Red Cross.

"A doctor from the Quarantine Office has to make sure no one with disease comes ashore," explained Dale.

At the dock, a barge was unloading hundreds of immigrant families. Some had only the clothes on their backs. Many had little children with hollow eyes as big as their faces, looking as if they had never eaten. But all of them, no matter how poor or exhausted, looked elated to be in the New World.

"Once they disembark, however," Dale went on drolly, "they face a different kind of parasite."

A dozen or so street hustlers descended on the immigrants, waving tickets and money like prizes from heaven.

"A few are simply agents of the railroads, the steamship

lines, the boarding houses, the money exchanges—they're looking to fleece the unwary. But others, the more vile ones, work for steel mills and coal mines and sweat shops—they're all looking for cheap labor. The idea is to put the immigrants in debt on the journey there, then make them work for months at slave wages to pay it off."

The men surrounded the immigrants and sweet-talked them in languages Nellie didn't recognize. Some of the immigrants, taken in by the friendliness and excitement of arriving in America, couldn't resist the men's entreaties.

"Emma took them on," Dale continued with deep admiration. "Her first day here, she shouted at two thieves fleecing a family, but they roughed her up and chased her away. The next day she came back with Governor Cleveland himself and shamed him into putting a stop to it immediately. No hustlers were allowed anywhere near Castle Garden, the outside was patrolled by police, and all immigrants were directed inside the building where government workers offered assistance on where to go and how to pay for it. And for those who by nature mistrusted bureaucrats, Emma wrote a Guide for Immigrants, translated into ten different languages."

Nellie watched a burly con man with muttonchops and a plaid suit speaking magnanimously to an immigrant family with a pregnant wife and five small children. He cast a dark look at another hustler trying to horn in on his business.

"Once Cleveland became President," continued Dale, "his attention shifted elsewhere and the vermin returned. Emma fought twice as hard, demanded the authorities maintain their resolve, and when they faltered, went to the press. Most of them ignored her, but Pulitzer published stories on these thieves, naming them and the people behind them. It kept them at bay until Emma became ill. After she died, there was no one to carry on the fight."

Nellie saw the con man offer candy to the immigrant children. Her ire got the better of her, and she strode up the planks.

"Where are you going?" asked Dale.

She approached the family. The agent was holding a ticket, and the father was about to hand him some crumpled money. Nellie could not make out much of the conversation, but she did hear the word *Atlanta*.

"Excuse me," she said to the father. "What is your destination?"

The father looked at her in confusion. He did not understand English.

"Where are you going? What is your destination?" asked Nellie slowly.

"What are you doing, lady?" asked the burly agent, irritated.

"Trying to help them."

"They don't need your help. Leave."

The agent said something to the father in a language she couldn't make out, indicating that Nellie was unstable and shouldn't be listened to. He handed the father the ticket and reached for his money.

"Do any of you speak English?" Nellie pressed the wife and children. They shook their heads.

The agent grabbed her by the arm. "I told you. Move along." He shoved her away.

"No, I won't move along."

She took a step toward the family when the thug smacked her across the temple with the back of his hand and knocked her down.

"Now stay the hell away from here." She lay there, dazed.

"Miss Bly. Are you all right?"

It was Dale, kneeling beside her. Nellie's head throbbed, and she tried to shake away the haze.

"Say something, Miss Bly. Are you all right?"

"I think so," she said uneasily.

Dale glared at the thug.

"You want to be next, sheenie?" said the man. "Come on. Say something. I can knock you right down with her and the two of you can moan together."

Dale held his tongue.

The burly man grunted with contempt, turned back to the

family, and grabbed the father's money. Suddenly he heard an unexpected voice.

"*Wohin gehten Sie?*"

It was Dale. The family perked up and looked at him like a long-lost friend.

"I'm warning you," said the burly man menacingly. "Stay out of this."

"Atlahnta," said the father in a thick accent. "*Wie haben freunde.*"

Dale stood and beckoned for the ticket. The father handed it to him.

"This says Chicago," Dale said to the thug. "They want to go to Atlanta."

"The ticket is to Atlanta, Illinois. It stops in Chicago."

Dale turned to the father.

"*Das ticket ist fur Chicago. Chicago ist der West, zwei thousand miles. Atlanta ist der Sud, zwei thousand miles. Das man ist ein gonef!*"

"*Ich nicht ein gonef—*" said the man, but the father angrily grabbed his money back and spit at the thug's feet.

"Hey. *Gibbe—*" said the thug and reached for the money. But the father began shouting.

"*Gonef! Mumzer!*" Other immigrants came over as if it were a distress call. The father began jabbering at them in Yiddish and pointed at the thug. The men began surrounding him with violence in their hearts. The thug took off as fast as he could, with some of the men in pursuit.

The father turned to Dale.

"*Danke,*" he said with deep gratitude.

"*Bitte. Zie helfen innen.*" He pointed toward the Garden. The pregnant wife helped Nellie to her feet.

"Thank you," said the woman in a thick Russian accent. Nellie smiled at her, still trying to get her bearings.

"Welcome to America," said Nellie.

The father hugged Dale. The mother hugged Nellie. Soon the kids hugged them both.

Dale pointed again toward the Garden.

"*Zie helfen innen.*"

The family nodded and squeezed their hands again and again and finally went inside. Nellie watched them go.

"If the public ever learns you are capable of such kindness, Mr. Dale, they will be very disappointed."

"I beg you not to tell them. Now you see why I took you here."

"So I would understand more of Miss Lazarus." Reading about Emma was one thing, but seeing firsthand what she fought against and what she accomplished was something else altogether.

"I wanted to see if you were capable of such understanding. And you did well." She appreciated the compliment. Those were rarities coming from Alan Dale.

"But I still need to know more of Mr. DeKay."

"And you shall, Miss Bly."

He took out two tickets from his breast pocket.

"He will be at the Metropolitan tonight, for the opening of the new Verdi opera. Judge him for yourself."

He handed her the tickets.

"But aren't you going?"

"I've seen the rehearsals and the performers. I already know what I'll write," he said and summoned a carriage.

CHAPTER SIX

METROPOLITAN OPERA HOUSE

On the carriage ride to Chelsea, Alan Dale described what awaited Nellie that night, both at the opera and with Charles DeKay.

"Five years ago, New York City society underwent a grand metamorphosis. Some considered the shift to be monumental, but others"—indicating himself—"viewed it as simply a new wave of pests infesting the land.

"Ever since the Civil War, Mrs. William Astor—Lina to her friends—ruled New York society like an iron-willed Victoria. With her sycophantic ferret from Savannah, she developed 'Mrs.

Astor's 400,' a list of the families blessed enough to be invited to her annual ball at her mansion at Thirty-Fourth Street and Fifth Avenue. Mrs. Astor and her four hundred had no use for lowlifes such as the Vanderbilts, the Morgans, the Rockefellers, and anyone else who made their fortunes in the messy world of business.

"The industrial millionaires and their wives, as you can imagine, smarted from the rejection. They felt entitled to the respectability that goes along with enormous wealth.

"And while they did build massive mansions that dwarfed the brownstones of the four hundred, Mrs. Astor and her list preserved the one bastion that the nouveau riche craved above all others: the boxes at the Academy of Music Opera House. The Academy hall had eighteen carefully guarded boxes strictly reserved for the city's aristocracy. Only those on the list of four hundred could enter the eighteen Academy boxes or attend the balls afterward.

"The wives of the industrialists refused to stand for this. Mrs. Alva Vanderbilt arranged for seventy shareholders to put up $1.7 million to acquire land and erect a new opera house at Thirty-Ninth and Broadway—mere blocks from Mrs. Astor's home. A glittering new theater—four times the size of the Academy of Music, with 122 boxes and 3,615 seats spread among three tiers—debuted one year later with a performance of *Faust*. All of New York rushed to see the new building and attend the operas, and with unlimited wealth at its disposal, the Metropolitan Opera attracted the finest performers in the world—on an exclusive basis, of course. Within two years, the old Academy of Music was forced to close. It is now a vaudeville house for sailors on shore leave."

Dale chuckled. Americans and their craving of respectability amused him no end.

"This is not to say that the atmosphere at the new opera house is any less stifling. As with the old Academy, the program at the Met is secondary to the company one keeps. And no one at the new opera house is more aware of his company than Charles DeKay."

"But DeKay has all the pedigree he needs. A Yale education, an arts critic for a newspaper, family in the literary world—"

"DeKay was born into an old New York family, yes. But when he was a young boy, his father lost the family fortune on a business venture and then drank himself to death. The mother took the three children to Europe—partly out of shame, partly out of economic necessity. With the help of friends, the family eventually made it back to America, but DeKay never forgot the humiliation of being looked upon with pity."

" 'The help of friends,' " thought Nellie with resentment. The kind of friends who were unavailable to her mother when they were tossed out of their house. Already she had no use for Charles DeKay.

"DeKay has a certain unctuous charm," said Dale, "and through family connections, he was admitted to Yale, where he concentrated on fencing and plagiarizing poetry. After leaving Yale, he was eager to make a mark and submitted a poem to *The Atlantic* that, it turned out, Longfellow had written for *Scribner's* forty years earlier. Because his sister and brother-in-law, Helena and Richard Gilder, were editors at *Harper's*, the matter was quietly dropped, apologies given and accepted. A year later, through Helena's intercession, *The Times* took him on as its arts critic."

"The political desk must have been filled," she said acerbically. Of all the papers Nellie had interviewed for her initial story, the *Times* had been the most adamant about not hiring women.

"It was his treatment of Emma that was truly vile. You see, DeKay stayed inseparably close to her in literary circles, to catch the reflected light of her brilliance, but in social circles he kept his distance because she was a Jew. Within months of Emma's death, DeKay announced an engagement to Lucy Edwaline Coffey, the daughter of a wealthy importer and the granddaughter of Robert E. Lee."

"But Lee was a traitor!" she said. Nellie's father had despised Lee. He would go on and on about it when she was a little girl. "Lee was the superintendent of West Point," her father would say when someone made the mistake of speaking favorably of the Confederate general, "and then he fought *against* the United States. Of the ten battles in the war with the most casualties, Lee led the Confederacy in six of them. *Two hundred thousand soldiers died in those battles*. He should be hung!"

"And when did DeKay meet Miss Coffey?" asked Nellie, sensing the answer.

"Well before Emma became ill. He remained with Emma so as to avoid her wrath and retain whatever access he had to the literary elite. The courtship of Miss Coffey was not made public until after the funeral—about the same time that DeKay suddenly began spending on extravagant items beyond his means."

"What a loathsome human being."

"Now you see why I was reluctant to talk about him," he went on. "If you were halfhearted about reporting the story, I had no interest in helping you."

"But why would Miss Lazarus be involved with such a man?"

"That, I am sorry to say, remains a mystery."

The hansom pulled up to a theater in Madison Square. It was shortly before six.

"Why are we stopping here?"

"You wanted to speak to Mr. DeKay, didn't you? You will be seated two boxes away from him at tonight's opera."

"But that's in just a few hours," she sputtered, glancing at the late afternoon sun.

"Is there a problem?"

"Of course there's a problem. For one thing, I have no escort." Nellie was an independent woman, but no woman went to an opera by herself, especially if she wanted to be inconspicuous.

"I'm sure you can think of someone." He snapped his fingers, and a boy—there were dozens on every Midtown street corner—came hurrying over. Dale took a paper and pen from the boy and offered it to her. Nellie hesitated. She and Ingram kept their relationship private. But she had no idea whom else to ask.

"Miss Bly," Dale said impatiently. "This is no time for propriety—especially one I suspect you don't subscribe to anyhow."

"All right." She took the piece of paper and pen and wrote out a short message, then folded it up and wrote an address on top. Dale handed it to the courier and gave him a coin.

"Be quick about it," he said to the boy. "Wait for a reply and bring it back to us. We'll be in there," he said, indicating the theater across the street.

The boy scampered off. "What else?" asked Dale.

"What do I wear to this opera?"

"My dear. That is why we're here."

He took her inside the Winter Garden Theater, where the crew was preparing for that night's show, a melodrama called *A Moral Crime*. He seemed to know everyone by name, and suddenly Nellie understood why Dale always made a point of mentioning the production side in all his reviews. It gave him unparalleled access to behind-the-scenes scuttlebutt, which his readers craved and which kept him as New York's best-read critic.

Dale walked over to the wardrobe director, a man in his late forties arranging last-minute adjustments to the costumes for the evening. The two greeted one another with a familiarity that Nellie instantly recognized as former lovers. Dale whispered something to the man, who dropped what he was doing and returned a moment later with a resplendent maroon velvet dress with matching arm-length gloves, a low neckline, and a tight bodice. With twenty minutes of tailoring, it fit Nellie perfectly. The director also chose a smashing hat and dazzling jewelry that looked beyond anything Nellie could ever afford. Ten minutes with the makeup and hair stylist, plus the right shoes and wrap, and she was ready for the opera. Dale, who'd tried to remain quiet during the fitting and jewelry selection, finally couldn't help himself and approvingly pronounced her "the envy of Alva Vanderbilt herself."

Nellie did not have time to go home or even eat before the performance; she barely was able to meet Ingram at the entrance as it was. She hurried (as best as one could hurry in a full-length opera gown) through the dozens and dozens of hansoms and formally dressed couples making their way inside. Ingram was waiting for her outside the eight-story opera house wearing a full tuxedo with tails and white tie. His eyes widened when he saw her.

"You are a vision, Miss Bly." She put her arm through his.

"Thank you, Dr. Ingram. And you look so handsome that if I were not working, I would whisk you off to your examining room."

"I have arranged to make it available for later tonight."

She handed him the tickets, and they started inside. At the door, Ingram showed the tickets to an usher in a long tuxedo coat who did not even bother to check the authenticity or the dates. The opera society crowd did not sneak into places.

"Third tier to your right, sir. Your box is fifth in from the stairwell."

"Thank you."

They walked inside, to a lobby with shiny oak floors, massive Oriental rugs forty feet long, and glittering crystal chandeliers that hung from a ceiling four-stories high. But the furnishings were mere backdrop. It was the most expensively tailored crowd Nellie had ever been near. All the men wore tails and white ties; all the women, long gowns and expensive jewels. And every woman over the age of twenty-seven adorned herself with wide diamond chokers to hide the wrinkles.

It was a warm evening. The women were fanning themselves, and the men were sweating profusely through their tuxedos. Nellie looked around in the stifling atmosphere and felt generations of ostracism and ridicule welling through her body. She had been raised to loathe these people. The resentment became so overwhelming that she stopped in her tracks.

"What's wrong?" asked Ingram.

"I don't belong here."

"What are you talking about?" She felt the urge to flee.

"I've never been to an opera before. I have no idea what's going on."

"My dear, don't you understand? No one is here for the opera."

He took her arm and tried to resume walking through the lobby, but she was frozen.

"We should leave."

"Nellie." He looked at her sternly, like a scolding parent. "You have a story to write. Besides, it took me two hours to get dressed."

That was what she needed: a firm hand to remind her of her purpose for being there. She took his arm, and they walked up the blood red carpeted stairs, past French Academy tapestries and royal blue curtains with braided gold tassels. She wanted to be at her seat, away from these people, but the going was slow as the women in their floor-length gowns and full slips could go up only one laborious step at a time. Stumbles were common, not so much from the challenge of making it up the stairs while weighted down with twenty pounds of slips and jewelry, but because everyone kept looking around to see who else was in attendance.

Something else was causing heads to turn.

"Why are they staring at us?" Nellie asked. She was getting uncomfortable again, fighting the lifelong fear that she would be pointed out as an intruder and forcibly removed. She didn't realize how striking she was and that people were trying to place her. Was she visiting royalty? A star of an upcoming performance? The daughter of a railroad tycoon?

"They know you're an impostor."

"Ingram—"

"My dear, you are the most beautiful woman here. The men are desirous and the women envious. If you weren't on my arm, I'd be staring at you, too."

He clasped her hand and resumed walking. She felt better— Ingram had that effect on her. She squeezed his arm in gratitude and kept her hand there. Ingram, as always, did his duty, nodding at the curious onlookers and smiling back inscrutably.

They finally made it to their box and beheld the new Manhattan Opera House. Above the main orchestra floor were five balconies, with boxes on the bottom three tiers. The stage was surrounded by a giant square arch with gold carvings and two statues of sentries on each side. An enormous red curtain with intricate gold embroidery hung over the stage. It was by far the largest and most plush theater Nellie had ever seen, and as she sat back to take it all in, she almost forgot why she was there. She looked over at the *Times* box, which Dale had said was two over from theirs. It was empty and remained so as the lights dimmed.

The opera that evening was Verdi's newest, *Otello*, based on the Shakespeare play. Nellie and Ingram both loved the spectacle and the music, and she had always enjoyed Shakespeare's tale of jealousy and deceit, but she could tell that the audience didn't know what to think. People were looking around for someone to tell them how to respond. But those who attended the opera primarily for social reasons had not arrived yet, and no one else's opinion much mattered. As the first act wore on, and the players poured themselves into their parts with heart and soul, Nellie could feel the audience's anxiety building. She realized for the first time the power of Dale and other critics. Not only did they tell people what to see, they also told them what to think.

The *Times* box remained empty until just before the first act curtain, when an immaculately tailored man in his late thirties, accompanied by an expensively coutured young woman in her early twenties, slipped into their seats. Charles DeKay was more striking than Nellie expected, dashingly handsome with an undeniable charisma that would overpower most women. He made no attempt to hide his tardiness; if anything, his manner suggested irritation that the show had not waited an hour for him to begin.

Nevertheless, as the house lights came up, signaling the end of the act, DeKay stood and applauded thunderously. Those around him, equally shallow though far less charismatic, took their cues and joined in. The standing and applauding spread outward, like a bad concussion.

Finally, after a two-minute ovation, the musicians began to leave the orchestra pit, while DeKay sat down and surveyed the concert hall to arrange his social agenda for the intermission. He glanced casually toward the *World* box, almost as an afterthought, but stopped when he saw Nellie. His eyes locked on hers, and he nodded firmly that he approved and would like to see more. She answered his nod with a smile that thanked him for his compliment and returned the expression of interest even more so. Suddenly the woman with DeKay, her fan flapping like a hummingbird, tapped him gently on the arm, signaling that she wanted some air. He helped her to her feet, glanced once more at Nellie, motioned his head ever so slightly toward the corridor, and escorted her out.

"Shall we?" said Nellie to Ingram.

"We mustn't keep the man waiting." He offered his arm, and they walked out the narrow entrance together to the crowded hallway. It was filled with people trying to see, or be seen by, those around them. Some of the staring was directed at Nellie and Ingram, a smashing couple with a prized box, but Nellie barely noticed. Her interest was in DeKay. She saw him making light conversation with some important-looking patrons, but when he spotted her, he preened, excused himself, took his companion by the elbow, and glided over for his conquest.

"Don't tell me Alan Dale is no longer with the *World*," he said to Ingram.

"No, Mr. Dale is ill, I'm afraid," said Ingram.

"I'm sorry to hear that. Are you reviewing the performance for him?"

"No," spoke up Nellie. "I am."

That surprised and pleased DeKay, giving him the opportunity to converse with her directly.

"Well, then. Welcome to a fellow critic. I am Charles DeKay from the *Times*. And may I present my fiancée, Lucy Coffey."

"It is very gracious of you to come over," she said. "My name is Nellie Bly. And this is my escort, Dr. Ingram."

The two men shook hands, though neither could hide his distaste for the other.

"I admired your pieces on the Bellevue asylum, Miss Bly," allowed DeKay. "Very bold. Congratulations." Flattery came easily to him. He used it to disarm and to dominate. But when it came to dealing with detestable men, Nellie was in her element.

"Thank you. A most valued compliment."

"You saw the articles, didn't you, darling?" DeKay commented to his fiancée.

"I'm sorry, I don't believe I did," said Lucy in a vaguely Southern accent. Lucy was a poor liar, and it was clear she had read the articles closely and even talked about them but was not about to offer praise to a woman as attractive as Nellie. "But I'm sure they were most engaging."

"I hope Mr. Dale's illness is not serious," said DeKay.

"It is not. He should be fine for his next review."

"Ah. The actors in New York will be disappointed with his speedy recovery."

"As well as the other critics."

"Oh, there is no competition between us, Miss Bly. Mr. Dale and I address our reviews to different readers. I write for those steeped in the arts. Mr. Dale writes more for those touring the arts."

Lucy chuckled at DeKay's show of wit.

"But some of the finest minds in New York are among Mr. Dale's readers," said Nellie. "I'm told that Emma Lazarus read Mr. Dale's articles religiously."

His eyes didn't even flicker at the mention of Emma's name. He was a cool one, thought Nellie.

"I wouldn't know," he said.

"Oh?" said Nellie. "I was given to understand otherwise."

Suddenly it dawned on him that Nellie was there as a reporter, not a critic. The walls shot up, though DeKay was too smooth and intent on impressing to retreat behind them completely.

"And what is your newest assignment for the *World*, Miss Bly?" asked DeKay, deftly changing the subject.

"The death of Miss Lazarus."

"But she died six months ago," he said evenly. "And of a difficult cancer. I'm not sure what story there is to tell. Unless Mr. Pulitzer is simply looking to keep you busy."

"No, Mr. Pulitzer is convinced the true facts of her death,

once uncovered, will make compelling reading. He wants me to devote all of my energies to the task. In fact, I was wondering if I might speak with you at greater length, since you knew Miss Lazarus well."

"Not that well." He stole an involuntary look at his fiancée. "We shared interests in poetry for a time but then drifted apart."

"Still, may I call on you at the *Times*, tomorrow perhaps? Around eleven midday?"

"Certainly," he said tentatively.

"Thank you—"

"Charles! There you are."

To Nellie's dismay, none other than Nathaniel Barker, the doctor she had seen with her mother a few days before, walked up to them in a formal tux.

"I've been looking for you. Agnes and I are entertaining at Delmonico's later tonight. You and Lucy simply have to attend—"

He glanced at the lovely woman with DeKay and recognized her immediately.

"Miss Cochran!" he said with surprise.

"Hello, doctor."

"You two know one another?" asked DeKay.

"Miss Cochran came to see me with her mother only two days ago. What an interesting coincidence."

"Yes," said DeKay. "It is. Do you know Miss Cochran's companion, Dr. Ingram?"

Barker, well acquainted with Ingram's low opinion of him, regarded him with hostility.

"Only by reputation." He turned to Nellie. "How is your mother feeling?"

"Much better, thank you."

"Barker, 'Miss Cochran' is Nellie Bly. The reporter who wrote the story on the women's prison at Bellevue."

Barker's attitude suddenly darkened.

"You said your name was Cochran," he snapped angrily.

"Cochran is my real name. Bly is my professional name."

"You should have told me."

"Or perhaps," blurted out Ingram, "*you* should have told *her* that your breast examination was completely beyond medical propriety. You should be thrashed."

The atmosphere had become tense. Both doctors' fists clenched.

"Perhaps we should return to our seats now," interposed DeKay.

"I agree," said Nellie. "I will see you tomorrow?"

"If you wish."

"Good evening, then."

She turned to go, but DeKay squeezed her arm and dropped his voice.

"Miss Bly. Or Miss Cochran. Whatever you want to call yourself. Be advised, you are treading on dangerous ground."

"But you said there is no story here."

Not amused by her challenge, his voice took on an even more ominous tone. "Just be careful. I will not warn you again."

Without another word, DeKay and his companions walked away.

"I am sorry I spoke out of turn," Ingram said to Nellie. "Forgive me."

"You did nothing wrong. But now that Barker knows who I am, I have lost the element of surprise."

"Not entirely. They don't know what you know and what you do not know."

"Nevertheless, I wish he had not seen us."

They returned to their seats. The lights dimmed. As the orchestra began the introduction for the second act, Nellie watched DeKay return to his box with Miss Coffey. As they sat down, he nodded curtly to Nellie, a small smile playing on his lips.

"He's a smug one, isn't he?" she whispered to Ingram.

"He certainly is."

But something didn't make sense.

"He should be worried," she said. "Yet he acts as if he hasn't a care in the world."

"The pomposity of the—"

They both realized it at the same time.

"We need to leave," she said.

"Immediately," he said. They got up from their seats and hurried out to the narrow hallway.

But they feared it was too late.

CHAPTER SEVEN

EMMA LAZARUS

There were no hansoms outside the Opera House. A half hour earlier, at intermission, there had been dozens. An hour later, after the final curtain, there would be more than a hundred. But with the start of the second act, the hansoms had driven off to trawl the streets for fares until the opera let out. Nellie and Ingram had to wait for ten maddening minutes until they could flag a carriage to take them to the Cancer Hospital.

Every passing minute, they knew, lessened their chances of stopping Barker.

The driver they finally hailed raced like the wind over the cobblestone streets and around dimly lit corners, and Ingram knew exactly where to direct him, but the sight of another hansom waiting outside the hospital's night entrance told them it was futile. Still they rushed inside, Ingram showed his credentials to the guard, and they hurried downstairs to the basement. Barker was just emerging from the double doors as they approached.

"Why, Doctor Ingram," he said, feigning pleasant surprise. "Miss Cochran. What are you two doing here?"

"Trying to preserve evidence before you destroy it," said Nellie, barely able to contain her rage.

"I have no idea what you're talking about—" They started past him through the double doors. "You can't go in there—" he said.

But they ignored him and went inside, to a room unlike anything Nellie had ever seen. It was a laboratory of a dozen marble counters, with Bunsen burners, thick blown glass beakers and flasks, electric lights, and copper piping. Ingram raced past the burners and flasks to the refrigeration area and pulled open the door. Hundreds of flasks of blood with white labels sat on shelves inside the refrigerator.

"How are they arranged?" he demanded of Barker. "By date or last name?"

"Both," said Barker, only too glad to cooperate. "First by date, then by patient."

"What was Miss Lazarus's date of death?" Ingram pressed.

"I'm sorry, doctor. I don't recall."

"November 19, 1887," chimed in Nellie.

Ingram found the right place on the shelves, then began working backward. He wasn't finding what he was looking for.

"When did she return from England?"

"In March of '87," she said.

Ingram went to that marked area but couldn't find anything. Once again he turned to Barker.

"Where are they?"

"Where is what?"

Ingram, fists clenching, looked around and spotted a large metal bin. He strode over and looked inside. Several broken flasks with blood lay on the bottom.

"What are these?" Barker looked in the bin.

"Those? We dispose of blood all the time, to make room for analysis of our newer patients."

"Were these samples from Miss Lazarus?"

"I have no idea," he replied innocently.

Ingram was livid.

"How could you do such a thing—?"

"I'm not sure I see the problem."

"I think you see it perfectly well."

"So now we will never be able to prove how Miss Lazarus died?" Nellie asked Ingram.

He shook his head. She turned to Barker in a fury. "I will

make sure the world knows you did this."

"Did what?"

At that point, the security guard came down the stairs. "Everything all right, doctor?"

"I think so, Hudson. Thank you." Barker turned to Nellie and Ingram. "Can I take you anywhere? I'm sure there is room in my hansom, and you may have trouble finding one at this time of night."

They were seething with frustration, but there was nothing to be done. "The Columbia faculty was right to reject you," said Ingram.

"I don't care about them. Look around you. Why would I need a faculty?"

"I will make sure the truth is known within the entire medical community. No self-respecting physician will ever refer a patient to you again."

"That's all right. I'll get plenty from the rest. Hudson, please see them out. I think I'll straighten up here."

"Certainly, doctor."

They had no choice and followed the security guard out. Their driver had waited, at Ingram's instruction. That was about the only thing that went right that evening, rued Nellie.

"Is there no other way to prove she was poisoned?" she asked.

"Not scientifically."

Ingram could see the wind go out of her.

"What about a witness?" he asked, trying to boost her spirits. "Or a letter?"

"No one has come forward as of now. I'm afraid someone suddenly appearing a year later would seem highly suspicious."

They rode on in silence. Nellie was now convinced that cancer had not killed Emma; Barker's hurried trip to the hospital during the opera was proof of that.

"Maybe if we stop thinking like scientists," said Ingram, "there is a way."

"I don't follow."

"Well, as a scientist, I deal in verifiable fact. But not everyone is so demanding before reaching a conclusion."

"Such as?"

"Such as readers and writers of newspapers. They embrace positions with the greatest of fervor when often there is no basis in logic for doing so."

"I suppose I should be insulted, but let me understand your point. You are saying if I wrote an article that was speculative but compelling, people would be as persuaded as if I had written one filled with facts?"

"Many people, yes. Most, in fact. And public opinion can be every bit as powerful as scientific opinion."

"I can't resort to innuendo, Ingram. I'm a reporter."

"Your readers trust you. If you are convinced there was foul play, they will give you the benefit of any doubt. And some of them may even come forward with supporting evidence."

She knew he was right. Readers didn't mind if you took liberties as long as you strove for the truth and treated them with respect. When she wrote about the working conditions in factories, she didn't have every fact right. But the picture she painted was accurate, and that was all people cared about. No one quibbled with details. And once the articles hit the streets, the paper was flooded with corroborating letters of mistreatment.

The purpose, as Ingram was saying, was to get to the truth. She knew how to write a story that would stir people. After tonight, she certainly had the raw material to work with. She was ready to write. She would have a story for Cockerill in the morning.

CHAPTER EIGHT

COL. JOHN A. COCKERILL.
MANAGING EDITOR "NEW YORK WORLD."

It took less than two hours to write it.

WAS EMMA LAZARUS MURDERED?

Poet May Have Died from Unnatural Causes

Emma Lazarus, the celebrated poet who passed away tragically at the age of 38 on November 19, 1887, may have died from other than natural causes.

Her doctor at the time of her demise, Nathaniel Barker, signed a death certificate stating the cause of death as cancer. Within the past several weeks, however, rumors have begun to circulate that Miss Lazarus may in fact have been poisoned with arsenic, and her cancer not as advanced as previously thought.

Upon her return from England in March 1887, Miss Lazarus was placed under the care of Dr. Barker at the New York Cancer Hospital. Dr. Barker, according to several sources, treated Miss Lazarus with arsenic, which he called a "wonder drug" that is "used extensively around the world" for the treatment of that disease. However, medical experts contacted by the World questioned the efficacy of arsenic when a patient suffers from advanced cancer and almost universally agreed that arsenic in an acute cancer patient can only accelerate death.

Attempts by the World to assess the amount of arsenic in Miss Lazarus's blood were to no avail. Normal protocol at the Cancer Hospital is to preserve blood of cancer patients for several years after death. When asked for samples of Miss Lazarus's blood, however, Dr. Barker said that all flasks containing her blood had been destroyed. Pressed for an explanation as to why hospital procedures were not followed, Dr. Barker offered none.

Dr. Barker's role as physician to Miss Lazarus has also raised serious questions. Dr. Barker acknowledged that he was not Miss Lazarus's normal physician but only became so at the behest of Mr. Charles DeKay, the arts critic for the Times, a close friend of both Miss Lazarus and Dr. Barker.

Although we may never learn the actual circumstances surrounding the death of Miss Lazarus, the World will continue to pursue all avenues regarding the demise of one of America's finest poets. Anyone with information on the matter should contact the editors at the World. Anonymity will be protected.

Nellie left Ingram's house just before dawn. He was in a deep sleep, and she almost crept away without saying good-bye but then caught herself. The story was his idea, after all, and she owed him a kiss of gratitude if nothing else. Once again she had to remind herself that Ingram was not like other men, who always kept an accounting. She kissed him, whispered thank you, and slipped out.

She took the Elevated up Ninth Avenue to Harlem. Very few women were on the train, none by themselves, and none in a formal opera dress, but she managed to make it home after contending with only some odd stares and nothing more. She changed clothes, awakened her mother, made breakfast for them both, then rode the Elevated and horsecar (a fifteen-foot carriage pulled by two horses along a rail embedded in the street) back to the office. Between writing the story, the robust lovemaking—she and Ingram were unable to contain themselves the moment they walked through his door—and the train ride back, she'd had very little sleep, but she was exhilarated. Barker and DeKay had thought they were free of worry. It would be a treat to watch them squirm.

She was already waiting for Cockerill when he arrived at his desk.

"Good morning," she announced as she handed him the piece.

"What's this?" he asked.

"The first Emma Lazarus story."

He was impressed. "I didn't expect something so soon." He sat down and started reading.

"Shall I come back?"

"No, no. Stay here."

She resumed her seat. Nellie wasn't used to an editor reading her copy while she waited. Most editors preferred time to gather their thoughts, but Cockerill was not one to dawdle. He sat at his desk, engrossed, nodding and even grunting now and then with approval. Finally he looked up.

"Well-written, Miss Bly. It makes the reader sit up and take notice."

"Thank you."

"I only wish we could print it."

Her heart sank. "What do you mean?"

"There are laws in this country against destroying a man's reputation."

She knew, of course, that a man's most valuable commodity was his reputation, and in a land based on opportunity and second chances, an attack on a man's reputation was an attack on America itself. It was only in the past thirty years that truth had become a valid defense in criminal defamation cases—you could no longer be thrown in jail for telling the truth. But protecting a man's reputation ought only go so far.

"There are also laws against men committing murder," she snapped.

"You don't know they committed murder. All you know is that a doctor at a hospital—one of New York's finest hospitals—threw away the blood of a patient seven months after she died."

"After hurriedly departing in the middle of a concert."

"Suspicious, I grant you. But we can't publish a story about a respectable doctor and a writer from a rival paper based on suspicion alone. Within twenty-four hours we would have a nasty lawsuit on our hands."

Nellie expected more from the editor of New York's most aggressive paper, especially since the assignment had come from Pulitzer himself. Suddenly it dawned on her that Cockerill might be considering factors other than a lawsuit.

"You're trying to protect them, aren't you?" she asked.

"Who? Barker and DeKay? I've never even met them."

"But you sympathize with them. You don't like putting them in a bad light," she continued with increasing vehemence.

"You have quite a tongue on you, Miss Bly."

"That's it, isn't it? You're protecting your own—"

"I am protecting no one other than this newspaper," he shot back with indignation.

"Then why refuse to publish this story? I have only so many means at my disposal to learn what happened to Miss Lazarus. I need to apply pressure to those who might be responsible and to draw out those who might know more about it. This story would accomplish both—yet you won't allow it. I don't see how I can meet Mr. Pulitzer's request if you won't publish this story."

"Well, you'll just have to find a way," he retorted.

And at that, he moved on to other work at his desk. For a moment she thought of going straight to Pulitzer and laying out the situation, but Cockerill would never forgive her, and as much as Pulitzer wanted to find out what had happened to Emma, he would never choose her over Cockerill, at least not until she had a much stronger case.

"Anything else, Miss Bly?" he asked, looking up from his work impatiently.

"No."

"Then that will be all."

There was no getting Cockerill to change his mind; that was clear. But Nellie was nothing if not resourceful, and by the time she returned to her desk, she had come up with another way to turn the screws, one that didn't require Cockerill's approval.

She proceeded to the *New York Times* offices for her meeting with DeKay.

At first she'd thought it would be pointless, certain that DeKay would not honor the appointment. Most people suspected of murder would keep their distance from a newspaper reporter. But she felt that DeKay, arrogant and confident that Nellie could never connect him to Emma's death, would savor engaging a celebrated investigative writer. And so Nellie kept their date, convinced something would come of it.

The New York Times was only thirty years old and very much a Republican paper. To establish itself among its older competitors, its owners had constructed the tallest and most garish building on Newspaper Row, an eight-story red building with twisted iron trim. Nellie shuddered as she approached the building—the *Times* had led the campaign against voting rights for Irish immigrants, famously proclaiming, "Only taxpayers should be able to vote." She was admitted immediately—a far cry from her treatment only months before—and shown into the plush downstairs sitting room, portraits of sober male editors and investors looking down at her from the dark wooden walls. DeKay was comfortably settled into a winged green leather chair, scanning his own review of *Otello* while an attentive steward poured him coffee.

"Good morning, Miss Bly," he said with a brilliant smile, rising to greet her.

"Good morning, Mr. DeKay," she returned with great poise.

"Please." He directed her to a matching winged chair and waited as she sat, ever the solicitous gentleman. As he relaxed back into his own chair, she observed that he had no fear of her whatsoever. Nor was he interested in lording the events of last night over her. He was here to charm her out of any mischief she might be up to and seduce her in the process if he could.

"I am so glad you kept our appointment," he said intently, his blue eyes focused keenly on her. "Barker told me you were upset when you left the hospital last night."

"I was. Very much so."

"I'm so sorry." He reached for her hand to console her. She let him take it.

"In fact," she allowed, "I was so upset that I wrote a story for today's edition."

"Oh?"

She took the story from her large purse and handed it to him.

"Mr. Pulitzer wanted to give you the opportunity to respond, to make the story as fair as possible."

A shadow flickered across his face, as she intended. As a member of New York's newspaper community, DeKay might trust Cockerill, the *World*'s editor, to protect him, but he could expect no such treatment from the immigrant half-Jew Pulitzer.

"My instructions," Nellie said with infinite politeness, "are to wait while you read it and write down whatever you say."

DeKay squirmed. He hadn't expected Nellie to write a story, and he certainly hadn't expected Cockerill to be powerless to stop it.

"May I?" he asked, reaching for the manuscript while trying to maintain his composure.

"Certainly."

He read it through without further conversation. She watched as his face soured and the arrogance disappeared. She had to move deftly now. A desperate DeKay might press Cockerill to get the story killed, and she needed to head off that possibility.

"I am to take down your reaction verbatim," she reminded him. "That was Mr. Pulitzer's directive." Nellie hoped that, in his panic, DeKay would let slip information she could use for the story. At some point, Cockerill *had* to publish it; he was still a newspaperman, after all, and loyalty to class went only so far. The stronger her case, the less choice he would have.

DeKay was unnerved. No longer a predator planning to beguile her, he was suddenly at her mercy.

"Well?" she asked.

"You cannot publish this."

"Why not? It's true, isn't it?"

"You make it sound like there was some type of conspiracy to kill Emma. Nothing could be further from the truth."

"Then what is the truth?"

He bit his lower lip and shook his head. "I cannot tell you."

"Then I will simply tell Mr. Pulitzer you refused all comment. Our printers will be grateful. They are already setting type for the story."

She gathered her things.

"Please," he said. "I implore you not to publish it."

"I'm sorry."

She put the papers back in her bag and stood up. DeKay's fists clenched. He wanted to stop her. She saw the look in his eye and suddenly became wary. Quickly she moved toward the door, but he blocked her way.

"Please, sir. Do not make matters worse for yourself."

"I will tell you the truth if you promise not to publish the story."

"I will make no such promise."

"You must!"

He grabbed her arm, but she pushed him aside and reached for the door, wanting distance from his desperation.

"We gave Emma the arsenic at her own insistence!"

Nellie stopped. "She *asked* you for it?"

"Yes."

"Did she know it was killing her?"

"Yes. That was the point."

She hadn't expected this. She looked closely at DeKay. His charm had evaporated, and in its place was a man revealing a most private secret.

"Emma knew she had the cancer," he said. "But a dark cloud had descended over her even before she went to England. It was something she lived with all her life. In fact, that is why she went abroad so often, to try and escape her mood. When the doctors in England diagnosed the cancer and prescribed arsenic, she saw an opportunity for the darkness to finally end. But as she became increasingly ill, the English doctors refused to continue the prescription, and the darkness returned."

"And that is where Barker came in."

"Yes. She begged me to find a doctor in New York who would obtain it for her. Her own doctor never would. Barker was an old friend, and I introduced her. She told him that if he did not give it to her, she would simply find someone else. Barker was convinced he could treat her with less pain than anyone else, and so he took her on."

Nellie, nonplussed, had never conceived of this. It made no sense. "Why keep it such a secret after her death?"

"Emma was revered, for both her poetry and her charity work. If people learned of a suicide, they would think less of her, and she worried their foolish biases would eclipse her accomplishments and causes."

Nellie was flabbergasted. How could she have been so wrong about DeKay? She studied his face for signs of lying or manipulation.

"A melancholia I understand," she said. "But suicide …?"

"You don't know how she suffered. You never saw such dark moods. Her friends would try to get her out of them, but they would last for months at a time. She fought them as long as she could, but the prospect of battling both her moods and a cancer was too much for her."

"That is why you had Barker destroy the bottles of blood."

"I wanted to protect him, but I wanted to protect Emma even more. I don't want this to be her legacy. This is not how the world should remember her … You won't write about this, will you, Miss Bly?" He spoke earnestly, without any flirtation or vanity.

"I don't know."

"Please. I beg you."

She was still a reporter, though she had surely come to admire Emma. "Who else knows about this? Who can verify it?"

"No one else knows she took her own life. It was a secret among the three of us. But ask her friends about her moods. Ask her family. Ask her editors. You'll see I'm telling the truth." He gazed at her directly, beseechingly. "You cannot publish this story."

CHAPTER NINE

JEWISH CEMETERY

At the *Dispatch*, Nellie had covered several suicides of both men and women.

Even though more men committed suicide in the nineteenth century than women—four times as many—the act itself was always associated with women. Suicide was seen as a weakness, a feminine malady. Women were even condemned for the *way* they killed themselves—usually by poison rather than something more assertive, such as a knife or a gun. Her editor had little interest in considering what might drive a woman to take her own life. Suicide was simply confirmation that women were the weaker sex.

And so, given the common thinking of the day, DeKay's narrative rang true, and it saddened her. In her struggle to enter a man's world, Nellie had begun to see Emma as a model, a hero. The literary accomplishments, the work with immigrants, the battles against the powerful and the corrupt against staggering odds ... if Emma could accomplish so much, then maybe Nellie could as well. That was the hope, the inspiration. But apparently it had proven too much for Emma. She had given up and practically welcomed the cancer because the arsenic provided her a way out.

Suddenly Nellie's aspirations seemed futile. With sentries manning the doors at every turn, from thick-headed Flaherty to wily Cockerill, the image of Emma had fortified her in taking them on. Now, no matter how ambitious and combative she was, it all seemed too daunting.

She would have to tell Pulitzer. She would do more investigating, of course, and not merely take DeKay's word for it, but she would just be going through the motions. Pulitzer would be furious and confuse the messenger with the message and want nothing more to do with her. It wasn't fair; she was just telling him the truth, but it would be human nature for him to hold it against her.

She tried to think of a way out. DeKay and Barker would have a convincing response to anything she managed to get printed. They would say it was a suicide, that Emma had taken her own life because she was overwhelmed with the cancer "and other problems"—code for female frailty—and people would doubtless believe them. DeKay would almost certainly use the *Times* to tell his story, after which Emma Lazarus would be totally discredited. Pulitzer would be even angrier, and Nellie would be relieved of her duties. If journalism were a true profession, she could simply write the truth as she saw it and let the chips fall where they may, but it didn't work that way. Newspapers wrote to their audience, gave them what they wanted to read. As a reporter, you delivered to that audience what the publisher wanted delivered, and Pulitzer had no interest in delivering up Emma Lazarus as a suicide.

Nellie left the *Times* building feeling sick and shattered. Worse yet, the fears she tried to keep at bay—that she was destined to wind up back in Pittsburg writing gardening and fashion stories the rest of her life—came roaring back.

Why did people kill themselves? Maybe that could be the story. To most people, suicide was simply the sign of a troubled soul, but there had to be more. She thought of going to see Ingram. He understood these things as well as anyone she knew. But she shied away, afraid of what he might say about women as a weaker sex and self-conscious of seeming helpless in his eyes.

Suddenly she had a thought, a wild, bizarre thought. Impulsively she went back inside, to the *Times* sitting room. DeKay had left. The steward was cleaning off the table.

"Excuse me," she said. "I need to go to Queens."

"What part, miss?"

"Cypress Hills. The Shearith Israel cemetery."

"The Number 14. Right outside."

"Thank you."

It was an hour train and ferry ride to the cemetery, even though Emma had lived a short walk from Newspaper Row. Burials in Manhattan had been outlawed for forty years; people who had never set foot in Queens or Brooklyn in life now resided there for all eternity in death. Going to the cemetery was a totally irrational act; she knew that as she boarded the train. She should be looking for proof that the death had not been a suicide, not wasting time visiting the gravesite. But maybe staring at Emma's tombstone would give her an idea or possibly a deeper understanding of the woman. She didn't exactly expect Emma to make a suggestion from the grave, but she was just desperate enough to be open to that possibility.

The ride only made her more fretful, she realized, as she finally stepped off the horsecar in a remote part of Queens. It was a small cemetery, no more than 120 plots. Despite the warm June weather, the ground was still a foot deep in snow, seven weeks after the Great Blizzard. A caretaker directed her to the tombstone, which was simple enough: granite, two feet high, inscribed with "In Memory of Emma Lazarus, Daughter of Moses and Esther Lazarus, Born July 22, 1849 – Died November 19, 1887." No religious markings, no reference to her as poet or champion of the poor. Nearby were the gravestones of Emma's mother and father, equally simple. Nellie thought of her own father's gravesite by the mill he had started in Apollo. She had no desire to be buried beside her half-brothers and sisters, who had made life so difficult for her and her mother. Her fantasy was to make enough money to buy the mill outright and keep the rest of the family away from her father. Only she, her mother, and her full siblings would be buried alongside him.

She stared at Emma's grave. "What happened to you, Emma?" she mused. "You didn't kill yourself. I know you didn't. Tell me what happened."

She felt someone watching her. She looked around and saw a man standing by a hansom, staring at her. A big, rough-looking man, he wore clothes several sizes too small for him, which made him look all the larger, and he made no effort to avert his eyes. He was intimidating, especially in this remote cemetery, yet he took no step toward her.

"No need to be afraid, miss."

"What do you want?" she asked. He stood between her and the only way out.

"I'm supposed to take you back to Manhattan when you're finished."

"Who sent you?"

"That you'll find out in due time, miss. I'll just wait here until you're done."

"Suppose I don't want to go with you."

"Then my employer would be upset, with both of us." He climbed up the hansom to the driver's seat. "You take your time, miss."

Nellie turned back to the grave and addressed the headstone.

"Emma," she entreated in a low voice, "what are you doing? What is happening?"

No answer. Nellie just shook her head and headed over to the hansom.

The driver took her to the northwest corner of Eighth Avenue and Twenty-Third Street and into the largest theater in New York, Pike's Opera House, a former burlesque venue made over into the offices of the most feared man in the history of Wall Street.

If Emma Lazarus represented all that was good in the human condition, Jay Gould represented all that was bad. The press dubbed him Mephistopheles only because they couldn't think of anything worse. At a time when the only punishable crime on Wall Street was outright fraud—and some would question if even that were the case—Gould made a fortune in stocks using insider information and spreading disinformation to buy low and sell high. At one point, he owned both of the largest transportation and communication companies in the country. But it was his methods more than his power that made him so despised. In 1868, at the age of twenty-eight, he had brought the great Cornelius Vanderbilt to his knees by bribing state court judges into awarding Gould the Erie Railroad, the main route from the Great Lakes to New York City. In 1872, he and his partner James Fisk set off a national panic and five-year depression when they cornered the gold market in the United States after bribing the brother-in-law of President Grant to keep the government's gold off the market. When the price of gold had tripled from its original level and Grant finally ordered the release of the government's gold, the brother-in-law tipped off Gould ahead of time, allowing him to sell at the peak while most of Wall Street's other investors, who had bought in as the price rose, were ruined. If Gould had cornered the gold market simply to become rich, that would have been venal enough, but later testimony before a congressional committee revealed his true intentions: with the price of gold rising and the dollar dropping, Midwestern farmers would want to ship more of their crops to foreign markets, and Gould, who had a virtual monopoly on the nation's railroads, would jack up freight rates and amass even more wealth.

While working at the *Dispatch*, Nellie had met Andrew Carnegie and Henry Clay Frick, phenomenally wealthy men in their own right, but they were manufacturing geniuses. They made things and managed people. Gould, though, was a financial genius. He bought and sold companies and bought and sold stock, with no interest in managing anyone. If one of his companies performed poorly, he was indifferent since it was usually a monopoly and he could already get top dollar for it.

Although the building at Eighth and Twenty-Third was garish enough, Gould's offices were modest, almost stately, and bore none of the trappings Nellie associated with robber barons. Nellie noted just two armed guards and a male secretary outside the door to the inner office. When the hansom driver escorted her in, the secretary at the desk merely nodded, rose, and glided into the interior office. A moment later, Jay Gould himself emerged to greet her.

"Miss Bly. Thank you for coming. My name is Jay Gould."

He was a small man in his early fifties, no more than five foot four inches tall. He had tiny, delicate hands; a full, black beard flecked with gray; a low forehead; and piercing, almost fanatical eyes. There was no glad-handing or charming banter. Jay Gould did not mince words.

"I trust my driver conducted himself properly," he said, directing her inside to a chair and sitting down behind the desk. Nellie felt the almost hypnotic power of his eyes and his mind. She barely even took in the office.

"He startled me and has taken me out of my way, but no, he did not mistreat me."

"I apologize for the inconvenience. He will, of course, take you home. Or to Dr. Ingram's. Whichever you prefer."

Nellie managed to cover her surprise at the pointed reference. "Why am I here, Mr. Gould?" she asked with irritation.

"I had hoped to delay our initial meeting, but your conversation with Mr. DeKay this morning forced my hand. I thought we should speak before you did anything rash."

How could he have known about her meeting with DeKay? She hadn't told anyone. Gould, a self-made man, would have no use for a weasel like DeKay, and no one else knew about it. Then she remembered the steward who had poured coffee in the sitting room. He had lingered in the back of the room, straightening up and tending to some editors in another corner. She had asked him which train would take her to the Cypress Hills Cemetery in Queens, and he directed her to the #14. The waiter must have passed along this information to Gould, who then would have dispatched one of his men to the cemetery. She nearly shook her head in admiration. That Gould would have an employee at *The New York Times* on his payroll impressed her, but only for a moment.

Given his reputation, she told herself, she should not have been the least bit surprised. "What was it about our conversation that forced your hand?" she asked.

"You are about to be the victim of a monstrous fraud, Miss Bly. Emma Lazarus would never have taken her own life."

MARSHALL GOLDBERG

For a man who had made an enormous fortune being coldly rational, Gould made his pronouncement with surprising passion.

"I didn't realize you were acquainted with Miss Lazarus."

"Few people did. We preferred it that way."

She studied him closely.

"There was nothing untoward about it, Miss Bly," he said. "I admired Miss Lazarus for several years. It was a pleasure to make her acquaintance."

Gould did not seem the kind of man to whom admiration came easily. "How exactly did you meet?"

"I take my daily constitutional every morning at five. It allows me to think in peace, without investors or lawyers pestering me. I began to notice a woman who also took walks in the neighborhood at the same hour. We would nod hello. One morning, I happened to see her emerge from a house three blocks from mine. I knew who lived there—I was aware of her father through common business associates—and when I realized who she was, I introduced myself."

"The two of you became walking companions?"

"You might say that."

A flash of almost boyish embarrassment crossed Gould's face. He was at heart a shy man, and he knew how preposterous it sounded that he and Emma Lazarus—poet, humanitarian, patrician—would be friendly.

"What was it you had admired about her, Mr. Gould? You don't strike me as a poetry reader."

"No, I don't have the patience for poetry. My wife is the poetry reader. I admired what Miss Lazarus did after the Union Hotel incident."

"I'm not familiar with that."

He looked at her with surprise and disapproval.

"How can you investigate her death if you know nothing about her?"

"I'm still learning, Mr. Gould. And if you can help in that regard, I would urge you to do so."

He stared out the window, recounting his thoughts. "There

was a banker named Joseph Seligman," he said, "a German immigrant and a Jew, who had provided valuable service to this country during the war. At President Lincoln's behest, he sold millions of dollars in government bonds to Europeans to finance the Union cause. Without him, the President could not have carried on the war, and the country would have dissolved. The President was so grateful that he awarded Seligman a Medal of Merit. Three years later, President Grant asked him to become Secretary of the Treasury, an honor Seligman graciously refused because of family obligations. Grant then received word that Mr. A.T. Stewart sought the position. Have you heard of *him* at least?"

A.T. Stewart was a household name. He had founded the first department store in America and gone on to be the largest dry goods retailer in the country. His stores became so successful that during the 1870s he was the richest man in America, richer even than Jay Gould.

"Of course."

"Grant was wise enough to seek Seligman's counsel on the matter. Seligman recommended against the appointment. He believed the nation's leading banker required more knowledge than how to sell clothes."

Nellie had to smile. Gould's tongue could cut like a scalpel.

"Grant heeded Seligman's advice," he continued, "and did not offer Stewart the position. Stewart took the decision personally and vowed to bring down Seligman. He died before any revenge could be exacted, but his successors took up the charge for him. Are you familiar with the Grand Union Hotel in Saratoga?"

"I'm afraid not."

"Nor, fortunately, am I. I'm told it is the largest hotel in the world, a favored summer spot for New Yorkers who can afford it. Joseph Seligman and his family took holiday there every summer. The Grand Union Hotel was one of many properties owned by A.T. Stewart, and it remained in the estate upon his death. Now, the executor of Stewart's estate was a small-minded man named Henry Hilton, who had been Stewart's personal lawyer. One of Boss Tweed's lackeys who'd bought himself a judgeship, he suddenly found himself a very wealthy man. The summer following Stewart's death, in 1877, when Seligman arrived with his family at the Grand Union Hotel, as they had for the ten previous summers, they were told that no rooms were available. Seligman protested that he had reserved several rooms, the same ones the family had always stayed in. But the manager said he had his orders: Judge Hilton had directed that no Jews be permitted to stay at the Grand Union Hotel."

He said it with such disgust, she wondered for a moment if Gould himself had Jewish blood.

"There was a great public outcry at such treatment of a man who had done so much for this country, while others said with equal fervor that it was Hilton's property—albeit inherited—and he could do whatever he pleased with it. Sadly, most of the press sided with Hilton, and the event unleashed a terrible amount of hatred against Jews in this country. 'Hebrews will knock vainly for admission' became an all-too-frequent sign at finer hotels."

Nellie wondered where exactly Gould, a laissez-faire stock manipulator, stood on this issue. Sensing the question, he answered it for her.

"My sympathies were with Seligman, for reasons more personal than philosophical. You see, Joseph Seligman was my banker, a man I trusted completely and whom I grew to respect immensely. The outpouring of venom in the press affected him deeply, and within a short time he was dead."

Gould's eyes had narrowed at the circumstances of his friend's death. He paused ever so slightly before going on.

"No one," he said, "knew quite how to respond to Hilton's pronouncement. Remember, this was a man who now controlled one of the largest fortunes in the country and had most of the newspapers on his side. And Jews, by their nature and history, shunned controversy. That is when Miss Lazarus stepped forward."

He leaned forward, sharing a story he clearly relished.

"She turned Hilton's argument against him. If he was free to decide who could stay at his hotels, well, then people were free not to shop at the A.T. Stewart department store. Miss Lazarus organized a boycott. No Jews, no immigrants, no Irish, no Italians—no one who had ever been slighted or whose parents had ever been slighted—should shop at A.T. Stewart's. And, of course, nearly every immigrant to this country had felt the terrible sting of bigotry. She managed to spread the word far and wide, and business at Stewart's department store began to plummet immediately. Miss Lazarus remained in the background—Hilton shared acquaintances with her father— but she was tireless in assembling her forces. Hilton stubbornly clung to his policy, and in fact with great fanfare organized the American Society for the Suppression of the Jews, urging other hotel owners and restaurateurs to turn away Jews. That only gave strength to the boycott. Within six months—only six months, mind you—the A.T. Stewart department store, the largest in the world, was forced to declare bankruptcy, and the man who had driven Joseph Seligman to an early death was publicly humiliated."

She could hear the approval, and even admiration, in his voice.

"When I realized that the woman on my early morning walks was Emma Lazarus, I introduced myself and told her I was a friend of Joseph Seligman. At that point, we became, as you put it, walking companions."

"She was indeed a remarkable woman, that is clear," said Nellie. "But DeKay said she also suffered from dark moods and seized the opportunity to consume arsenic. Why are you convinced he is lying?"

"I make my living judging character, Miss Bly. Every investment I have ever made is based on an assessment of character. And I am wholly convinced that Miss Lazarus did not take her own life."

"You think DeKay poisoned her?"

"You suspected him of involvement until this morning."

"Yes. But why would he want to see Miss Lazarus dead? And why would he poison her when he knew she was only months from dying as it was?"

These were the questions that had plagued her the entire day. But Gould had no hesitation in answering.

"To curry favor with Henry Hilton."

"I don't understand—"

"Mr. DeKay is looking to elevate his status in New York society," Gould said impatiently. "In your brief time around him, surely you have seen that. Nothing is more important to his ilk than social standing. Nothing."

"I'm not sure I see the connection—"

"In his pursuit of respectability, DeKay has become the protégé of Henry Hilton."

"The enemy of the woman he loved?!"

"As much as he is capable of love, yes."

"But Charles DeKay and Henry Hilton … The two of them joining forces seems so out of the question."

"Never underestimate the lust for social advantage, Miss Bly. People will do anything to achieve it: betray friends, spy on family, murder lovers—"

"You think DeKay poisoned Miss Lazarus at the behest of Judge Hilton?"

"I have no doubt of it."

"But that would be monstrous. And then to claim it was a suicide—"

"You've spoken with him. Would *you* credit Charles DeKay for integrity?"

DeKay was a cad, that was beyond question. And he arranged for Barker to destroy the blood flasks. But he had seemed so sincere, even sorrowful, that morning. And to murder his companion of ten years?!

"What did Hilton offer him?"

"Sponsorship in a social club. Invitations to dinners and balls. A summer cottage in Newport. An ambassadorship to Germany—Hilton has spent a great deal of money to assure President Cleveland's defeat this fall. With the business and social contacts acquired through such a position, DeKay would live comfortably for the rest of his life."

"And in return Hilton would see the demise of the woman

he despised?"

"Yes."

It was a murderous trade with the devil, and yet Nellie had no trouble imagining Charles DeKay—the one she had seen at the opera—making it.

"You see, Miss Bly, these men are scoundrels. If you wrote a news article they found threatening in any way, I am certain harm would come to you. That is why I summoned you here. You need to know exactly what is in store should you continue. Though I would like nothing more than to see these men brought to justice, you must think long and hard before pursuing this matter and appreciate its gravity."

She beheld him sitting there, the most notorious man in New York, perhaps in the entire country. A man who had destroyed thousands of lives in his financial maneuvers, and yet he was warning her. She wondered if he was just manipulating her like some railroad stock. There was certainly a good chance of it. But DeKay *did* strike her as craven enough to do all Gould had described. She had no idea what to do. If she wrote about DeKay and Hilton, they would try to destroy Emma's reputation and, if Gould was to be believed, harm Nellie herself as well. But if she did nothing, two men who ended the life of a remarkable woman would get away with murder.

"There is no firm evidence as to how Miss Lazarus died," she said, "let alone whether she was murdered. It is pure conjecture."

"Most of life is conjecture, Miss Bly. That is one thing you understand at my age. The challenge is to reduce the conjecture to likelihood."

"I don't know whom or what to believe—"

"Then dig deeper. Sit down with Henry Hilton. Press him for answers. After speaking with him, you'll know what to do."

He wasn't trying to sway her, Nellie thought; he was clever enough to simply leave it to her to decide. She found herself flattered by his vote of confidence. No doubt it was one of his ways of manipulating her.

"I have a few questions for you, Mr. Gould," she said. "Please

… How did you express your admiration to Miss Lazarus?"

"Excuse me?"

"You admired her for the boycott that vindicated your friend. I'm sure you expressed your gratitude in ways other than words."

He was thrown by the question. That didn't happen often with Jay Gould.

"I paid for food and shelter for dozens of immigrants and did what I could to find them work."

"Miss Lazarus appreciated that?"

"Very much so."

That made sense, she thought to herself. Emma would use the opportunity of Gould's companionship to help her cause.

"And what did you ask in return?"

"In return? Nothing. She had vindicated my friend. I was glad to help her in some small way." He sounded almost offended at the question.

"A man in your position does not get there by providing gifts, Mr. Gould. Life for you is bartering. What did you receive in return for your philanthropic gestures?"

Gould nodded wanly.

"She passed along information about her father's sugar refineries, information I used in market purchases and in setting rates on my railroads."

Nellie smiled ever so slightly, as did he. She stood up.

"No one can know about this conversation, I take it? Not even Mr. Pulitzer?"

"No one. That can only make your task more difficult. But like me, Hilton has sources in many places."

He took her by the elbow and leaned close as he led her to the door. "She was an exceptional woman, Miss Bly. Please do her justice. I will assist you in any way I can. But know I am unable to protect you."

CHAPTER TEN

JAY GOULD

Nellie had Gould's driver take her back to Harlem. She had barely seen her mother the past two days, and Nellie didn't like to leave her alone too long. Mary Jane's mind was slipping, and Nellie worried she would hurt herself or wander out on her own and get lost in this strange city. During the ten days Nellie had spent in Bellevue, she had paid the landlady to look after her mother, but she couldn't afford that forever. One of her sisters could move to New York, but that would be one more mouth to feed, and the room they rented was too small as it was. Now that Nellie was getting busy on the Emma story, she would have to figure her way out of the conundrum.

It was a good thing she did go home because Mary Jane was in a tizzy over a telegram that had arrived from Nellie's younger sister Alice. The court case they filed three years ago against the First Pennsylvania Bank was proceeding to trial in two days.

Nellie had waited her whole life for this moment. All the times she had lain awake at night vowing revenge, all the hardships she and her mother and sisters had been forced to endure … she remembered every single one. Her family's life had been deeply damaged by the bank and its president, Colonel Thaddeus Jackson, who had embezzled all their money and then declared bankruptcy. The bank had refused to make amends and fought all attempts to compensate them, averring that a widow was not entitled to any inheritance and that the children were minors and unable to sue. After living in tenements as a child, Nellie had managed to make ends meet through odd jobs and eventually writing for newspapers, but she'd never lost her hatred for the First Pennsylvania Bank.

The day she turned 21 she filed a lawsuit against it for mismanaging the family funds.

The case had taken three years to make its way through the Armstrong County Court of Common Pleas, and now, finally, it was ready for trial.

Nellie had no illusions about the challenge she faced. Unable to afford a lawyer, she would have to represent herself and her sisters in court. The case would be before a judge who was a part-time lawyer and frequently employed, in all probability, by the First Pennsylvania Bank. The jury would be composed of men who did business with the bank and depended on it for their livelihoods. Both judge and jurors would undoubtedly know Colonel Jackson and want to protect his reputation, as Jackson had commanded the Eleventh Pennsylvania Reserves in the Civil War. And even though he was its president at the time, state agency law would permit the bank to deny all financial responsibility for the actions of Colonel Jackson.

Nevertheless, Nellie was not about to back down. These people had cheated her family and made their lives difficult and cruel. She wanted justice. The cause was not totally hopeless, as she saw it. She had some weapons of her own. But she had to move quickly; two days was not much time. She would also have to put aside the Emma story for a week or two.

"Mother. We have to leave tomorrow."

Mary Jane was confused. "For where, dear?"

"For home."

"I don't understand—"

"The lawsuit against the bank is going to trial."

"What will they do to us, dear?" asked Mary Jane, cowering. "Will they throw us out of our house again?"

"No, Mother. They can't hurt us anymore."

"Are you sure? Perhaps we should just stay here."

Mary Jane had been irreparably scarred from losing her husband and her home and then living in poverty while raising young children. It had been disruptive to move to New York, but it was also a blessing in that it helped Mary Jane begin to put the awful experience of the past fifteen years behind her. Now, though, she was frightened at the thought of facing those same vicious people again.

"Can you start packing without me?" asked Nellie. "And fix yourself dinner? I need to tell someone I'm leaving."

"Will you be long?" Mary Jane asked anxiously. It was pitiful, thought Nellie, what life had done to her.

"An hour or two. I will come right back. I promise."

"All right, dear. But do hurry."

On Tuesday and Thursday evenings, Ingram worked at the Bellevue Hospital, so Nellie rode the streetcar south to First Avenue and Twenty-Seventh Street, then took the ferry to Blackwell's Island and the hospital.

Like her mother returning to Apollo, Nellie shuddered at the thought of setting foot in Bellevue. Even more than reliving bad memories, she half-worried the authorities would find a way to keep her there, only this time Pulitzer's lawyer would not be able to get her out. She would have waited and chosen anywhere else in the city to meet Ingram, but she had to leave the next day and needed to see him before she departed.

The place was as dreary and dank as she remembered. The guard at the elevated front desk, a brutish man in his early forties named Jenkes, whom Nellie had described in her story as "a cold, heartless ogre, a most suitable public face for Bellevue," snarled when he saw her.

"What do you want?"

"I'm here to see Dr. Ingram. He is expecting me."

Jenkes grunted resentfully, got up from his chair, and unlocked the door. He didn't bother to open it for her. She had to let herself in. He started to follow her.

"No need to take me back. I know my way."

"I don't trust you," he said.

"And I don't trust you." The women inmates had warned her never to be alone with any of the male guards, especially Jenkes.

"Suit yourself."

He locked the door and returned to his chair.

"Tell me, Jenkes. Did I spell your name right in the newspaper? The *World* wants me to do another story on Bellevue, to see if things have changed. I wouldn't want to misspell it again."

He got the point. He didn't like it, but he got it. He trudged over and unlocked the door. After he walked back to his desk, she opened the door.

"One of these days someone's going to get you alone on the street, missie," he said. "And you're going to get all you have coming to you. That'll be a glorious day."

"Perhaps so, Jenkes. It's a pity that someone won't be you."

As she stepped inside to a poorly lit brick corridor at least fifty feet long, she shivered involuntarily from her confrontation with Jenkes. She had expected him to be fired after her story, but his sister was the wife of John Kelly, the current head of Tammany Hall, and Kelly was notoriously ruthless—he had betrayed Boss Tweed and arranged for him to be sent to prison fifteen years earlier. The City Council might be outraged by what they saw of Bellevue, but no one thought it worth the trouble to take action against John Kelly's brother-in-law.

Ingram was in his office at the end of the corridor. Through the small window she could see him poring over a file. She tapped on the window. He looked up, surprised to see her, and unlocked the door.

"Miss Bly."

"May I come in?"

"Of course."

She walked inside and sat down by his desk. He closed the door behind her.

Although they were almost magnetically drawn to one another, there was no embrace. They had to be careful in the hospital, as a scandal could ruin them both. He joined her at the desk. Even though the door was closed, they spoke in quiet tones.

"What's wrong?" he asked.

"I must go away tomorrow, to tend to some matters at home." She didn't tell him what they were, and he didn't ask. She kept her past to herself. Whenever Ingram asked even innocent questions about life before they met, she ignored them. He had stopped asking altogether.

"When will you return?"

"I'm not sure. Within ten days, I suspect."

She started to reach for his hand, but he shook his head. Physical contact between them was out of the question.

"I was afraid I wouldn't see you."

He nodded. It took enormous willpower on both their parts to restrain themselves.

"What happened with the story?" he asked. "It was not in the afternoon paper."

"Mr. Cockerill declined to run it."

She told him about the meetings with Cockerill, and then DeKay, and then Gould.

"DeKay insists it was a suicide, and Gould is just as insistent it was a murder."

"Which one do you believe?"

"Gould."

"Why?"

"He believed Emma was incapable of taking her own life, and I agree."

Ingram was skeptical. "There is no scientific connection between character and suicide. Lincoln was a brooder given to dark moments, yet it was his effervescent wife who repeatedly tried to take her own life."

"Then I really am wasting my time," she said in frustration. "There is no way of telling how she died."

"Not necessarily."

She looked at him, puzzled. "Assuming we could actually show she died of arsenic poisoning and not cancer, how could anyone prove it was a murder and not a suicide?"

"Arsenic is a very unpleasant poison. One looking to kill herself would want to do it quickly to shorten the suffering. One wanting to commit a murder, on the other hand, and have it appear as a cancer would administer it over a much longer period of time."

"But how could I show which of the two it was?" she asked.

"If you could get me any clothes she wore during the last several months of her life, I could tell you."

"I don't understand."

"The body expels arsenic any way it can—through the hair, through the skin, through sweat glands. That, plus the fact that arsenic can be detected after months, even years, means that we could tell how much arsenic was in her system even a year after her death."

"Simply by examining a dress?"

"We live in an age of science, my dear. Our microscopes can detect almost anything."

"So," she said excitedly, "if a nightshirt she wore three months before her death had no arsenic, and one she wore right before her death had a large amount, that would suggest suicide."

"Exactly. And if the shirt she wore three months before dying had a small amount, and the one before her death had the same or a slightly larger amount, that would suggest a murder."

She grasped the possibilities.

"Then I have to get my hands on her nightclothes."

"Or a bed sheet. Or a blanket. Or a chair she sat in, a napkin she used. Anything she touched would reveal the level of arsenic in her system. Remember, however, that she died a year ago. You would have to find items that were not washed or given away."

"But *if* I found them, you would be able to tell?"

"Yes."

"Once again, Dr. Ingram, you have given me hope." She wanted to add "and more," but lost her nerve.

"That is how doctors like to think of ourselves, Miss Bly. As purveyors of hope."

She stood up. "Thank you."

"Glad I was able to help."

He opened the door for her. She brushed against him on the way out and looked into his eyes. It was almost too much to ask, to keep their hands off one another.

"Good day, Miss Bly."

"Good day, Dr. Ingram."

She gave him a warm smile and passed closely enough to graze against his thigh. Her heart leapt, and she paused to look at his face when a patient's frightened scream cut through the asylum. He nodded and started to reach for her arm but held back.

She left, to the sounds of the woman screaming.

CHAPTER ELEVEN

ARMSTRONG CO. COURT HOUSE - KITTANNING, PA.

Nellie and Mary Jane took the sixteen-hour train ride from New York to Pittsburg. The sight of snow still piled high from the Great Blizzard was replaced by soot and gouges of hundreds of mine shafts probing for coal in central and western Pennsylvania. Because soft coal was the nation's primary source of energy for locomotives and steam engines and the giant steel-producing furnaces around Pittsburg, it was sought after like gold. No matter that it was so dirty that train passengers and residents living near railroad tracks found themselves covered with soot, even with all the windows closed and curtains drawn. Or that coal miners and nearby residents inhaled poisonous dust that shortened their lifespans by fifteen to twenty years. The country's energy demands were simply too great to accommodate such trivialities. And with no unions to jack up wages or prevent companies from charging workers for equipment or making them buy all their food and necessities in company-owned stores, coal producers made phenomenal profits. The richest man in the country was Henry Clay Frick, who controlled the coal industry, and the second-richest was Andrew Carnegie, who controlled the steel industry.

The train ride made Nellie sad and even weepy. Her fondest childhood memories were of her father taking the family on long train rides through forest-covered mountains to Philadelphia or for long picnics through a quiet countryside of rolling hills and farms. Now smokestacks spewed yellow-brown ash into the gray skies, while beneath them gangs of soulless miners and equipment mutilated not only the hillside but her fondest memories of childhood as well.

Nellie spent most of the train ride reading everything Emma Lazarus had ever written. She was in awe—that was the only word for it—at the breadth of Emma's talent.

She read the first set of poems Emma had published as a teenager, the ones that brought her to Ralph Waldo Emerson's attention, about the upheaval of the war. Then, as a young woman, came book reviews about love and the mysteries of the heart. In the late 1870s, after the incident at Saratoga and the boycott of the Stewart Department Store, Emma had shifted to poetry with more religious and political themes, decrying Christian cruelty and the treatment of Jews throughout history. She made a passionate and persuasive case for a Palestine homeland for Jews, and her poem "1492," contrasting Columbus sailing for America with Jews dying during the Inquisition, was perhaps the finest poem Nellie had ever read. Then came deeply affecting essays on the plight of immigrants to America and reviews of the Yiddish theater. Surveying this body of work, Nellie felt a profound sadness that so prodigious a writer had met death at such an early age. The writings inspired her all the more to continue her investigation once the trial was finished.

After reaching Pittsburg, their clothes filthy and skin blackened with soot, Nellie and Mary Jane rode another two hours to Apollo, arriving just after midnight the night before the trial. Nellie had hoped to see her younger sisters, but one had married a steelworker in Carnegie, and the other worked fourteen-hour days in a sewing factory in McKeesport. If things went well, she might see them on the way back to New York.

Manufacturing had replaced agriculture as the leading industry in Pennsylvania, but the wave of prosperity had not yet reached Apollo. That town remained a farming community with a sprinkle of textile mills, and technology was leaving the citizenry behind. Bitterness had set in, though perhaps it had always been there and Nellie simply hadn't noticed it before. Mary Jane's sister Lucy met them at the train station and took them to the tenement where Nellie grew up. It was not a pleasant ride. Lucy thought Nellie was wasting time, money, and Mary Jane's health with the lawsuit and told her so. The legal world was a man's world—no women lawyers, no women judges, no women jurors. Juries were made up entirely of white men who owned property. What was the point of all this fuss?

But Nellie was convinced she could gain the sympathies of any jury once they heard what the bank had done to her family. Most farmers and merchants in Armstrong County had been mistreated by the First Pennsylvania Bank at one point or another, and all of them would surely find its behavior toward her family unconscionable.

Her confidence grew the next morning when she saw the dozen men serving on the jury. Some she had known as a little girl; at least two had worked in her father's mill, and her father had taken care of their families during hard times. She took pains to dress modestly and not put on city airs. The citizenry in Apollo resented big-city Pittsburgers, New Yorkers even more so. Nellie presented herself as pure Apollo. Her western Pennsylvania accent, which she had worked hard to lose in New York, came back loud and pronounced in Apollo. The worst thing that could be said about someone who left Apollo was "they changed." Nellie wanted to show that she hadn't changed at all.

The presiding judge, Henry Ratkin, Esq., was a balding man whose stooped shoulders and pained expression accurately reflected his lack of backbone. Like many judges, Ratkin practiced law and farmed tomatoes and wasn't very good at either. The attorney representing the bank was Frederick Shaeffer, a stiff, humorless, properly dressed man in his early fifties. The most successful lawyer in the county, Shaeffer handled most of the bank's legal business and consequently was disliked intensely by the jury members, as nearly all of them had been sued, or had friends who had been sued, by Shaeffer and the bank at one time or another. Normally Shaeffer appeared only in front of judges, invariably a sympathetic audience, as he would throw bank legal business the judge's way after a favorable ruling. But the fact that the current case was before a jury was of little concern to him since the judge still controlled the ground rules.

Some things, however, Judge Ratkin could not control. The courtroom itself was circular, not to produce an intimacy or artistic effect but to maximize the warmth from the room's centrally located gas heating lamps. This meant that both Nellie and Shaeffer were in close proximity to the jury, a factor that worked strongly in Nellie's favor. Ratkin also could not control that all the wives in Apollo were familiar with what had happened to Mary Jane and the girls and were sure to be furious if their husbands issued a verdict for the bank. Most significant of all, however, was that while he could control what the jurors were permitted to hear and the way it was presented, Ratkin could not control what came out of the witnesses' mouths.

And so, as Ratkin called the proceedings to order, Nellie was far from despairing.

"Miss Cochran," said the judge sternly, "you are representing yourself and your sisters in this case?"

"Yes, Judge."

"Please address me as 'Your Honor.'"

"I'm sorry, Your Honor. I've never been in a courtroom before."

"What about getting sent to Bellevue?" interrupted Shaeffer, looking to put her on the defensive.

"Oh, that wasn't a real courtroom. That was New York." The jurors laughed. Ratkin started to laugh, too, but stopped when he saw Shaeffer frown.

"Call your first witness, Miss Cochran."

"I call Thaddeus Jackson."

"Objection!" said Shaeffer, indignantly rising to his feet.

"What's the problem?" asked Nellie. "He embezzled our money. He admitted it." She glanced at the jurors, who wondered the same thing.

"But there is no evidence the *bank* participated in any embezzlement. And your lawsuit is against the bank," said Shaeffer pedantically.

"Jackson is *president* of the bank. And he was at the time."

"Simply because he was the bank president doesn't make the bank responsible for his mistakes." Shaeffer sat down. As far as he was concerned, that was the end of it.

There were murmurs, even among the jurors, at the twisted logic.

"I think we should let the jurors decide that, Mr. Shaeffer," she said. "Unless, of course, you don't think they're up to the task."

That was exactly what Shaeffer thought and was unable to disguise it. The jurors naturally took umbrage and looked to Ratkin to see if he felt the same. Ratkin squirmed.

"The jury will hear from Colonel Jackson," he intoned. "Have Colonel Jackson come in."

Nellie glanced at the jury as the clerk went to summon Jackson. Nearly all of them were staring at her the way men stare at women. She winced. She didn't want them fantasizing about her, not now. As a reporter, it might help on occasion, but she needed them to sympathize with her. Like a good daughter, she walked over to Mary Jane, sitting in the front row.

"Are you okay, Mother?"

"Yes, dear. Thank you."

"Do you need anything? A glass of water?"

"No, dear. I'm fine. Thank you."

Suddenly the door opened, and Thaddeus Jackson walked into the courtroom. He was a tall man in his late fifties, ramrod straight, with deep-set, severe brown eyes, mutton chops flecked with gray, and the assured, condescending air of someone who routinely held the fate of others in his hands and felt perfectly comfortable crushing them. When she saw him, Nellie felt a surge of anger so intense her fists clenched. She counseled herself to stay calm.

"Good morning, Colonel Jackson," said the judge deferentially.

"Good morning, Mr. Ratkin," Jackson replied, remaining standing.

"*Judge* Ratkin," corrected Shaeffer.

"Excuse me," said Jackson, annoyed with the charade. "*Judge* Ratkin."

"Place your hand on the Bible, please."

The clerk placed a Bible in front of Jackson. He placed his left hand on it and raised his right hand as Ratkin administered the oath. Jackson vowed to tell the truth and sat down. He was as remote and cold as Nellie had imagined.

"Proceed, Miss Cochran."

"Thank you, Your Honor," said Nellie and approached the witness stand.

"Good morning, Miss Cochran," said Jackson, stiffly trying to be gracious.

"If you say so," said Nellie, her voice dripping with contempt. That got the attention of the jurors. They were accustomed to treating Jackson as a superior.

"Mr. Jackson, you are president of the First Pennsylvania Bank in Apollo?"

"It's *Colonel* Jackson," he corrected.

"No, it's *Mister* Jackson," snapped Nellie. "Anyone who steals from widows and children has forfeited his right to a military title. Even the term *mister* is too good for you."

The jurors sat up. This woman had backbone.

"Your Honor," protested an indignant Shaeffer. "The man

was a commissioned officer—"

"—And a convicted felon!" shot back Nellie.

"A war hero—"

"—who belongs in jail!"

"Stop!" said Ratkin. "You may address the witness as mister, Miss Cochran. But get on with it."

"Thank you, Your Honor." She turned to face Jackson, no more than three feet away, fearlessly crowding him. "Now, *Mister* Jackson," she began, as he smoldered at the insult. "When my father died, all the money meant for my sisters and me was placed in your bank?"

"With me. Yes."

"Because he knew you personally and had served in the war with you."

"That's right." Jackson squirmed. He was a proud man and did not like shining a light on his mistakes. But Nellie was in no rush to let him relax.

"And what happened to that money?"

He said nothing.

"What happened to the money?" she repeated sharply.

"I used it for myself." He said it softly, almost inaudibly.

"Louder, Mr. Jackson."

"I used it for myself."

"You built a new house in fact, correct?"

"Among other things, yes."

"The biggest house in town."

"Yes." Nellie had been by the house that very morning. Not that she needed the extra incentive, but she wanted every detail vivid in her mind.

"And where did you live while you were building this house?"

Shaeffer was on his feet. "Objection, Your Honor. Relevance."

"The relevance will be clear when he answers the question, Your Honor."

"I don't think so, Miss Cochran. Objection sustained."

Nellie pursed her lips. She wanted the jurors to know that while Jackson was using her money and her sisters' money to build his mansion, he was living in the house their own father had built specifically for them. It was diabolical and cruel. The jury should know all about that.

"Miss Cochran?"

No matter, she assured herself. *Stay with the plan you rehearsed thousands of times.*

"Now, this money you used for yourself, did you ever pay it back?"

"I did not." He was surprisingly unabashed about it.

"Why not?"

"I made some poor investments and was forced to declare bankruptcy."

"And now you are back on your financial feet?"

"Yes."

"You are even the president of the bank again."

"Yes."

"In fact, the entire time, even after your arrest, you remained the president of the bank."

"The stockholders showed remarkable faith in me, and I appreciate it."

"No doubt it helped that the shareholders were your immediate family."

"Objection!"

"Sustained. The jury will disregard that remark."

Nellie didn't mind the interruption. Nothing was going to slow her down now. "How many people did you steal from, Mr. Jackson?"

"I don't know."

"Five? Fifty? Five hundred?"

"I can't say."

"You mean you won't say. When you pled guilty to embezzlement, you acknowledged stealing from the accounts of sixty-five people."

"Yes."

She glanced at the jury to make sure they heard. They definitely heard. They were hanging on her every word, and despite his power, they loathed him.

"Did you pay back anyone whose money you stole?"

"No."

"That included soldiers who fought for you, their widows, my sisters, myself—"

"That is what happens with bankruptcy, Miss Cochran," he snapped. "It is a public humiliation. It also wipes the slate clean."

"Only your slate, Mr. Jackson. It wipes your slate clean, but everyone else's is still a mess."

"Objection!" cried Shaeffer, getting to his feet.

"Sustained."

The anger was taking over now, and her momentum increased.

"Did the bank pay back anyone whose money you stole?" she continued.

"No, it did not."

"Why not?"

"The bank did not know what I was doing."

"But you were the president."

"I was an officer. No one else knew about it."

"Even your family members who worked there?"

"That's right."

"They simply enjoyed sleeping in larger rooms and wearing fancier dresses—"

"Objection!"

"Sustained. Miss Cochran, save your arguments for later."

She returned to Jackson. "Did you ask the bank to pay back any of the money you stole?"

He swatted unconsciously with his hand as at a gnat. "Why would I ask the bank to do that? They had nothing to do with it."

"So you are saying the bank is not responsible for the actions of its president?"

"Or any of its other employees. You can't expect the bank to be responsible for everyone who works for it. Otherwise a bank could not conduct commerce."

Nellie suddenly walked over to the counsel table, sat down, and began writing. The only sound in the room was her scribbling on the paper.

"Miss Cochran?" said Ratkin.

"Just a moment, Your Honor," said Nellie, dipping her pen in the inkwell and writing.

"Miss Cochran. What are you doing?" asked Ratkin more sternly. She looked up at Jackson.

" 'You can't expect the bank to be responsible for everyone who works for it.' Do I have that right, Mr. Jackson? Is that what you said?"

"Yes."

" 'Otherwise a bank could not conduct commerce.' Do I have that right as well?"

"Yes."

"Thank you."

She wrote down a few more words and then looked up at him.

"Your waistcoat. Would you describe that as dark gray or more of a speckled black?"

"Objection!" said Shaeffer.

"Miss Cochran," said Ratkin impatiently. "What are you doing?"

"Writing a newspaper story about how a bank employee stole all the money my father left for his family. That Mr. Jackson as the bank president takes no responsibility whatsoever for the actions of his employee—in this case himself—and shows no concern whatsoever for the financial ruin of his many depositors, including the daughters of a longtime customer and fellow Union soldier. I will be saying that every customer at the bank should expect similar treatment, and only a fool would put even a single penny into Mr. Jackson's bank."

"You write that and I will sue you for everything you own," snarled Jackson.

"Well, that won't be for very much, Mr. Jackson," Nellie shot back, "thanks to your thievery. But at least everyone who reads the *New York World* will be aware that Thaddeus Jackson and the First Pennsylvania Bank of Apollo are nothing more than common thieves."

"I strongly advise you not to do that."

"Oh? And why is that?"

"I shall sue Pulitzer and everyone else connected with the paper, and I will make sure the case is heard right here in Armstrong County, where there is little regard for Hungarian Jews."

Nellie's jaw dropped.

"What does Mr. Pulitzer have to do with this?"

"He publishes your paper. He would be party to ruining the bank's good name."

"Mr. Pulitzer publishes a dozen newspapers. He will know nothing about this story until he reads it along with everyone else."

"Then I imagine he will be very upset with you."

All the stuffing seemed to go out of Nellie. "That is not fair, Colonel. This is between my family and your bank. Leave Mr. Pulitzer out of this," she pleaded. "He has been my godsend. Without him I have no work, and my family has nothing."

Jackson enjoyed watching Nellie squirm. He loved nothing more than an enemy begging for mercy. "I will not leave him out of this, young lady. He is accountable for the reckless actions of an ill-intentioned employee, and I intend to hold him as such."

"No!"

"Yes, Miss Cochran! Yes! So go ahead and print your story." Order was restored in Jackson's universe. Once again, he had the upper hand.

Suddenly Nellie smiled.

"Thank you, Mr. Jackson. That was my only point. And you made it very well."

A puzzled look flooded Jackson's face as it dawned on him that he had stepped into a trap. Nellie returned to the desk and resumed writing.

" 'A man is responsible for the reckless actions of an employee, and we should hold him accountable as such.' A most succinct statement of principle. Thank you."

She turned to Ratkin.

"I have no more questions for *Colonel* Jackson, Your Honor." The room fell silent. Jackson glared at her murderously.

"You think you're smart, don't you, young lady?"

"No, I'm not smart, Mr. Jackson. I just don't like thieves." The word hung there for all to take it in.

"Mr. Shaeffer?" said Ratkin. "Your witness."

Shaeffer stood up to contain the damage. But Jackson had had enough. In a fury, he got up and stalked out of the courtroom, leaving Shaeffer standing there flummoxed.

"I'm guessing he has no questions, Your Honor," said Nellie. The jurors laughed.

"The witness is excused," said Ratkin with a twinkle, looking at the empty chair and producing more laughs. "Your next witness?" he said to Nellie.

"I have no more witnesses. I see no reason to impose further on the jury's time."

"Mr. Shaeffer?" said Ratkin.

Shaeffer knew the jurors had made up their minds. Anything he said or did to prolong the trial would just make them angrier. It was time to minimize the damage.

"I have nothing, Your Honor."

Closing arguments were pointless, and everyone knew it. The outcome was a fait accompli. A family had placed all of its money with the bank, the president had stolen the money, and no matter what anyone said, the bank was responsible. The logic was unassailable.

"I believe we can dispense with closing arguments, Your Honor," said Shaeffer, rising to his feet. "The bank will acknowledge its responsibility for Colonel Jackson's actions."

A gasp went up in the courtroom. In the gallery, Mary Jane threw up her hands and yelled, "Glory be!" Tears welled up in Nellie's eyes. It had been such an arduous struggle, trying to get justice after all these years. The money would not bring her father back or remove the awful memories, but at least, for the first time since she was a child, they would be out from under terrible financial pressures.

"Then I direct a verdict in favor of the plaintiff," said Ratkin.

"Without objection, Your Honor," said Shaeffer.

"Miss Cochran?"

"No objection, Your Honor," said Nellie. She just shook

her head. All these years they had dragged it out and then had just given up. She glanced at her mother, who was praying and giving thanks to God.

"Writ of inquiry as to damages, Your Honor," said Shaeffer.

"So ordered," said Ratkin. "I will direct the sheriff to begin the process." Shaeffer sat down and began gathering papers.

Nellie was confused. "I don't understand."

"A defendant has the right to an independent assessment of damages," said Ratkin.

"Isn't that what the jury is for?"

"Not this jury. Once a plaintiff is found entitled to damages, a defendant can ask for an independent assessment by the sheriff and twelve jurors of his choosing."

"What does the sheriff have to do with it?" asked Nellie, sensing disaster.

"The sheriff is the law enforcement officer in charge of collecting all debts."

"But this jury just heard the case. They can decide what the bank owes us."

"Not if the defendant asks for a writ of inquiry. The bank owes you money, Miss Cochran. That is clear. The writ of inquiry panel will determine how much they owe you."

She could see her victory slipping away. Everyone in the courtroom could.

"Is the sheriff elected or appointed?" she asked.

"The sheriff is appointed, by the county council."

"They pay his salary?"

"That's right."

Then it hit her. "Is Mr. Jackson on the council?"

"He is the chairman of the council. But the sheriff will act independently." Ratkin turned to the jury. "Gentlemen of the jury, thank you for your time. You are dismissed."

"You mean that's it?" the jury foreman, a mill worker in his forties, asked indignantly.

"Your work is done here."

"But what about the money that's owed to Miss Cochran and her family?"

"That is none of your concern—"

"Of course it's our concern. She's entitled to it!"

"This court is now adjourned." Ratkin tapped his gavel and left the room. No one else moved. Nellie just sat there stunned. Shaeffer put his papers in his pouch and walked over to her.

"Congratulations, Miss Cochran," he said and walked out, unable to suppress a smile.

CHAPTER TWELVE

"Should we get the wagon? Or do you want to keep making an ass of yourself?"

Nellie had always hated her aunt. But she had to admit that Lucy was right. Of course the bank would never allow her to win. She should have realized that before she'd ever set foot in the courtroom.

The jurors had come over one by one and offered condolences as if it were a funeral, which in many ways it was. She was burying the last vestiges of hope. The powerful would always control the weak. That would never change. The stories she had written about women and children in factories and slums and asylums didn't really matter. That was the stark truth of it. The inertia of the world was too great. There might be outrage for a week or two, but once the public moved on to the next story, things would remain as before. The rich would get richer; the poor would struggle and die early.

That was the real reason she had resisted working on the Emma Lazarus story, she realized. It would bring home this most unpleasant truth yet again, and she just didn't want to face it anymore. Even if she could somehow show that Emma had been murdered, what difference would it make? The people who killed her would not be brought to justice. Pulitzer might publish a story in the *World*, and there might even be a hue and cry, but Hilton and DeKay and Barker would go unpunished.

She was better off writing about gardens and fashion for the *Dispatch*. The pay was better, and this way she would be nearer to her sisters, who could help take care of her mother. Working for the *World* was exciting, yes, but it was a false excitement, like trying on a dress you couldn't afford and no one would let you wear anyhow.

"I think we'll go to the train, Aunt Lucy."

They arrived at the livery, a large two-story building with a balcony up top.

Nellie dreaded the thought of seeing her sisters. In their letters they had been so hopeful that their time working sixteen-hour days in the factories would come to an end. The last time Nellie had seen them, they looked so worn down, they could have passed for ten years older than Nellie instead of three and five years younger.

An attentive man in his early twenties with a thick mustache, earnest eyes, ragged suspenders, and a shirt several sizes too large jumped up from his bench outside the stable.

"May I help you?" he asked in a thick Eastern European accent.

"Yes, Hunkie," said the aunt condescendingly. "Bring my wagon around."

To Lucy, everyone from Eastern Europe was a Hunkie. All the Irish Catholics were micks, the Italians wops, the Jews kikes, and, of course, the few blacks in Apollo niggers. Nor did Lucy think her own ethnic group, the Black Irish, was any better. Lucy resented anyone trying to get ahead, as if managing to move up the economic ladder was proof of her own shortcomings.

The man brought the horse and carriage around to the entrance. He had rubbed the carriage seat clean of dust and brushed off the horse. He proudly held the reins tight as Lucy climbed up to the driver's seat.

"Well," said Lucy, looking down at Nellie and Mary Jane, "get a move on."

Mary Jane balked at climbing up. Nellie realized they had forgotten the footstool at her aunt's house.

"Do you have a footstool?" she asked the attendant.

The man look confused.

"Do you have a *footstool*?" Lucy said with impatience.

He still looked confused. Nellie realized he didn't speak English. She pointed to her feet and mimed climbing on to the carriage. He caught on and motioned for her to wait a moment. He hurried inside the livery and brought out a stool, setting it down for Mary Jane and then helping her into the carriage. Then he took the stool and walked around to the other side, beckoned Nellie to come over, and helped her into her seat. She smiled at his solicitous manner.

"Thank you," she said kindly.

"You're welcome," he said with pleasure in a thick European accent and handed Lucy the reins. She clucked and the horse began walking. The man waved good-bye.

"Nice fellow," said Mary Jane.

"I think the only words he knows in English are thank you," said Lucy sourly.

"Well, if that's the case," said Mary Jane, "he should go far."

Nellie agreed. With that kind of energy and eagerness to please, the man *would* go far. She thought back to the immigrants at Castle Garden. They had such courage, risking their lives to make a weeks- or months-long journey in wretched conditions to a place where they knew no one, had no money, and couldn't speak the language. And the whole system was set up against them: thieves, con men, bureaucrats, and angry nativists awaiting them on their arrival. Still they came, by the hundreds of thousands, fueled by nothing but hope for a better life. Nellie understood why Emma had fought for them.

How did she do it? Nellie wondered. Where did she get the hope, the faith that she could actually change things? Yes, Emma came from wealth, but that didn't protect her from the enemies she was taking on, the parasites at Castle Garden or the hateful heir to the most successful department stores in America. The chances of prevailing in any of those situations had seemed impossible, but Emma had persevered—more than that, she'd actually succeeded. Emma saw an injustice and was willing to fight it, whatever daunting forces lurked on the other side. Nellie admired that so much. She didn't have that kind of fortitude. Oh, she had worked hard to get a job in New York and managed to land the Bellevue story and a position on the *World* staff, but she had been fighting discouragement the whole way and had nearly given into it dozens of times. If Emma ever felt discouraged, she certainly never succumbed to it.

Suddenly Nellie didn't feel quite so alone. The struggles to work in a man's world or to fight a bank that cheated her family had been so lonely. No one really understood what that was like, not even Ingram. But the trails Emma had tried to blaze were every bit as rugged as Nellie's. In her own eyes, Nellie fell short by comparison, but at last she had a guide, a beacon, someone who would have understood all she had to go through.

For the first time, Nellie saw why this assignment was so important to Pulitzer.

They *had* killed her, and letting Emma Lazarus die without getting to the bottom of what happened was like letting her die by the side of the road and then walking away. Emma, above all people, was entitled to a proper burial, and that meant exposing how she'd died. Justice would not come easily. Her murderers would almost certainly not be brought to legal justice. They were too powerful, too well-protected. But they might at least be brought to social justice.

She couldn't wait to go back to New York.

CHAPTER THIRTEEN

WOODLAWN PARK

The sensible next step, Nellie knew as she rode the train back to New York, was to take Ingram's suggestion and get hold of a piece of Emma's clothing, verify that the death was a murder, link DeKay definitively to the crime, and then link DeKay to Hilton. But after the travesty in the Apollo courtroom, Nellie was too angry with powerful men like Henry Hilton to be patient and methodical. She wanted to confront Hilton and let him know she knew exactly what he had done to Emma and that she wouldn't rest until the rest of the world knew it as well. It was a foolhardy and even dangerous approach, which she rationalized by thinking it might pressure Hilton into making a mistake. The nub of it, though, was she wanted to punch the bully in the nose and show she wasn't afraid of him.

Arranging to see him, however, would not be all that easy. Hilton loathed the press. With unending ridicule, both Republican and Democratic papers would point out how he had colossally mismanaged and bungled the immense fortune he'd inherited and lost more money than all but a handful of men in history had ever earned. As a result, Hilton had essentially closed off all communications with the fourth estate. He particularly despised the *World* and Joseph Pulitzer, for the additional transgression of trumpeting one of the sensational crimes of the century, a crime that had brought pain and embarrassment to Hilton and the family of A.T. Stewart.

It was a story well-known to anyone who worked at the *World*, alluded to often in the newsroom. On June 2, 1878, two years after Stewart's funeral, the body of the department store magnate suddenly disappeared from its two-story crypt, with only a ransom note for an undisclosed sum in its place. "The Missing Corpse Grave Robbery" generated twelve-point banner headlines for days and became the talk of the entire country. The public found the story of "the lifeless body of the richest man in American history, held for ransom by common thieves" abhorrent, sacrilegious, and, needless to say, riveting. A massive hunt for the corpse ensued, with the New York City police force and Pinkerton detectives pursuing every possible lead twenty-four hours a day. Then suddenly, two weeks after the corpse-napping, Hilton announced that the body had been found and returned to its grave, and the search was called off. No one was ever arrested and no ransom sum ever disclosed, and Hilton refused to say anything more on the matter.

But much of the press, especially the *World*, refused to let the story die. Had Hilton actually paid the ransom? Had the grave robbers been found, and if so, why hadn't they been arrested? Was the entire matter a hoax, to distract the public from Hilton's enormous business losses? Through it all, Hilton remained silent, and the more he stonewalled, the greater and more outrageous the speculation. He pleaded with the press to leave Stewart's family alone, but Pulitzer knew he had a compelling story on his hands and refused to drop it, doubling and even tripling the number of reporters assigned to it. In front-page editorials, Pulitzer even wondered if Hilton had simply taken an unclaimed body from the Manhattan morgue and placed it in the Stewart crypt to put an end to the matter and free himself from exorbitant ransom demands. When Hilton, through a friendly publisher, attacked the *World*'s speculations as "malevolent," Pulitzer demanded to know exactly how much had been paid to "the purported thieves"—the *World* always referred to the story's grave-robbers as "purported" or "so-called"—and called upon Hilton to produce them. The public devoured the coverage, and the *World* sold more papers relating to "The Missing Corpse Grave Robbery" than any other story in the entire nineteenth century. Hilton became so outraged at the coverage that he brought a criminal libel suit against Pulitzer—which, of course, only prolonged the controversy and sold yet more copies of the *World*. (The charges were dismissed. The *World* headline the next day: "Court Finds for *World*, Hilton Can't Find Corpse.")

As a reporter for the *World*, it would be next to impossible for Nellie to meet with Hilton if she identified herself, particularly regarding a story on Emma Lazarus, and given his reclusive life and layers of security, even more difficult for her to talk her way in with a false identity. But she was absolutely determined to see him, and she knew exactly how she would approach him if she ever got the chance. Hilton, like most men with power, enjoyed ignoring rules. It was a sign of special status that he could get away with things no one else would dare try, that his money and connections could transcend accountability. One reason Hilton hated Pulitzer so much was that he had no sway with Pulitzer; this immigrant son of a Jewish mother had held his feet to the fire with the corpse-napping, against all common decency. Emma Lazarus had treated him the same way. Nellie sensed that if she could get Hilton going on this subject, he might build a head of steam so great that he'd edge into bragging about poisoning Emma—which would only make the story that much more convincing and sensational.

But how to get in to see him? She considered possibilities the entire train ride back from Pittsburg, discarding each one as either too transparent or too shabby to win her a visit with the man who had sued the *World* and its publisher. Finally, as they approached the massive railroad yard of New York's Pennsylvania Station, she came up with an idea. It wasn't perfect, and she could use it only once, but it would get her face to face with Henry Hilton.

She hurried to the *World*'s archives and found exactly what she wanted. Not long after inheriting A.T. Stewart's money, Hilton had constructed one of the largest and most lavish mansions in America, Woodlawn Park, outside of Saratoga Springs. Although the property was already among the grandest in New York State, Hilton immediately added six hundred acres of surrounding land and stocked it with expensive show animals, including sixteen prize-winning stallions upon whom nothing was spared. "They have their own private train car, which takes them from the door of the home stable at Saratoga to all the principal horse shows," wrote the *Times*. "They are rubbed and fairly polished by expert grooms, and their beds are immaculately clean straw." Hilton enjoyed owning horses so much, he expanded his stock farm to dozens of Holstein and Guernsey cattle, Southdown sheep, poultry, and purebred dogs.

The house itself was extraordinarily elaborate. Its entrance included an eight-foot-high marble statue of Hiawatha created by the legendary Augustus Saint-Gaudens. The grounds had fifteen thousand trees and nearly as many bushes. (Hilton entertained thoughts of a flower garden to rival that of Versailles, but roses made him sneeze, so he kept it at a more modest level.) When first completed six years before, the grounds had been mentioned, though not reviewed, in New York's newspapers. Since then, however, much landscaping had been added, and the gardens were now fully mature. For once, Nellie's experience as a garden reporter would come in handy. She approached Hilton's office in Manhattan and, using the name Elizabeth Cochran, told them she wanted to write a story on Woodlawn Park's handsome gardens ten years later. They wired back the same day that Mr. Hilton was amenable to the story and would be delighted to show Miss Cochran the gardens himself the following day.

Nellie accepted the offer immediately. She had hoped to see Ingram first—she missed him terribly during her time in Apollo—but she had to seize the opportunity and spent much of the night reading all she could about Henry Hilton.

She took the ninety-minute ride to Schenectady on the first

train out and was met at the station by one of Hilton's employees, a brawny man with massive hands and a surly demeanor. In the hansom ride to the estate, Nellie considered engaging him in conversation to learn what she could about Hilton, but he kept leering at her, so she decided to look away and say nothing.

"Uppity, aren't you?" he said a few minutes into the ride.

"Excuse me?"

"High airs because some newspaper hired you. You'll be back begging for it before long. You'll see."

The man scared her. She could sense that the violence in him was barely under control.

"Yes, I suppose I will," she said and continued to look away. That seemed enough to appease the man, at least for the moment.

They arrived at Woodlawn Park after riding up a half-mile-long driveway from the main road to the largest house Nellie had ever seen. A house servant met her and took her inside to a foyer that itself was bigger than any house she had ever set foot in. On the lemon yellow walls, underneath giant chandeliers and fifty-foot-high ceilings, hung huge tapestries of knights on a crusade, and off to one side was an enormous ballroom with floor-to-ceiling mirrors that made it look even larger.

"Miss Cochran."

Henry Hilton came down the steps to meet her. He was a tall, thin man, with a pointed nose and sunken cheeks and thick, white muttonchops that extended down to his jaw. Nellie had seen a photograph of A.T. Stewart and noted that Hilton dressed and styled himself similarly. Apparently Hilton hoped that if he looked the part of Stewart, he might develop the economic touch as well.

"How was the journey from the city?" he asked expansively.

"Very comfortable, thank you. Though I did not expect so grand a destination."

"Well, we will have to make your visit a memorable one. Would you like a cup of tea? Or something to eat?"

Hilton was much more hospitable than she had expected, almost solicitous. She knew beneath the surface he was a wretch, yet he could not have been warmer.

"Perhaps we could tour the grounds first and then have some tea?" she suggested.

"Excellent. Harold, please have some tea ready when we return."

"Very good, sir." The butler beckoned to a maidservant, who quickly headed to the kitchen. It was not efficiency that was driving the woman, Nellie saw, but fear.

Hilton extended his arm to escort her. "Shall we?"

She smiled and took his arm as they headed outside to stroll between two rows of tall oak trees that led out to a meadow of flowers stretching as far as the eye could see. It was a beautiful summer day and the gardens were magnificent, but with her arm in Hilton's, she felt only revulsion. Fighting it, she played along and endeavored to put him completely at ease, listening intently as he bragged about his gardens, lord of the manor.

"I suppose you are wondering why I agreed to give a personal tour to a reporter from the *World*," he said as they walked underneath a canopy of branches.

"You are proud of your grounds and welcome interest from any paper, even one with a publisher you hold in low regard."

"That would make sense, Miss Bly, if the person touring my grounds was not looking to involve me in a murder."

He stopped and faced her, dropping her arm. His voice had turned cold, his manner no longer inviting.

"If you suspected that was the reason for my visit," she said, recovering as best she could, "why did you agree to see me?"

"Because I have something to offer you, something that will become the biggest story of the year, even bigger than your account of the Bellevue Women's asylum. Or anything to do with Emma Lazarus." He paused for effect, struggling to contain his excitement. "The defeat of Grover Cleveland in the presidential election."

Since day one of his administration, reformist President Grover Cleveland had taken on the monstrous forces of American big business and just the year before had signed into law the Interstate Commerce Act, which asserted long-awaited government control over railroad barons. He had also waged a battle to reduce protective tariffs, a position that resonated with the newly emerging middle class but that manufacturers claimed would wreck American industries. Republicans despised Cleveland and felt he had to be stopped, and indeed he received more death threats, and greater security, than any other president had ever received. Although populists had their issues with Cleveland, most Americans recognized him as an honest man, and he was expected to win reelection. Yet here was Hilton saying he had the means to defeat Cleveland.

"And how exactly would you do that?" asked Nellie.

With trembling hands, he withdrew a letter from his waistcoat and proffered it to her. It was written on official British Government stationery and addressed to a Charles F. Murchison of Sacramento, California.

> *Dear Mr. Murchison:*
>
> *Thank you for your inquiry, as a former Englishman, as to my advice on your vote in the U.S. presidential election in November. Because of his favorable position on free trade, President Cleveland is the Crown's preferred candidate.*
>
> *I hope I have been of assistance and wish you all good fortune.*
>
> *Sincerely,*
> *Sir Lionel Sackville-West*
> *His Majesty's Ambassador to The United States of America*

Politics was not one of Nellie's primary interests, but even she recognized the explosive nature of the letter in her hand. The Irish were the critical swing vote in any national election. In 1884, Democratic candidate Cleveland, the governor of New York, was headed for certain defeat when, at a dinner in New York City for his opponent, James G. Blaine of Maine, a Presbyterian minister had proclaimed to deafening applause, "We are Republicans, and we don't propose to identify ourselves with the party whose antecedents have been rum, Romanism, and rebellion." The Irish population, outraged at the "rum, Romanism, and rebellion" reference, turned out en masse for

Cleveland and produced a narrow victory in New York State and thus the nation.

Hilton, Blaine's biggest financial supporter and a cheering anti-Roman member of the audience that night, learned his lesson well. Britain, of course, opposed U.S. tariffs, as did Cleveland. Hilton's political operatives had apparently gotten someone in California to pose as a British expatriate and write His Majesty's Ambassador inquiring which candidate he should support. Incredibly, the Ambassador had delivered an honest reply. Because the Irish detested all things British, the letter Nellie held in her hands would do to Cleveland what "Rum, Romanism, and Rebellion" had done to Blaine—cost him the Irish vote and therefore the election.

Hilton beamed at his handiwork.

"Why are you offering this to me?" asked Nellie. "Why not publish it in a paper more to your liking, like the *Herald* or the *Times*?"

"Because the Irish, to the extent they can read at all, read your paper," Hilton said with contempt.

Nellie suddenly shared the loathing so many others had felt for Hilton.

Generations of Irish oppression at the hands of the English were coursing through her veins. She wanted to give him a tongue-lashing, rip up the letter, and get to the train station and as far away from him as possible. But she was there for important information. Hilton's comeuppance would have to come later.

"Why me?" she asked. "Why not use a reporter who writes about politics?"

"Because you are ambitious and more likely to make sure the paper publishes it."

But Hilton had misjudged her. To Nellie, everyone in politics was corrupt. She was indifferent whether the letter was published in the *World* or anywhere else. Clearly, though, the election mattered a great deal to Hilton, and she intended to use that fact to her advantage. She studied the letter. If authentic, it would put a Republican back in the White House and end any possible reforms.

"Before I take this to my editor, I need to know the role you played in Miss Lazarus's death."

"I don't think so, Miss Bly. You will take this letter and be grateful you've got the story of the year in your hands."

"It may be the story of the year, but it will be an even bigger story if it comes out in the *World*. Otherwise the Irish will doubt its authenticity, won't they, Mr. Hilton? And you know that your antipathy toward Mr. Pulitzer is mutual. You're counting on my ambition to be so great that I will persuade him to do whatever you ask. But the truth about Miss Lazarus means much more to me than the election this fall. So if I am to do your bidding, you must do mine. I need to know what role you played in her death."

She handed him back the letter. Hilton took her measure and knew she meant every word. Inwardly she smiled. His actions, and his face, only confirmed that he had invested too much in his plan to stop now.

"I had no role in her death," he said.

"I have sources who say otherwise."

"Oh?" Again he bridled at being contradicted. "And what do your sources say?"

"That you frittered away Mr. Stewart's fortune through incompetence, but in your mind it all began with Miss Lazarus's boycott of the downtown department store. Since then, as you steadily lost millions of dollars every year, you blamed her for your losses when in fact all the responsibility is yours."

He went flush. No one ever spoke to him like that, certainly not a woman.

"Your sources are jealous of my wealth."

"Not at all. One source is wealthier than you are and earned it through his own labors. He is convinced you arranged for the death of Miss Lazarus."

He stared at her, incensed that someone would make such a charge with impunity. "Gould. You have been talking to Gould."

Nellie said nothing, but Hilton knew he was correct.

"Well then, I shall have to extract my revenge on Mr. Gould

in other ways."

"I would be careful about taking on Mr. Gould. He said you would lose a fortune if you ever tried to engage in serious business."

She enjoyed tossing those words his way and watching him grow flush.

"We shall see about Jay Gould and his predictions. But if I am so inept, Miss Bly, why are you here? Apparently I was able to succeed at something."

The meaning of the "something"—Emma's untimely death—was unmistakable. All traces of a smile disappeared from Nellie's face. She became stone sober once again.

"Did you hire Charles DeKay to poison Miss Lazarus?"

He hesitated. And in that flicker of hesitation she knew she was right and that Gould had been right. But she needed him to say it.

"I know how much you loathe Mr. Pulitzer," she said. "I know how difficult it must be to offer something that will mean more sales for the *World* and more money in his pocket. That merely demonstrates your desire that I show him your letter. But I will show him nothing if you do not answer my question about Mr. DeKay."

"That would be tantamount to admitting murder."

She said nothing. He looked at the letter. Nothing would happen to him, he assured himself. No one in civil authority would dare lift a finger to challenge him. And the presidential election was hanging in the balance.

"I was aware of Mr. DeKay's close relationship with Miss Lazarus, and Mr. DeKay and I have attempted to help one another in social and financial matters in a mutually beneficial way. There. I have answered your question."

He had done her bidding; now it was her turn. He handed her another envelope.

"Here is a copy of the letter. I will provide the original when Pulitzer agrees to publish it."

She took the envelope. She felt sullied.

"Tell me," she said. "How much did it please you to see

Miss Lazarus dead?"

"Immensely."

Nellie could not stand to be in his presence a moment longer. She placed the envelope in her purse and turned to leave.

"I will summon my driver," he said.

"No, thank you. I prefer to walk." And she headed for the long driveway.

"You know," said Hilton matter-of-factly, "there was one thing that never made sense to me. When I turned away the kike Seligman from my hotel, I said that other Jews who had been here for generations were still welcome. I specifically mentioned the Lazarus family. And yet she gave me the back of her hand."

"I'm surprised she gave you even that much."

CHAPTER FOURTEEN

EMIL KRAEPELIN

Cockerill was looking over the layout for the afternoon edition when Nellie walked in.

"Good afternoon."

"Good afternoon, Miss Bly," he said without looking up. "I trust that all went well with your personal business at home?"

"Yes. Thank you."

She stood there waiting while he continued to read. Things were still cool between them since he had declined to publish the story about DeKay and Barker.

"Do you need something?" he asked.

"I have something for you."

He looked up and saw her holding an envelope.

"Set it down, if you would. I'll have a look later on."

"I think you might want to see it now."

He caught the imperative in her voice and began reading the letter. It did not take him long to grasp its import.

"Where did you get this?" he demanded.

"From Henry Hilton."

"How did you come to see Henry Hilton?!"

"I went to his office and asked to see him, and he agreed."

Cockerill was not easily taken by surprise. "Why did you want to see Henry Hilton?"

"I had information that he may have been involved in Miss Lazarus's death."

Cockerill knew full well Hilton's attitude toward the press, especially the *World*. "What exactly did you say to Henry Hilton that he agreed to see you?"

"I told his secretary that I wanted to write a story on the gardens at Woodlawn Park, and Hilton invited me up the next day."

He grunted in admiration. "And the letter?"

"His condition for talking to me."

"Well, I need to learn more. This could affect the entire election—"

"I suggest you check with the British Ambassador. They can most likely attest to its authenticity."

She turned to walk away. Her utter lack of interest perplexed him. "Miss Bly. Don't you realize what you have here?"

"I do."

She walked away, leaving him shaking his head.

Ingram and Nellie avoided meeting in his office whenever possible. Although the setting was comfortable and intimate, Mrs. Fairley, the receptionist, could make trouble if her suspicions were aroused. The Harlem room where Nellie stayed with her mother was out of the question for a variety of reasons, including a rule prohibiting gentlemen callers from setting foot in any of the sleeping rooms. Many unmarried couples were in a similar predicament, of course, and the free market system had come up with its natural solution. On Forty-Fourth Street in Manhattan, between Broadway and Sixth Avenue, hotels sprang up that rented rooms by the hour. Unlike the seedy rooms for streetwalkers and their johns on Canal Street, the inns on Forty-Fourth Street catered to a decidedly upscale clientele. A man or woman would arrive separately, be shown discreetly to their rooms, then depart by separate entrances. Nellie and Ingram had a particular hotel, The Hudson, that they visited at least once a week, usually on Thursdays around four, after Ingram had finished seeing patients. They became acquainted with the desk clerk, and Thursday afternoons he always set aside the same room, with flowers freshly cut that morning.

They hadn't been together since Nellie left for the trial outside of Pittsburg. She had missed him terribly and wished for his companionship and to make love and lie nestled in his arms. She was so eager to see him, she arrived fifteen minutes early. She paced the room, straightened the flowers, undid the bed, and checked herself in the mirror. She decided to remove her underskirts so they could begin making love more quickly. She considered undressing altogether to be lying in bed under the blanket when he walked in. That would definitely surprise him, but Ingram was too earnest for that, she thought, at least now. She would make him playful soon enough.

A key slipped into the lock, the door opened, and Ingram walked in. She rushed to him and practically jumped into his arms. He held her tight, both of them too happy even to speak. It felt wonderful to embrace him, even more than she had imagined.

"I missed you so much," whispered Nellie. She surprised herself at her boldness.

She was so happy to be with him. He sensed her trust, her exquisite vulnerability, and touched her head gently, kissed her hair. She could feel his love. His breathing was even faster than usual. Tears welled up in her eyes.

"So many times I wanted to ride the train to see you," he said.

"I'm glad you were spared my humiliation."

"I wish I had been there to comfort you." She felt such desire for him. She could feel dampness between her legs. She took his hand to lead him over to the bed.

"I have some news for you," he said.

She stopped and looked at him. He had a boyish eagerness to share a secret. "I cabled Miss Lazarus's doctors in London."

She did not expect that. The transatlantic cable had only recently reached the point where an office could transmit and receive 120 words per minute, at fifty cents a word.

"It's so expensive."

"I wanted to know the answer myself."

"What did you learn?"

"Miss Lazarus stopped receiving arsenic treatments six months before she returned to the United States."

"Six months?! So any arsenic in her system came solely after her return."

"Yes."

Now Nellie absolutely had to obtain an item Emma had worn after returning. That would make it all the easier to prove that her death was a murder.

"Thank you for doing that."

"It was my pleasure."

"In that case I am curious to see what you will call this." She began unbuttoning his shirt and stroking his chest with her fingers. She wanted him so badly, and not only sexually. She wanted to feel his soul against her.

"I received another cable from Europe."

He said it haltingly. Something was wrong.

"An invitation from Emil Kraepelin, to study at his hospital in Germany."

Kraepelin was the leading psychiatrist in Europe and a pioneer in the new field of mental illness. Ingram had corresponded with him regularly, sharing observations from Bellevue and his own practice. Kraepelin, like Ingram, classified his patients by symptoms and had begun developing different approaches for each disorder, and he had met with meaningful success.

All Nellie's joy and anticipation of seeing him suddenly dissipated. "That is a marvelous opportunity," she said.

"Yes."

"You must accept it." He nodded.

"How long will you be gone?" She dreaded the answer.

"A year."

The words sliced through her heart to the core. Nellie needed Ingram, more than she had ever needed anyone. She had only begun to acknowledge that in the past few weeks. Life had been so lonely, as long as she could remember. One skirmish after another, one enemy after another, one trial after another, always leaving her alone and mistrustful. Ever since her father died and life became so difficult, she wanted to be close with a man, but they had always let her down, starting with Thaddeus Jackson, continuing with teachers and policemen and employers and union organizers and the publisher at the *Dispatch*. The men either wanted her for sex or menial tasks; no one had ever really cared about her as a person or given her any credit. No one until Ingram.

"When will you go?" she asked.

"Within the month. As soon as I can find a suitable replacement at the hospital."

A month?! She needed him longer than that. She needed him for the story—to analyze the clothes Emma wore, the clothes DeKay wore, the items DeKay touched. More than that, she needed him to talk with, to bolster her courage when she felt overwhelmed and alone.

He took her hand in both of his. "Come with me," he said solemnly.

"I'm working on this story."

"Join me when it's finished. We can marry over there."

She gasped. Other women called attention to the inherent unfairness of marriage, but Nellie wasn't like them. She was an Irish girl through and through, and part of her longed for a husband and a family and a home where you could tell stories at night and laugh with your children and make passionate love with your husband. Deep down, try as she might to give up that dream, she still clung to it. But this was not the way.

"I can't."

"Please, Nellie—"

"I am responsible for my mother. And my sisters. I need to keep working."

"I'll take care of you. I'll take care of your entire family, for the rest of your life."

He meant it. She could see that. But her father had made the same promise to her mother, to take care of her and their children forever, and the moment he died, their lives had fallen apart. How could she explain to Ingram what it was like to be thrown out of your house as a child? She had vowed never to rely upon a father or husband for her well-being ever again. She had worked hard to get a job, a very good job, and she could not give that up. It had nothing to do with ambition or pride or independence of mind—she simply could not put herself in a position where she and her family were dependent on a husband for their survival.

"No." She was adamant.

"Please, Nellie. Marry me." He squeezed her hand tight. "Spend your life with me."

She shook her head, an act of will to keep away the temptation.

"Will you at least wait for me?"

He was asking her to be like a wife waiting for her soldier husband to return from war or her fisherman husband to return from a long sailing trip, but she didn't want to be like those women. She had gone without for long enough. She wanted Ingram in her life day in and day out.

"I don't think so."

He suspected as much. He knew the history and the fears. Still, he had hoped.

"I'm sorry," he said.

"No, no. I am very happy for you."

"I will miss you terribly."

She didn't know what to say. She had pulled back from him. They were no longer touching. She began putting on her underskirts.

"Please understand—" He looked so wounded.

But she didn't care. "I do understand."

She dressed as fast as she could. Neither knew what to say. Finally she stood up, straightened her dress, and slipped on her coat.

"If you can locate any samples before I leave, I would be glad to take a look," he said.

"Thank you. If it is not too much trouble."

"No trouble at all."

She walked to the door and stopped. "Congratulations

again on your invitation," she said.

His heart was breaking. "Please don't rush off—"

She walked out and closed the door behind her. And burst into tears.

CHAPTER FIFTEEN

STEREOGRAPH OF NEW YORK WORLD BUILDING

After leaving the Hudson Hotel on Forty-Fourth Street, Nellie decided to return to the paper. She was too sad to go home. Her mother would immediately see something was wrong and press her, and she wouldn't know what to say. Or her mother would be disoriented and notice nothing at all, which in some ways was even worse. She was still crying when she got off the streetcar in front of the *World* offices a half hour later.

Perhaps that was why she didn't notice the onrushing hansom that nearly ran her down and splattered her skirts and bodice with slush when she stepped into the street. The traffic laws of the day required all hansoms to stop when passengers alighted on the right side, but this one seemed to speed up when Nellie reached the road. If the conductor hadn't pulled her back, she would have been trampled and probably killed.

The near-accident jolted Nellie back to reality and the tasks at hand. She carefully crossed the street and headed up the steps. She was so busy composing herself, she walked past sentry Flaherty with neither an insult nor a word of greeting.

She wiped off her dress as best she could and walked into the newsroom. As she lifted her skirts above the spit and tobacco juice and made her way gingerly along the floor, the place grew quiet. That happened every time Nellie walked in. The reporters still didn't know what to make of a woman reporter, and an attractive one at that.

"Miss Bly!"

She turned and saw Cockerill heading toward her.

"We sent a messenger to your house," he said impatiently. "Where were you?"

"It doesn't matter. You have me now. What is the problem?"

"The letter you gave me. Mr. Pulitzer wants to speak to you about it."

"I told you all I know, Mr. Cockerill. I want no credit for the story. I simply agreed to bring you the letter in exchange for Hilton giving me certain information. Do with it what you want."

"Mr. Pulitzer does not want to leave it at that. He insists on seeing you."

"I need to speak with Mr. Dale first."

"I'm afraid Mr. Dale will have to wait," he said sharply.

He turned on his heel and headed out of the newsroom, expecting her to follow. She knew she had no choice, but time was suddenly important in the Emma story. She needed to meet with Emma's sisters, retrieve some of her clothes or blankets, and get them to Ingram before he left for Europe. She wished she could avoid seeing him altogether, but there was no one else she trusted as both a scientist and confidant.

When she walked into Pulitzer's office, his mood was markedly different from what it had been three weeks before. Then he'd been effusive and charming, but now he acted like a tyrannical father dealing with an incorrigible child.

"What were you doing talking to Henry Hilton?" he demanded in his thick accent.

"I was pursuing a lead on the Emma Lazarus story."

That surprised him, but he was so worked up it barely blunted his impatience. "And what lead would that be?"

She glanced at Cockerill, who averted his eyes.

"I became convinced that a former male companion of Miss Lazarus had something to do with her death. Then I learned that he was acting at the possible behest of Judge Hilton. I wanted to ask him about that."

The repeated mention of Emma Lazarus, and the fact that Nellie had been pursuing the story and actually getting somewhere, finally calmed Pulitzer.

"Why was I not told about this?"

She knew she could get Cockerill in serious trouble if she answered that question honestly.

"I wanted to develop more substantial information before I shared anything with you. What I had before were simply theories. I am much further along now."

Pulitzer did not notice the softening on Cockerill's face. "So this election story … that is not why you saw Hilton?"

"No. Not at all. It took me completely by surprise. I'd gone there to talk about Miss Lazarus."

Pulitzer eyed her closely, saw she was telling the truth. He sat down and motioned for Cockerill and Nellie to do the same. He was back in the role of supportive publisher.

"Did Hilton give you what you wanted?"

"Yes. I had to agree to deliver the letter, but he convinced me I am on the right track. I need to find more, but I know what the story will be."

Pulitzer allowed himself a smile. He liked what he was hearing, and he liked Nellie's determination. The shift in his moods was dizzying.

"You know that Henry Hilton is an enemy of this paper?" he asked.

"Yes."

"You need to be careful. He would like nothing more than to embarrass us."

"I realize that, Mr. Pulitzer—"

"And that is why I will not be publishing this letter." Both Nellie and Cockerill reacted in surprise.

"But it appears authentic," she said.

"It *is* authentic," said Cockerill. "The British embassy said it was."

"I am still not publishing it."

Nellie could not help herself.

"I'm not a political reporter, Mr. Pulitzer, but wouldn't this be an enormous story for the paper?"

"Yes, Miss Bly, it would," said Pulitzer, chuckling. "It must have frustrated Hilton no end to give it to a reporter from the *World.*"

"Actually, he enjoyed the idea of you helping his candidate win the presidency."

"I am sure he did. And he is right about the impact of the story. The Irish might hear about it in other papers, but in our paper they would read it for themselves and know it was genuine. But now they must read it elsewhere."

She looked at Cockerill. He was confused as well.

"I will not be publishing this," Pulitzer went on, "for two reasons. One, I do not trust what Hilton is up to, no matter what the British embassy says. And two, I do not want the *World* to help him in any way, no matter what it costs us."

"You hate him that much?"

"Even more so, now that I learn he may have been involved in Miss Lazarus's death."

There was something about Pulitzer's loyalty to his friend, so powerful that it transcended even his business or political interests, that resonated with Nellie. It inspired her, motivated her, made her all the more determined to give him what he wanted.

"That is your final decision, sir?" asked Cockerill.

"Yes."

"May I be excused now?" Nellie asked. "I have a story to work on."

"Of course. And keep me informed. I want to know everything."

"I will, Mr. Pulitzer." She stood up. "One more thing, sir."

"Certainly."

"Will I be reimbursed for expenses related to this story? It will affect the way I go about it."

"What types of expenses?" asked Cockerill warily. But the notoriously cheap Pulitzer dismissed the concerns with a wave of his hand.

"Miss Bly will not be reckless, Cockerill." He regarded Nellie earnestly. "But you must be careful. If someone did kill Emma Lazarus, they will not hesitate to harm you in order to protect themselves."

She suddenly remembered the hansom that had almost run her down and realized the strong possibility that it had not been happenstance. She thought about DeKay's cold arrogance, both at the theater and in lying to her so brazenly at the *Times* the following day, about Barker blithely destroying the vials of blood in the laboratory, about the fear among the workers at Woodlawn Park. Pulitzer was right to be worried. And if she hadn't despised DeKay and Hilton so much, she would have been more worried, too.

"I will be careful, Mr. Pulitzer. But I intend to get to the bottom of this."

"I know you will, young lady. I have no doubt of that."

CHAPTER SIXTEEN

WEALTHY MANHATTAN NEIGHBORHOOD, 1880s

Nellie took the Sixth Avenue Elevated up toward the Lazarus home at Forty-Ninth Street and Fifth Avenue. Down below her the foot traffic was thick, now that the snow from the Great Blizzard had finally melted away. From thirty feet above, on a stifling summer day, she was reminded of animals in a stockyard awaiting slaughter. But as the train rolled into the city's more well-to-do neighborhoods, traffic in general thinned out considerably—due in no small part to Pinkerton guards stationed on each corner from Forty-Third Street up to Sixty-Third Street to discourage the unwashed.

She walked four blocks to the Lazarus home on upper Fifth Avenue, a large brownstone with a dozen chimneys and a two-story balcony edifice over the entrance, which fit nicely among the other large mansions in the most expensive neighborhood in the city.

Nellie had decided to visit Emma's sisters unannounced, fearing that if she sent a telegram or sought permission some other way, they would simply decline to see her. Cockerill said the family had almost disowned Emma for the embarrassment she'd provoked by working with immigrants. Nellie suspected the sisters would want nothing at all to do with a newspaper reporter inquiring about Emma and a possible murder. But it would be harder to turn her away in person.

She walked up the dozen granite steps and rang the bell by

the large cast-iron portal. A moment later, a gruff maidservant in her fifties opened the door.

"Yes?" asked the woman uninvitingly.

"I am here to see Miss Anne Lazarus and Miss Josephine Lazarus."

"They are not expecting anyone."

"The matter I wish to discuss came up suddenly."

She handed the maidservant a calling card. The woman frowned when she saw it.

"Miss Anne and Miss Josephine do not speak with the press," said the maidservant. "May I suggest you write and ask for an appointment?"

"I have important information about their sister, Emma."

"Perhaps you might mention that in your request."

"I have reason to believe she was murdered."

That shook the woman out of her impassive demeanor. "I will wait here," said Nellie.

The maidservant went back inside. Nellie looked around at the sidewalk below. The lamps were powered by electricity and had bulbs rather than gas lanterns. Nellie had read about such streetlamps in Paris and London, but this was the first time she had ever seen them for herself. Any New York neighborhood wishing to change over to electric lights had to pay for the lamps and generator itself, and so far only the wealthy area bounded by Fifth and Madison, from Forty-Eighth to Fifty-Second, had done so.

Two homely women in their early thirties, in conservative attire that left only the hands and face uncovered, appeared at the door, trailed by the maidservant.

"Miss Bly?" said the taller one. "I am Josephine Lazarus. And this is my sister, Anne." Josephine was the harsher-looking and more commanding of the two. Anne struck Nellie as gentle but intimidated by her older sister.

"Thank you for seeing me," said Nellie.

"What's this about a murder?"

"May I come in?" The sisters hesitated. "It is not a matter to be discussed on a stoop in this neighborhood," said Nellie.

"All right." Josephine reluctantly turned to the maidservant. "Sarah, we will be in the library."

The sisters retreated inside, leaving Nellie standing there. No invitation to have tea, no offer to take her coat. The maidservant held the door open, and Nellie stepped into a giant foyer with tapestries of French battle scenes. The fifteen-foot-high walls were papered seamlessly in a gray pattern, and silver candelabra gleaned on marble counters.

Nellie recalled her first memories of her family house in Apollo, then the newest and largest in town. There was such joy in that house. This one, by contrast, seemed to have been completely drained of joy. She followed the maidservant to a room off the main hall, a library with shelves two stories high and a balcony fifteen feet up. The room itself was littered with loose papers and open books.

Josephine motioned her in, pointed to a chair, and closed the door behind her. "Now, what is this assertion you have concerning Emma?" she asked, sitting across from her on a French Louis XV hand-carved walnut sofa with a lime-colored damask, resting on six exquisitely carved cabriole legs.

"I have reason to believe your sister was poisoned."

"Miss Bly," said Anne, "she saw the finest doctors in England. They were perfectly clear she was dying of cancer. I know that because I was with her at every visit. And the illness proceeded exactly as they described."

"I have no doubt she suffered a cancer, Miss Lazarus. But her death was accelerated and ultimately caused by poison. Specifically, arsenic."

"Arsenic? That's impossible," said Josephine.

"Is it? Why?"

"Anne or I were with Emma at virtually every moment for eight months."

"No friends or acquaintances kept watch while you left the room? One of you was with her at all times? Are you absolutely sure?"

"There may have been a few moments here or there. But who would have wanted to kill Emma? And why? The doctors all agreed she would be dead within months."

"Both of those questions I hesitate to answer until I have actual proof she was murdered."

"And how would you obtain such proof? She has been dead for nearly a year." Josephine's skepticism made clear she considered the conversation a waste of time.

"I have a scientist who believes he can determine the true cause of her death if presented with a piece of your sister's clothing."

"Her *clothing*? How would that help him?"

"He believes that traces of the poison would remain on the clothing. He is highly respected, Miss Lazarus. And I am convinced he is right."

Josephine shook her head. "We mourned our sister's death for nearly a year, Miss Bly, and now occupy ourselves with her legacy, an anthology of her poems." She indicated all the loose papers in the room. "We plan to have two volumes to the printer by the anniversary of her death. There is no point in spending time examining her demise."

Nellie had not expected this.

"But what if she was, in fact, murdered?"

"Emma presented us with enough of the sensational in her own lifetime," said Josephine. "I see no reason to continue that into ours."

"Surely you want to know if your sister's death came at the hands of another—"

Josephine stood up abruptly. "Thank you for visiting, Miss Bly. We won't detain you any longer."

Nellie stared at her, completely at a loss. It made no sense that someone would have no interest in learning how her sister was killed.

"May I at least borrow a nightgown she wore in her final weeks? Or a blanket she used?"

"No. As I said, the matter of Emma's death will stay at rest."

Josephine strode toward the door. But Anne's curiosity got the best of her. "Miss Bly. Whom do you suspect of arranging this poisoning?"

"Mr. Henry Hilton. He despised your sister."

"Yes, he did." Josephine glared at Anne for prolonging the discussion. "But their problems occurred more than ten years ago."

"Mr. Hilton's fortune has shrunk every year. He holds your sister, and Jews in general, responsible."

"Mr. Hilton went to great lengths not to include our family in his criticism of Jews. He wrote a letter to our father, personally inviting him to stay as his guest at the Grand Hotel. He would never have committed violence against one of our family."

The naïveté and ignorance of these women was stunning.

"Please excuse us, Miss Bly," said Josephine. "We have work to do."

"Yes. The anthology," said Nellie, looking at the papers strewn about the room.

Nellie was not prepared to leave empty-handed. It was imperative to come away with an item for Ingram to examine. She wracked her brain for some other way to get through to the sisters, but Josephine interrupted, as if she could see the gears turning.

"Let me explain, Miss Bly. The circumstances of Emma's death are of little interest to us. Anything about her in the newspapers at this point should be related to her poetry, not the manner of how she left this world."

Something didn't make sense about the anthology. Nellie finally realized what it was.

"Your sister wrote hundreds and hundreds of poems. Why only two volumes?"

"We omitted poems, if you want to call them that, when Emma meandered on to one of her political tangents. We are putting forth only more traditional poetry."

"Those will have the most enduring legacy," added Anne.

"May I see the table of contents?"

"Certainly."

Anne proudly handed her a piece of paper, hoping for a compliment. Nellie perused the list and noted the most glaring omission.

"What about 'The New Colossus'?"

"That will not be included in the two volumes," said Josephine tartly.

"But it is a masterpiece. I have never read anything so stirring."

"I am glad it moved you, Miss Bly. Perhaps someday we will include it in a collection of her more zealous poems," Josephine said with a chill.

Nellie, astounded by the bowdlerization of Emma's canon, observed that "1492," an epic poem comparing Columbus's discovering America with the Spanish Inquisition, was not there. Nor were Emma's passionate reviews of *Daniel Daronda*, George Eliot's masterpiece of an Englishman discovering his Jewish roots, which Emma wrote had changed her life.

"We really should get back to the compilation. Sarah!" The maidservant appeared at the door.

"Please show Miss Bly out."

Nellie brusquely walked past the sisters and the maidservant without a thank you or good-bye. Without an item of Emma's clothing, she had no idea where next to turn.

She reached to open the front door.

"Miss Bly!"

It was the maidservant, Sarah.

"The door can be peculiar sometimes. Please."

Sarah opened the front door for her. As Nellie walked past, Sarah deftly slipped a folded-up piece of cloth from under her apron and handed it to her.

"This was the covering for Miss Emma's pillow," she whispered. "It has not been washed since her death. In fact, her entire room has stayed the same since the day she died."

Nellie looked at her with surprise. The woman could lose her job for something like this.

"Miss Emma was a lovely girl," she said in a low voice filled with emotion. "I knew her since she was a child. If she was murdered, the world should know of it."

Nellie slipped the pillow covering inside her coat. Mixed in with determination was a look of fear on Sarah's face.

"I will not say where I got this. I promise," Nellie whispered and walked out.

Sarah closed the door behind her. Nellie proceeded down the steps, the pillowcase hidden in her jacket, her left arm pressing against it. She dared not move it until she was safely away from the house, lest the sisters were watching from the window.

She had gotten what she wanted.

"I'm not surprised," said Alan Dale.

The sisters' attitude had confounded Nellie. How could anyone not care if their own sister was murdered? She hoped that Alan Dale, as a Jew and a friend of Emma's, might enlighten her, so she stopped to see him before taking the pillowcase to Ingram.

"To you and to me, Miss Bly, Emma Lazarus was a person to be revered. To her family, she was nothing short of an embarrassment."

"That was the very word they used this afternoon. I don't understand. Her poems were admired around the world. She had audiences with royalty. She devoted herself to the poor. How could such a woman possibly be an embarrassment?"

"You need to understand that the Lazarus family has already suffered several major scandals and wants to avoid all mention in the press. One uncle was brutally murdered and no arrest was ever made. His brother, who was suspected of the murder, was shot by a prostitute and barely survived. A third uncle was a justice on the New York Supreme Court and forced to resign after being implicated in a Tammany Hall scandal. The sisters grew up in this public ignominy. The last thing they want is more of it."

"But Emma was practically a saint. They seemed almost ashamed of her."

"Miss Lazarus's family were Sephardim," said Dale with a shrug.

"Sephardim?" Nellie had never heard the term.

"Jews who lived in Spain before the Inquisition and then fled to Portugal and the Portuguese colonies. Several thousand of them came to America in the 1600s, when those colonies were no longer safe. At first they encountered persecution here—"

"Mr. Cockerill mentioned that. But in a short time, the Lazaruses made a fortune."

"Indeed. But what Cockerill no doubt failed to tell you was that like most Sephardim, the Lazarus family kept their Jewish identity to themselves, unveiling it only at their homes or in their synagogues. They had a public life and a private life, an arrangement that worked well for Jews in Colonial America. But eventually a new wave of Jewish immigrants arrived in this country, from Germany and Central Europe, who looked and sounded very different from the Sephardim of Iberia. They were poor and had Germanic names and accents and practiced a much different brand of Judaism, and the Sephardim looked down on them. Sephardic daughters were forbidden to marry or even converse with German Jews. Sephardic men avoided doing business with German men. Joseph Seligman, the man Hilton turned away from the hotel in Saratoga, was a German Jew, and truth be known, many Sephardim had no problem with what Hilton did to him. They would have done exactly the same, given the chance."

"But he was still a Jew."

"He was a *German* Jew, which to many Sephardim meant he was no Jew at all. Emma's family was outraged when she organized a boycott on behalf of Seligman, but they put up with it, in part because President Lincoln and President Grant had treated him as a war hero. But her work at Castle Garden ... that was simply unacceptable."

"She was helping the poor."

"Yes, but it was the nature of these particular poor that so upset the family. These new immigrants were below even German Jews. They were *Russian* Jews."

None of this was making sense to Nellie.

"You see," Dale continued, "in Russia and Poland, Jews were poor farmers, with little education. In Germany at least they could function as merchants. After Tsar Alexander, who had provided protection for Jews, was murdered in 1881, hundreds of thousands of Jews in Russia and Poland were slaughtered and their villages burned to the ground. Those who survived fled to Germany and France and England, but those countries were overwhelmed by the numbers—one hundred thousand immigrated to Britain alone. The Hebrews in Europe wrote their brethren in the States, asking them to take in some of the poor souls, but the Jews in America turned them down cold." Dale recounted the history with total disdain.

"For what possible reason?"

"They claimed there was no place to put them. They said the new arrivals could not make it as farmers—the crops here were too different from those in Russia and Poland—and the Lower East Side was already as crowded as a rat's nest. They were too big a burden for the community, and the Jewish leaders here refused to take them."

"How could they refuse?" Nellie asked incredulously.

"You're Irish, aren't you, Miss Bly?"

"Yes. But I don't see—"

"How would your well-to-do Protestant friends feel about taking in a bunch of Catholic beggars from Dublin?"

"The Catholics would not bother to ask because they would know the answer. But the Jews have such a history of persecution. To turn their backs on their own—"

"They didn't *forbid* them from coming; they simply said they would not look after them. The immigrants would have to survive with absolutely no support—and with no knowledge of English, no way of earning a living, no way to feed their families. It was disgraceful, and Emma Lazarus refused to accept it. She went to her friends in the press—including Mr. Pulitzer, I'm proud to say—and publicly shamed the more prominent Jews here, many of them members of the same synagogue as her family. She raised money to provide for the immigrants and found them work and shelter and gave them an appropriate welcome. But the family was horrified and wanted to disown her. In fact, if the father had not had a prolonged illness, the sisters *would* have disowned her. He was the only one in the family defending her."

That explained why so few poems were part of the compilation, Nellie realized. The sisters wanted the history of Emma's life to stop before the incident at the Union Hotel in 1877. As far as they were concerned, the Emma after that time could be buried forever.

"So you see, Miss Bly, Emma has brought the Lazarus family quite enough attention from the press for a while."

Mrs. Fairley, the receptionist in Ingram's office, was as sullen as ever.

"Good afternoon, Mrs. Fairley," Nellie greeted her with insincere good cheer.

"Good afternoon, Miss Bly," returned Mrs. Fairley with a marked lack of enthusiasm.

"Is Dr. Ingram available?"

"He is with patients."

Nellie knew that was the case, of course, and in fact timed her visit so she would not see Ingram. His plans continued to wound her deeply and constantly, and she was not at all sure how she would react if she saw him. She decided she would meet with him after he had done the chemical analysis. There was no need before then.

"I have something for him." Nellie set the pillowcase, wrapped in newspaper and tied with twine, on the desk. "He is expecting it."

Mrs. Fairley took out her scissors.

"Do not unwrap it, please. It is of scientific import."

"He prefers me to open packages—"

"He prefers nothing of the sort. I have told him that the paper seams are marked in ink, and he will become very upset if the package has been opened."

Mrs. Fairley's cheeks flushed with color.

"You listen to me, young lady. I am his assistant—"

"Not in his laboratory, Mrs. Fairley. Only in his reception area. In Dr. Ingram's scientific work you have no place. And should that ever change, I will take my inquiries elsewhere."

Mrs. Fairley had never been spoken to like that, certainly not by a woman twenty years her junior. But Nellie was fed up, and with Ingram about to leave her life, she saw no reason to suffer Mrs. Fairley's ill-mannered judgments any longer.

"That should be no problem," snapped Mrs. Fairley. "I'm sure you have many doctors who see you in the late afternoon."

Now it was Nellie's turn to go flush. This woman observed more than Nellie thought and lacked the good taste to be quiet about it.

"Please have him inform me when he has the results," she said and left.

Nellie's impatience with Mrs. Fairley stemmed from more than Ingram's impending departure. Almost immediately after obtaining the pillowcase from Sarah, Nellie had realized it would be of limited value. The fabric would confirm whether or not Emma was murdered, and in that sense it was helpful, but without someone to attest that it had actually belonged to Emma—in other words, unless Sarah was prepared to lose her job—Nellie could not use it to make a convincing case to the public. She would be asserting that the most famous poet in America had been murdered and asking the readers to take her word for it. The pressure to disclose the source for the story would be enormous. But asking Sarah to identify herself publicly was out of the question.

Employment for women of any age, particularly Sarah's, was hard to come by, and as much as Nellie wanted to see that story in the paper, she could not bring herself to consider making such a request.

Ingram had said the item need not be an article of clothing. It could be anything she held or sat on or leaned against. Nellie asked herself who visited Emma frequently those last three months. Her family, of course, but they would be of no help. Charles DeKay, but he too had to be eliminated, for obvious reasons. Surely, thought Nellie, Emma must have had friends concerned for her health whom she would have insisted on seeing. But how could Nellie find them?

Her only hope was the *World's* archives. She asked to see copies of all New York newspapers within two weeks of either side of Emma's death. At first, the archivist balked, uncomfortable with assisting a woman and especially being alone with one in the isolated stacks of old newspapers. He quickly relented, however, when Nellie threatened to summon Pulitzer himself, who would no doubt take great exception at the waste of his time and probably relieve the archivist of his duties on the spot. The archivist then dutifully brought her copies of all the New York newspapers during the period requested.

The *World*, befitting Pulitzer, had a laudatory obituary quoting Emma's poetry extensively and detailing her charity work, but it contained nothing like the traditional "those in the company of at time of death." The *Times* piece, which was most likely written by DeKay himself as the current arts editor, was a strange mix of rhapsodic admiration for her poetry and petty criticisms of her character: "Devoted to study and by nature extremely fastidious and critical, Emma Lazarus had comparatively few intimates, but they were constant and warm." It, too, made no mention of those at the bedside at time of death. Nor did the *Herald* and *Sun*, though they discoursed at length about Emma's literary and charitable accomplishments. Interestingly, it was the *Tribune*, the greatest exponent of anti-Semitism in the New York press, that provided the information she wanted.

"... she was surrounded by her sisters, Anne and Josephine, her editors at the *Atlantic*, Helena and Richard Gilder, and friends, most notably the poet and philanthropist Julia Ward Howe."

Julia Ward Howe?! Nellie had to read the item several times to make sure she wasn't seeing things. The composer of the most famous song in America, "The Battle Hymn of the Republic"? Every schoolchild and every adult knew that song by heart. It was sung in churches and theater halls, at picnics and family gatherings, and even popped into Nellie's mind at the sight of the composer's name.

Julia Ward Howe was the great moral force of the United

States. It was impossible to overstate the esteem held for her in most of the country, especially by women. She was active in causes throughout the nineteenth century, from abolishing slavery to promoting women's suffrage to helping Russian émigrés to founding the nation's first school for the blind. She was as close to royalty as existed in the country, and people from all over the world went to her Portsmouth, Rhode Island home to pay tribute. Now that she had reached seventy, she left Portsmouth only for a summer home in Newport and rarely left her beloved New England at all. Yet she had visited Emma's sickbed and attended her funeral.

Nellie hurried to Cockerill's desk.

"I need to send a telegram to Portsmouth, Rhode Island."

Nellie had proved her mettle by covering for him with Pulitzer. Cockerill now viewed her as one of his reporters, and he would do anything to help her.

"We have a reporter in Providence," he said. "He can arrange it. Portsmouth is twenty miles away."

"I need it delivered immediately. It involves Emma Lazarus."

"I'll send it to him myself. Do you have the address?"

"No. But the person is well-known in Portsmouth. Mrs. Julia Ward Howe."

Cockerill looked at her in surprise.

"What is her connection with Miss Lazarus?"

"Mrs. Ward Howe is known for never leaving New England. Yet she was by Emma's side when she died."

Cockerill took out a piece of paper and a pen.

"Bring a suitcase tomorrow morning and an extra coat. Long Island Sound can be chilly this time of year."

CHAPTER SEVENTEEN

JULIA WARD HOWE

Nellie had never ridden on an ocean ferry. In fact, prior to moving to Manhattan, she had never been on water in anything larger than a rowboat, and that was at age eight. Fortunately Long Island Sound was so calm and the New England light so clear that she could lean over the rail and practically touch the enormous schools of fish swimming alongside.

Breathing in thick salty air for the first time, she sat on the deck and looked over the newspapers she had bought that morning for the ride. The big story in all of them (other than the *World*) was the publication in the *Los Angeles Times* of the letter from Lord Sackville-West, the British ambassador to Washington, to "Mr. Murchison of California," stating Her Majesty's Government's preference for the election of Mr. Cleveland rather than Mr. Harrison to the American presidency. Every newspaper had an editorial comment. If one didn't know better, one would have thought from the outpouring of indignation that all the publishers were Irish.

Nellie knew that for the next two months, until the election, the *Sun* and *Herald* and the rest of them would unrelentingly proclaim that "Grover Cleveland is Britain's truest friend in America." No self-respecting Irishman would ever vote for Cleveland now. The Republicans would be returning to the White House.

And yet Nellie did not think the election much mattered. Elected politicians, even the president himself, did not have the real power in the country. That lay with the rich, people like Carnegie and Frick and Hilton. The politicians simply did their bidding and diverted public attention from the real goings-on. Elections were a bone tossed out to entertain the populace.

The real reason she didn't pay much attention to the stories, however, was that she could think only about the Emma story. She had high hopes for her journey to New England. Mrs. Ward Howe had written back immediately, handing her reply to the *World* reporter who had delivered the telegram: "Will meet you tomorrow at Newport harbor. Take the morning ferry. Eager to hear about the women's asylum." Nellie was flattered to be recognized by such an iconic figure but more pleased that Mrs. Ward Howe was so willing to cooperate. Nellie had been hoping simply for an item to verify the poisoning. Now she might obtain some insight into Emma's personal life as well.

Julia Ward Howe was a particular hero of Nellie's. Ward Howe had started the phenomenon of women's study clubs, which initially began as reading groups but eventually transformed into community service organizations throughout the country. After Howe had established the New England Women's Club, the *Boston Transcript* had warned that "Homes will be ruined, children neglected. Woman is straying from the home." It was the absurdity of that proclamation, in fact, that spurred Nellie to join the women's study club in Pittsburg.

She was puzzled, however, as to why Howe had chosen to meet in Newport. Mrs. Howe was already in Portsmouth, her home. Newport was thirty miles away, an unwelcome journey for a woman in her seventies. What was the point of meeting there? It was mid-October, and the summer crowd would have left Newport weeks ago.

As the ferry approached Newport, Nellie saw immediately why those who could afford it would flock there every summer. It was an emerald jewel island in the middle of a beautiful ocean, surrounded by a ring of brilliantly colored hills, the leaves already turned on a breathtaking fall day. The light was as clear as any she had ever seen, with none of the yellow-gray skies of eastern cities. In fact, she couldn't even spot a smokestack on the entire island. Newport was the playground of the wealthy, and nothing as base as manufacturing would sully their holiday.

A stringpole servant in his late fifties, in black waistcoat and tails, approached her as she stepped off the dock.

"Miss Bly?"

"Yes?"

"Good day, miss. My name is Mathews. I am employed by Mrs. Howe." He reached for her bags.

"Thank you, Mathews." He led her along the dock.

"Tell me," she said, "is it far to Mrs. Howe's home?"

"About twenty minutes, miss. But I'm not sure what madam has planned. You can ask her yourself."

At the end of the dock, a horse and carriage was parked on the street. Seated in the back was an elderly, pear-shaped woman with a ruddy complexion, piercing almond-shaped eyes, floppy dark bonnet, and black dress with high collar.

"How was your journey, my dear?"

"Excellent, Mrs. Howe. Thank you."

The older woman extended her hand to help Nellie up into the carriage. Her grip was surprisingly strong.

"Your stomach is heartier than mine. I never cared much for the ocean. Mathews, take us to Potter's Inn. Miss Bly must be famished."

The carriage started away from the docks and turned on to Thames Street, a thoroughfare of shops that ran along the water. Because the summer season was over, most of the shops and markets were closed.

"I enjoyed your stories on the women's asylum, my dear. You showed remarkable ingenuity."

Nellie was genuinely flattered. "Thank you—" was the best she could muster.

"I assume you are here to look into dear Emma's death."

Nellie hadn't mentioned anything about that in her telegram.

"I may live a long way from New York," Howe explained, "but some things are clear even to an old woman like me. You are obviously exceptional at ferreting out the truth. Pulitzer would not send you up here to write about Emma's poetry. And it was perfectly apparent that something was terribly wrong with her besides the cancer."

"How so?"

"Emma was an inveterate writer. Whether abroad or at home or summering here, she was always writing poems, letters, essays. Yet she stopped completely those final three months. Hardly a word. Something was making her too sick to write, and I know it wasn't the cancer."

A pall of hope and anxiety swept over Nellie.

"Did she write *any* letters to you during those final three months?"

"I brought them for you," she said, tapping at her purse, much to Nellie's relief. "So whom do you suspect?"

This woman had a way of getting right to the point. Nellie hesitated to reveal what she knew, but there was something about Julia that made her throw caution to the wind.

"Henry Hilton."

"Excellent, my dear." Julia nodded approvingly and took Nellie's hand in both of hers. "We are going to have a lovely afternoon. I hope you like fish."

They stopped at an inn with narrow wooden doors and a sign with a poorly painted fish over the entrance. Mathews helped them both down to the cobblestones, and they stepped inside to a room with half a dozen tables, a bar, and a low fire. The place was thick with the smell of fish, an aroma Nellie had her fill of on the boat ride to Newport, but fortunately it was also redolent with potatoes, onions, and steaming milk, smells she was more accustomed to. A gaunt man with gnarled hands and a face sculpted by a harsh wind greeted them.

"Good afternoon, Mrs. Howe."

"Good afternoon, Harold. How is the fish soup today?"

'I've outdone myself, if you will pardon the immodesty."

"I will not only pardon it, Harold, I will reward it. A bowl for my companion, and one for myself."

Julia, apparently having the run of the place, walked over to a table in the corner and sat down. For the first time, Nellie was able to see her face. She had deep wrinkles from character more than age, yet there was a fire and youthful twinkle in her eyes.

"We have less than three hours, my dear. So let's get straight to it, shall we?" Julia saw Nellie's disappointment immediately.

"Three hours will be enough time. I promise. And I will not be much use to you after that, if I'm not asleep before then."

"I was hoping to hear you sing the 'Battle Hymn.' "

Julia smiled. "Now I see how you got to the bottom of the asylum story. Perhaps in a while. Tell me, what is it you want to know?"

"First, may I have the letters? A friend is convinced he can perform a scientific analysis that will prove Emma was murdered."

"I have seen enough of science not to doubt its possibilities." She handed Nellie a half dozen letters tied with a ribbon.

"That was simpler than I expected," Nellie said with relief.

"What is your next question?"

"Why are you so sure Judge Hilton is involved?"

Julia looked at her in surprise, her bushy eyebrows sinking into the cracks of her forehead.

"Who else could it be? She was making his life extremely difficult. He despised her for it."

"That's what I don't understand. The boycott happened eleven years before her death. After all that time, why would he accelerate her death when she was about to die anyhow?"

"This was not about the boycott," Julia scoffed. "This concerned the tribal land at Montauk."

Nellie looked at her, mystified.

"You don't know about this?"

"No."

The innkeeper brought two bowls of the fish soup. "Here it is, Mrs. Howe," he murmured. "I'll stake my reputation on this one."

"Your reputation would survive even that soup they serve down the street."

Pleased to be praised by the great woman, he set down the bowls and left.

"Are you aware of a man named Austin Corbin?" Julia

asked Nellie.

"He owns railroads."

"He holds a monopoly on train transportation on Long Island and in much of New England. Mr. Corbin is a very wealthy man and a very twisted man. He and Judge Hilton share a hatred for Jews. The American Society for the Suppression of Jews is their joint enterprise."

When Nellie had read about Judge Hilton in the *World* archives, she came across numerous stories about the organization that turned her stomach. "We pledge ourselves to spare no effort to remand the Jews to the condition that they were in the Middle Ages or to exterminate them utterly," Corbin and his supporters had proclaimed.

"Judge Hilton, as you must know, squandered much of the fortune he inherited from A.T. Stewart—himself also a person not to my liking—and received an appropriate amount of ridicule for it. Apparently he was determined to prove the world wrong and demonstrate he could make a success of himself in ways beyond the good fortune of inheritance. He approached his friend Corbin and offered to supply him with capital he might need for any venture of his choice. Corbin, I'm told, had one in mind, a project so ambitious it was beyond even his means. I'm not sure what it was exactly, but Emma apparently stumbled across it and incurred their wrath."

"She never mentioned it to you?"

"No, only that a young woman had written seeking her help, and that the woman's cause was legitimate. She said that Hilton, in his crude way, even confronted her on the street about it when she was walking with her sisters. Here she was barely able to stand, and he began screaming at her, in threatening and coarse language. What a horrible man. How is your soup?"

"Excellent." Nellie made a point of eating around the fish and concentrating on the potatoes and onions. "And you have no idea what the venture was?"

"She never told me. Only that it involved the Montauk tribe on Long Island."

"I know nothing about them."

"Well, you will find out all you need to know soon enough, my dear. There is a ferry from Newport to Sag Harbor in a little over two hours. I have arranged for the woman who sought out poor Emma to meet you at the dock. She and I have been in correspondence since Emma's death."

Suddenly Nellie glimpsed the depth and intelligence of Julia Ward Howe. "That is very kind of you."

"Not at all. Now, during these next two hours I thought we would finish our lunch and then I would show you some items of Emma's past. The more you know about the dear girl, the better your story will be, I imagine."

"As long as I hear a verse before I leave."

"If you insist, my dear."

"I do."

"How did you become so close with Miss Lazarus?"

They strolled along Thames Street, arm in arm, with the carriage trailing behind.

"You know about Emerson taking her under his wing?"

"Yes."

"He urged me to invite her for tea. She was only fifteen at the time, but her brilliance outshone everyone in the parlor. I suspect she found me boring."

They stopped at a white Colonial building with two rows of four arched windows on each side and a Jewish star in front.

"This is the Touro synagogue, the oldest in North America," said Julia. "Emma's great-great-grandparents were the founding members."

They walked up three steps and inside to a large meeting hall with dark red carpeting and a balcony supported by twelve pillars. Over the ark on the east wall was a hundred-year-old painting of the Ten Commandments.

"After the Revolution, when the country first achieved independence, Emma's great-great-grandfather invited George Washington to visit the congregation. Their exchange of letters is the most stirring I have ever read. Washington's reply is by the side wall."

Nellie walked over to a glass case near the staircase leading to the second floor. In the case was a letter, handwritten in ink on parchment paper.

> *To the Hebrew Congregation in Newport Rhode Island.*
> *Gentlemen,*
>
> *While I receive, with much satisfaction, your Address replete with expressions of affection and esteem; I rejoice in the opportunity of assuring you, that I shall always retain a grateful remembrance of the cordial welcome I experienced in my visit to Newport, from all classes of Citizens.*
>
> *The reflection on the days of difficulty and danger which are past is rendered the more sweet, from a consciousness that they are succeeded by days of uncommon prosperity and security. If we have wisdom to make the best use of the advantages with which we are now favored, we cannot fail, under the just administration of a good Government, to become a great and happy people.*
>
> *The Citizens of the United States of America have a right to applaud themselves for having given to mankind examples of an enlarged and liberal policy: a policy worthy of imitation. All possess alike liberty of conscience and immunities of citizenship. It is now no more that toleration is spoken of, as if it was by the indulgence of one class of people, that another enjoyed the exercise of their inherent national gifts. For happily the Government of the United States, which gives to bigotry no sanction, to persecution no assistance requires only that they who live under its protection should demean themselves as good citizens, in giving it on all occasions their effectual support.*
>
> *It would be inconsistent with the frankness of my character not to avow that I am pleased with your favorable opinion of my Administration, and fervent wishes for my felicity. May the children of the Stock of Abraham, who dwell in this land, continue to merit and enjoy the good will of the other Inhabitants; while every one shall sit in safety*

*under his own vine and fig tree, and there shall be none to
make him afraid. May the father of all mercies scatter light
and not darkness in our paths, and make us all in our
several vocations useful here, and in his own due time and
way everlastingly happy.*

G. *Washington*

"That was Emma's heritage, and she took it seriously. I
remember the first time she visited here, as a girl of seventeen.
She was never the same. And if that weren't enough …"

Julia walked up three short steps to the *bima*, the lectern
overlooking the congregation, and pointed to a square piece
of carpeting.

"Miss Bly, do you mind lifting that?"

Nellie bent down and found a seam in the carpeting. She
lifted the cloth and saw the handle to a door in the floor.

"Open it, if you would," said Julia.

Nellie lifted the door and saw a large room paneled with
wood and benches.

"This was used by Patriots fighting the British and then
by runaway slaves before the Emancipation. Congregants would
hide them here, and if the authorities ever came by, there were
tunnels that led to escape. Emma treated it as a calling. Her
poems switched from odes to love and life to the plight of her
people, the plights of all peoples. Oh, her family did not like
that, but no matter. Eventually came the boycott with Hilton
and the Stewart Department store and then her work with
the immigrants."

"Apparently her sisters were not similarly affected."

"No."

"They showed no interest whatsoever in her death. They
would not even discuss it, as if it would embarrass them."

"I'm not surprised. Come."

They walked outside to the carriage. Julia held on to Nellie
as they walked down the steps. The moment they were on flat
surface, Julia sped up again. Nellie had trouble keeping up.

"Mathews, the Beeches, on Bellevue Avenue."

Mathews helped Julia into the carriage, followed by Nellie.

"Not long after Washington's visit, the capital of Rhode Island moved to Providence, along with the seaworthy traffic. Many of the Hebrew families left Newport and moved to New York. That included Emma's family, in the 1830s. But the family wanted to maintain a connection to Newport. And so they built the Beeches."

"Their home has a name?"

"All the mansions in Newport do, my dear. But theirs was the first."

They rode along Bellevue Avenue and arrived at a three-story mansion with a wraparound porch and deck that Nellie estimated from the number of windows to have eight bedrooms. It was one of the largest homes she had ever seen.

"This was their *summer* home?"

"When Emma was a young girl of twenty, we would have tea and parlor games here every Monday. The house was very warm in those days, filled with laughter. The war was over and everyone was free of serious worries. But then Mr. Gould tried to corner the gold market, a great panic set in, and the mood turned somber again."

Nellie thought better than to tell her that she had met Gould and he had actually provided useful information.

"And then came the incident with Mr. Seligman," said Nellie.

"Yes. And her work with the immigrants. Emma rarely made it back here." Julia referred to the house with a sweeping gesture.

"This is the dichotomy of the Lazarus family, and indeed of many families in America. You have the side that helps patriots and runaway slaves and the other that lives like robber barons. And each is embarrassed by the other."

They arrived at the dock for the ferry to Orient Point with little time to spare. On the carriage ride, Julia had indeed sung a verse of "The Battle Hymn of the Republic" but insisted Nellie sing along with her. Julia's voice was strong, the conviction coming from deep inside, on this song that Nellie had sung hundreds of times. Nellie's heart swelled at the experience, and her spirit soared like never before with "His truth is marching on."

Just as Nellie was about to leave Julia to walk onto the ferry, Julia took her by the arm and spoke earnestly.

"Your task will not be an easy one, my dear. Hilton and Corbin are powerful men. But do not despair. If we could defeat slavery, anything is possible."

CHAPTER EIGHTEEN

MONTAUK INDIAN

On the ferry ride to Long Island, Nellie read Emma's final letters to Julia. The steady hand of the manuscripts at the Lazarus home was now shaky and weak. All the spirit and strength had been sapped. The last letter was particularly heartbreaking:

My Most Dear Mrs. H.:
    Please excuse my brevity. I lack the strength to convey all that is in my heart, and for that I shall never forgive myself. I so appreciated your recent visit. Your kind smile and even kinder eyes eased my discomfort beyond description. You have always provided such joy and inspiration.
    Though I sadly fall short of your example, know that I shall always remain, Your faithful servant,
    Emma L.

A wizened older woman with chestnut skin, pencil-thin wrists, and weather-beaten features had met Nellie at the ferry in Sag Harbor, the main fishing village on eastern Long Island. Though her clothes were tattered and her belly protruded from malnutrition, Maria Pharaoh had a royal dignity about her, with an erect posture and direct gaze. Nellie offered to treat her to a meal or some cider in a whaling inn, but Maria did not want to spend their time searching for a place that would allow her inside. Her guess was there would be none. Instead they sat on a wooden bench by the dock on a chilly fall day and even so drew sullen stares from the white fishermen.

Maria waited silently while Nellie read through a packet of newspaper clippings Emma Lazarus had compiled for Maria to show to receptive strangers. The shameful history of Maria's people was set out in black and white.

Unlike the American West, where the natives congregated in distinct tribes, the Indians of New England and Long Island shared a similar language and culture. Europeans assigned them names based on the Indian names of where they lived—Shinnecock, Pachogue—but the major differences among the native groups were mainly of dialect and accent. The most important of these tribes, the Montauks (as the white men called them), lived on the easternmost part of the southern fork of Long Island. The medium of exchange among the Indians of New England, and then among the Indians and the white settlers in the early Colonial era, was the wampum, and there was more wampum on eastern Long Island than anywhere else in the colonies. The Montauks were the keepers of the wampum as economic high priests for the natives in the northeast, and as such they enjoyed a noble place among the natives—and a targeted position among the whites. In a remarkably short period of time, the whites managed to steal Montauk land and take possession of the Native American currency.

By the early 1880s, they had succeeded. In 1871, a New York state court referee ruled that the Montauks had no property rights that white men were obligated to respect. In affirming the referee's decision a few months later, the New York Supreme Court held that the Montauks were "trespassing" on their own land. To mute any public outcry, the Montauks were then placed on a reservation—predictably located on the least inviting parts of eastern Long Island. But soon that, too, became valuable property for railroad owners, fishermen, and white land developers. In October 1879, a man named Arthur Benson petitioned the New York state court to sell him the reservation land at "auction," and for $150,000, Benson was awarded the entire parcel.

Maria took up the narrative from there. "After they stole

our land and placed us on the reservation, my nephew David came forward to lead us. He had worked for the Union Army and observed the white man's ways, and he understood them as a child understands a pet. He knew the whites would ignore him if the tribe referred to him merely as their leader, so he asked them to make him king. He did not know exactly what it meant to be king, only that the whites treated you differently if that was what you were called. The newspapers wrote about him as king, and with this title he went to Albany to ask the government of New York to give us back our land. David had served with some of the men there in the cavalry, and they offered to help him. But Mr. Hilton would not allow it."

Nellie perked up. "Mr. Hilton? Henry Hilton?"

"Yes."

"How was he involved?"

"Mr. Benson had sold much of the land to Mr. Hilton—"

"And Mr. Corbin?"

"Yes. To Hilton and Corbin."

"Go on. Please." Nellie could sense the pieces about to fall into place.

"The men in Albany became afraid to help David, even though he had saved their lives, and would no longer speak with him. Some said it was because our tribe now had African blood because they hated the Africans, and this allowed them to say our blood was no longer pure, though of course that was a lie. David found a lawyer, another soldier he had fought beside, to tell a judge about all the stealing, but then something terrible happened."

The older woman, stolid in recounting all the injustice, paused to gather herself. "My sister, David's mother, was murdered in her home. David found her."

The old woman handed Nellie a tattered clip from *The Brooklyn Eagle*. "The back of her head was crushed in."

Nellie read the clip.

Aurelia Pharaoh, mother of King David Pharaoh of the Montauk tribe of Indians, was found dead on the floor of her cabin. Foul play was suspected, but the jury settled that by a verdict she had died from "a visitation of Almighty God."

"They thought that would be the end of it. David would be so upset and frightened that he would stop his efforts to regain our land. But David was not afraid. He was devoted to his people. He suffered from the loss of my sister, yes, but that only made him stronger. And so they murdered him, too."

The old woman handed Nellie another clip from *The Brooklyn Eagle*, frayed and browning around the edges like the first one.

David Pharaoh, the King of the Montauk Indians, is missing, under suspicious circumstances. His hat was found on the deck of a schooner, and as he was known to have a large amount of money, foul play is suspected. He is the last of the Montauk tribe.

"And so they killed them both, Aurelia and David. My sister and my nephew."

Nellie felt terrible for the old woman. There was not a doubt in Nellie's mind that she was telling the truth.

"But he was not the last of the Montauks," said Nellie.

"No."

"And after they killed him, you went to see Miss Lazarus."

"Yes. Some people from a faraway land, who had crossed the great ocean, settled near here. They told me she had found them food and shelter and a place to live. They said her heart was good. And so I went to see her at the docks in Manhattan, where those who cross the ocean walk onto the land."

"What did she say?"

"She said she would help me. She wanted me to meet a lawyer. I said I had no money for a lawyer, but she told me not to worry, that she would pay the lawyer."

"Did you tell Miss Lazarus about Hilton's involvement? And Corbin's?"

"Yes. She was not surprised. She said they were bad men.

But she would try to stop them. She said she had beaten them before and would have ways to do it again."

"Then what happened?"

"Miss Lazarus crossed the ocean."

"And the lawyer?"

"He watched the grass grow by the cobblestones near his office."

Nellie had to smile.

"So he did nothing unless Miss Lazarus was around?"

"Nothing."

"And when she returned?"

"She was weak from the cancer, but she became very angry with him. And he did bring some papers to the court, asking for the return of our land. She still held hope and would write to me. But soon she lost all strength. And then she died."

"And the lawyer?"

"He said he could no longer work on the case."

"But she had paid him."

"Yes. But he wanted nothing more to do with me."

Something wasn't making sense to Nellie. "Miss Pharaoh, do you know why Hilton and Corbin were so determined to keep your tribe away from Montauk?"

To the old woman it was obvious. "They want our land."

"Yes, but why? Corbin already has the sole railroad to Sag Harbor. No one else could build one farther east without connecting to his. If they tried to build their own, it would be prohibitively expensive."

"There are many things I do not understand about white men. Their greed, their violence. They stole our land and moved us to a reservation with great praise for their own kindness, then took that land for themselves as well. When we protested, they killed my sister and my nephew. What can there be to understand about people such as this?"

CHAPTER NINETEEN

SAG HARBOR

"What can there be to understand about people such as this?"

On the train from Sag Harbor to Hunters Point, and then on the ferry ride back to Manhattan, Nellie tried to answer that question, and some others. Whites could kill Indians and take their land because they knew there would be no consequences, in the same way whites could kill blacks and take their land without consequence. But for Hilton and Corbin to kill Emma Lazarus, there was no simple guarantee of impunity.

Emma had powerful friends—Julia Ward Howe loved her like a daughter, as did Joseph Pulitzer and possibly even Jay Gould. Arranging for her murder would be a very risky matter. It would have to be extremely well-planned and worth the extremely serious risk. What were they planning that the two of them were willing to jeopardize their fortunes and their freedom?

Whatever it was, Nellie realized, had to do with the Montauks and their territory on Long Island. It was only when

Emma became involved with Maria Pharaoh that her life had been placed in real danger. What could possibly be at stake that Hilton and Corbin would act so brazenly? Once again she mentally reviewed: they already had deeds to the land and, more importantly, controlled the only access to the land with Corbin's monopoly of the Long Island Railroad. Nellie finally gave up thinking about it because she was getting nowhere.

Perhaps she was way off base. Perhaps Emma was not murdered after all, or there would be no way of proving it. Perhaps ... she caught herself. First things first. She would have to get an answer from Ingram.

It had been a long day. She had left for Newport at dawn, had lunch with Julia Ward Howe, took the afternoon ferry to Sag Harbor, arrived in the early evening for her meeting with Maria Pharaoh, then took the train back to Hunters Point and the ferry to Manhattan, arriving just after midnight. She should have gone straight home, but she needed to take this story out of the realm of conjecture as quickly as possible. She took a carriage from the Thirty-Fourth Street ferry terminal to Ingram's house.

A light was on in the basement: Ingram, to her relief and trepidation, was working. She knocked hesitantly on the door and heard him hurry up the stairs and to the front door. He opened it quickly and stared at her without a word. He looked even more tired and drawn than usual.

"Forgive the intrusion."

"No intrusion at all."

He looked as if he hadn't eaten for days. She wanted to hold him and hug him and comfort him and make love to him, but she couldn't. He would be leaving in a matter of days.

"Are you all right?" she asked.

"Yes. I was working. Please. Come in." He opened the door wide. She walked in. "Would you like some tea?" he asked.

"Please. Thank you."

She followed him into his kitchen. A fire burned in the fireplace. He filled the tea kettle and put it on a shelf over the fire.

"Are you hungry? Would you like some food?"

"No. I'm fine. Thank you."

She hadn't eaten since lunch and was famished, but she wanted to stay no longer than needed. In her fatigued state, there was no telling what she might do or say. He stoked the fire to increase the heat.

"Don't you want to know why I'm here at this hour?" she asked.

"No. I am happy you're here whatever the reason."

She watched him prepare the tea. He avoided looking at her. "I conducted the analysis for the pillowcase," he said.

She had almost forgotten about the pillowcase Sarah had given her. In his presence, she had almost forgotten about the case entirely and, watching him tend to the fire, could think only of his gentle touch on her inner thighs. She could feel resistance abandoning her.

"The concentrations of arsenic were high," Ingram began, "approaching a fatal level but well below a suicidal level. She would be terribly sick and, without proper treatment, would expire. A person with this amount of arsenic in her system was not intent on killing herself, nor could she have ingested it by accident. The only viable conclusion is that it was ingested without her knowledge."

"So it was murder."

"Yes."

"I have another item for you, this time from someone who will publicly attest to it." She took out Julia's letters from her satchel. But he shook his head.

"No."

"Ingram, I need these analyzed for arsenic."

"I know you do, but I must decline," he said, staring at the fireplace.

"Because I will no longer share your bed?" She was shaking with anger. "I must prostitute myself in order for you to help me? You who know the extent of the corruption here? Look at me, for God's sake! Answer me!"

He looked up at her slowly, with mournful eyes.

"The pillowcase confirmed my worst suspicions, that you

have stumbled upon a murder—committed by powerful and ruthless men. Should the people who killed Miss Lazarus think for even a moment that you pose any threat to them, they will not hesitate to harm you. I will not be a party to that. I would never forgive myself."

He looked at her with a kind of love and tenderness she had never known in all her life. She could feel the pain in his heart as if it were her own. In that moment, she realized she loved him the same way. Tears pricked her eyes.

"I cannot stop my work on this story. If you will not help me, I will find someone else. It may be difficult, and it may take time, but I will find a chemist somewhere."

"I assumed you would say that. And so I have a proposition for you. I will do all the chemical analysis you need and even testify if need be, if—and only if—you and your mother will move here in the morning. I will have the maid make up the rooms."

"I don't think that is necessary—"

"It is absolutely necessary. I will worry myself to death if you refuse me." He was insistent.

"What about Mrs. Fairley?"

"The rooms are in a separate part of the house. You will never see Mrs. Fairley unless you seek her out."

"My mother may be aghast."

"Not when she sees the size of the rooms. And the presence of a guard on the street will put her at ease."

A guard? He had thought this through completely. She was overwhelmed at his desire to protect her.

"But Dr. Kraepelin and your trip to Europe—"

"I will contact him and delay my visit until this business is finished."

"Ingram, you can't."

"I must. I have no choice. Just as you had a painful lesson that shaped your entire outlook, I had mine, as a doctor in the Indian Wars. I saw men lose their lives in an instant. I realized how fleeting life can be and that one must never put off what is truly important."

She stood there, not knowing what to say. She wanted to go to him and tell him how much she loved him and beg him not to leave her ever. He wanted nothing more than to take her in his arms, but he understood, yet again, that she would have to make the first move.

"That is extremely generous," she said. "Thank you."

"Then you will accept my offer?"

"Yes."

Inside Nellie was a war between her desires and her fears. Her fears prevailed. "I should go home and see about mother."

He nodded. He had anticipated this. But the fact that she agreed to stay at his home was enough for now.

"Should I send someone in the morning to help with your moving?"

"That would be most helpful. Thank you."

"Not at all."

She turned and opened the door. "Good night, Doctor Ingram."

"Good night, Miss Bly."

CHAPTER TWENTY

Charles DeKay strode into the Montagne Hotel, just down the street from the inn Nellie and Ingram used for their trysts. Though life was breaking his way and he had more than his usual swagger, he was wistful. His wedding was in less than two weeks, and he would not

NEW YORK HOTELS, 1880s

be having many more of these afternoon visits. Oh, he would still have some—marriage did not necessarily consign one to a monastic existence—but he would need to be discreet. He was about to become more prominent and would have much more to lose. Ah, the price one paid for moving up in the world.

He stopped at the front desk where the clerk, a go-getter in his forties wearing a light green tweed suit, greeted him warmly.

"Good afternoon, sir."

"Good afternoon, Simmons. My appointment is waiting for me?"

"Yes, sir. One I suspect will please you immensely."

The two men smiled at their own private double-entendre as Simmons let Charles know he'd chosen well among the street women for that afternoon.

"And you provided proper refreshments?"

"Enough to last for a good while, sir. Depending on the appetite, of course."

Charles paid Simmons for the room and a little extra as usual for his trouble, then headed to his customary meeting place. He hoped this one would be especially good; today would most likely be his last dalliance before the wedding. Simmons had decent taste—a little more genteel than he preferred, but the girls always seemed to sense what he wanted and loosened up right away. A prostitute had to be pliable in more ways than one, he always said. Otherwise they wouldn't last.

As he approached Room 17 at the end of the corridor, his pulse quickened and his step lightened. This was his favorite part of the rendezvous: the anticipation and the mystery. He had no idea what awaited him on the other side of the door, just that he wanted it to be wonderful and take his breath away.

He tapped on the door.

"Are you decent?" he asked in an authoritative voice.

"You'll be the judge of that."

A witty one. And a flirt. He smiled and opened the door. But the smile soon froze.

Standing there alone in the room, fully clothed, was Nellie Bly. "Good afternoon."

Charles glowered. For one of the rare times in his life, he was speechless.

"You look disappointed."

"What are you doing here?" He was not amused.

"I needed to speak with you."

"I have nothing to say to you—"

"Oh, I think you do. Or else your fiancée will have a great deal to say to you. You have made quite a name for yourself among the prostitutes in this neighborhood. They don't like that you may be taking your business elsewhere."

She watched DeKay try to regain the advantage. She could practically read his mind. The two of them were alone, after all. Simmons would cover if there was a disturbance. The man was practically on his payroll. DeKay closed the door.

But Nellie tapped twice on the wall. From the room next door came two taps.

"And someone is next to this room as well. I really do need you to answer some questions."

He was trapped. But he retained that confident air. He would dance nimbly around her questions, just as he had the previous time. He had been doing it all his life.

"What is it you want to know?"

"Why you poisoned Emma Lazarus."

"I didn't poison her."

"Please. No more lies. I know she didn't kill herself. We have proof of that."

"If you are convinced it wasn't a suicide, what are you waiting for? Go ahead and publish your story."

"I will keep your name out of the story if you tell me why Hilton was so intent that Emma die right away. Why couldn't he wait a few more months?"

"I don't know. He just approached me and asked me to do it. *Told* me to do it, I should say."

"And so you did. You poisoned her."

"No."

Nellie scoffed.

"Right. I forgot. She poisoned herself. You may be oblique with me, Mr. DeKay, but I suspect that option will be unavailable to you with Miss Coffey. Her family will insist on direct answers."

There was no point in evasion. The woman was determined. But he still did not have to tell her everything. It was his nature to withhold information.

"Barker had prescribed arsenic for her right after she returned from England. He thought it would help her with the cancer, but it only made her more ill, so he stopped. Neither he nor I gave her arsenic again."

"Someone did."

"Yes. Without our knowledge. The symptoms persisted, and she became weaker and weaker. He analyzed her blood, and there was much more arsenic than he had given her. Barker was afraid someone would blame him for the death."

"That's why he destroyed the blood samples when we saw him at the opera?"

He nodded. "The protocol at the hospital required him to keep flasks of her blood. He wasn't worried about it until you began asking questions. At that point he feared a scandal."

"How did the additional poison get into her system?

"I don't know. I honestly don't." He stumbled over the

word "honestly," as if it was unfamiliar to him. Nellie didn't know whether to believe him.

"But you were happy to take credit for it with Judge Hilton."

"Yes."

He made no attempt to defend or excuse himself. There was no need. This was how the world worked in New York.

"Why did Hilton want Emma dead?"

"I don't know."

They both knew he was lying.

"You want the prostitutes to visit your fiancée? And her family?"

"I swear. I don't know."

She had worried he would protect Hilton no matter what, even at the cost of his marriage. She knew she wouldn't be getting any more from him. She sighed, grabbed her coat, and headed for the door.

"I don't suppose you would care for some wine," said DeKay. "It seems a pity to let all this go to waste."

"Perhaps you can serve it at your wedding." She walked out.

CHAPTER TWENTY-ONE

The offices of *Scribner's Monthly* were just off Union Square on Fifteenth Street. Along with *Harper's* and *The Atlantic, Scribner's* was the most admired magazine in America. In 1880, it had officially changed its name to *The Century*, after the club of its new publishers and editor in chief, Richard Gilder. Before the arrival of Gilder and his wife, Helena DeKay Gilder, *Scribner's* had been considered a third-tier publication among the nation's intellectual magazines. The Gilders, however, managed to attract the great writers and illustrators of the day, from Mark Twain, Henry James, and Edith Wharton to James Whistler, Edward Penfield, and Winslow Homer. Helena had more of the artistic eye, at a time where the public valued illustrations as much as text, and Richard more of the literary and business eye. They were, in the competitive world of publishing, a formidable team.

Helena DeKay Gilder was by all accounts Emma Lazarus's closest friend. With a shadow cast over Emma's death, it was only natural that Nellie would meet with Helena, and ordinarily a woman would have cooperated fully to bring the killer of her best friend to justice. The problem, of course, was that the person who may well have carried out that murder was Helena's brother, Charles. Helena's efforts in landing Charles a position at the *Times* made clear where her loyalties would fall if forced to choose between her family and justice for a friend.

Nevertheless Nellie thought Helena could be helpful. Nellie needed to know more about Charles and Emma, Helena's brother and best friend. As an editor, it would go against Helena's nature to refuse to speak with Nellie altogether. She would be coy and oblique rather than flatly uncooperative. In fact, from what Nellie had heard of Helena's pride of wit, and from what she had seen of Helena's brother, Charles, Helena would enjoy sparring with Nellie and tying her up in verbal knots.

To prepare for her meeting, Nellie had scoured the numerous biographical accounts of Helena that had circulated when she joined *Scribner's* and, of course, that had accompanied her marriage to Richard Gilder. Both were seminal events in the literary world. Helena, like Charles, had spent her early years in Germany, then attended a girls' boarding school in Connecticut where the class notes described her as "strong-willed" and "independent." She studied for four years at Cooper Union, where she became an accomplished artist, then settled in New York City, where she shared a studio with her close friend from college, the western illustrator and author Mary Hallock Foote. In 1872, she married Richard and started a family of her own, raising a boy and a girl. Richard was the son of a clergyman and the only male student at his father's female academy outside of Flushing. He had fought at the Battle of Gettysburg and following the Civil War had entered the literary world, moving easily among the salons and editorial rooms. Well-known writers trusted him with their work, and yet he could speak as easily to businessmen and held positions on numerous civic and social organizations. Where Helena was artistic but flighty, Richard was grounded, a man of the business world. Friday nights at their New York apartment, nicknamed the Studio, were the most sought-after invitations in literary New York.

The one thing that struck Nellie in all the news articles was that both men and women seemed to fall hopelessly in love with Helena DeKay Gilder. Winslow Homer used her likeness in a dozen paintings, including "Waiting for an Answer" (depicting a young man awaiting a romantic decision from a young woman), and was said to have been devastated when Helena declined his offer of marriage. Charles Dudley Warner, Mark Twain's co-author of *The Gilded Age*, said to Helena, "I'm not going to Egypt! I think you are the finest girl I ever saw." Mary Hallock Foote had serialized a rhapsodic portrayal of Helena as a fictionalized main character in what would eventually become the novel *Edith Bonham*. Richard Gilder had won her favor with sonnets published in *Scribner's* before they were married. Flirtatious charm must run in the family, thought Nellie.

The *Century* offices were not particularly large. The printing warehouse was located in Queens, and the editorial side of the enterprise was a medium-sized brownstone just off Union Square. The reception area was the foyer, with lush European area rugs and stained oak shelves holding first editions from the magazine's many authors. On the walls hung past covers of *Century* and *Scribner's*. Nellie almost stopped in her tracks wide-eyed when she saw a drawing by Winslow Homer on a magazine cover, trumpeting the latest story by Mark Twain.

"May I help you?" asked a young woman Nellie's age, whose accent and dress clearly reflected her privileged class.

"I am here to see Mrs. Gilder."

"Your name, please?"

"Miss Nellie Bly. She is expecting me."

"One moment," the young woman said with condescension, eyeing with distaste the mud on Nellie's skirt hem. "Please remain here."

Nellie felt like an applicant for a custodial job. She was used to similar dismissal from men in such situations, but haughtiness from a woman her own age made her bristle. As she reviewed the supercilious people she kept encountering in this investigation—Hilton, DeKay, Barker—her temper started roiling, but she forced herself to suppress it. She had worked too hard to get to this point to allow snubs or pettiness to interfere. She could take it out on all of them later, in the story that would expose just how vacuous and vile they all were.

"Good afternoon, Miss Bly."

Nellie turned to behold one of the most beautiful women she had ever laid eyes on. Helena DeKay Gilder was in her early forties but possessed the kind of beauty age would never touch. Her emerald green eyes, shimmering and alive, took in everything. Her auburn hair, piled atop her head, made those heavenly eyes all the more pronounced. The sharpness and excitement of the eyes was offset by a soft mouth and a ready smile that was perfectly symmetrical and brightened the entire house. *Lustrous.* That's what she was, thought Nellie. Radiant and lustrous. Helena's beauty went far beyond anything Nellie could capture in writing. It was a task best left to artists. And, Nellie realized, Helena had only said hello.

"Good afternoon, Mrs. Gilder," said Nellie. She wished she had come up with something more winning, but "Good afternoon" was the best she could muster.

"Would you like some tea?"

"No, thank you."

"Do you mind if I have some? We'll make enough in case you change your mind. Martha, some tea for myself and Miss Bly."

"Right away, Mrs. Gilder."

Helena beckoned to Nellie. "Please."

Helena turned away from the reception area and, with a walk befitting royalty, led Nellie into what was originally a parlor room but now served as Helena's office. By the window was an oak desk with manuscripts piled high. Near the fireplace was a chartreuse couch with tassels on the bottom, a royal blue wing chair, and a finely polished table for tea or coffee. On the walls were paintings of museum quality, including one of Helena done by Homer himself.

"I was pleased to receive your telegram," said Helena. "I had been thinking of approaching you to write something for our magazine."

"I'm well below your literary level, Mrs. Gilder. I write only for newspapers."

"You have set New York journalism on fire. Your modesty suggests you are not a good judge of literary talent."

Nellie saw a framed magazine cover on the wall. She walked over and peered at it closely.

"Edward Penfield?"

"Yes. Are you an admirer?"

"Very much so."

The etching showed ladies on a train, with ruffled bonnets, reading books. It was early Penfield; the artist would not achieve real fame for several more years. But to those fortunate enough to be exposed to him, his ability was undeniable.

"He submitted a drawing to a newspaper where I worked," Nellie said, studying it closely. "I urged the editors to buy it, but they refused—"

She turned around and caught Helena staring at her. Not at her face but at her waist and hips, the way men eyed her. Helena was not the least bit embarrassed. She made no attempt to avert her eyes, as if perusing Nellie's body was the most natural thing in the world. As if she were entitled to do it.

"Refused what, my dear?" asked Helena.

"Refused to go along," said Nellie, recovering her train of thought. She walked back to the couch. Helena continued to appraise her physically, and with approval. Nellie wondered if Helena was simply trying to make her uncomfortable. If so, she was succeeding. Yet Nellie had to admit a certain pleasure that such a beautiful woman would look at her admiringly.

"I gather you are here to talk about Emma."

"Yes."

"Charles told me your theory that she was murdered."

"It is more than a theory. We have a scientist who can prove it."

"Dr. Ingram."

"Yes." Nellie regretted that Ingram had been dragged into this. Another mark against Charles, she thought, for telling Helena all about Ingram.

"I am not surprised," Helena nodded unexpectedly, as if her worst suspicions were confirmed.

"Oh?"

"When someone so young and vital as Emma passes away suddenly, one naturally thinks the worst."

"Then you suspected someone of taking her life?"

"I did. But certainly not Charles."

"Why 'certainly not'?"

"Charles was devoted to Emma. He admired her and protected her. He would never have harmed her."

"Judge Hilton is under the impression that Charles is responsible for her death and has even rewarded him for it."

"Yes, I am aware of that," said Helena without skipping a beat. Her aplomb in the face of disquieting facts was disarming. "Charles has a great deal to gain from his association with Judge Hilton. If the judge believes he is in Charles' debt, I see no reason for Charles to disabuse him."

"In that case, you won't mind showing me Emma's manuscript."

"Her manuscript?"

"The one that she gave you before her last trip to England."

For the first time, uncertainty crept into in Helena's manner. "There was no such manuscript."

"I met with a Montauk tribeswoman whom Miss Lazarus was eager to help. Right before she left for Europe, Miss Lazarus told the woman that she was using every means at her disposal to seek justice."

"That could mean anything—"

"No, not when she was about to embark on a long journey. Miss Lazarus had taken her cause to heart. She would have relied on what she did best: writing something for publication, with her name attached to it."

"But why give it to us? This is a literary magazine."

"I agree; Mr. Pulitzer would have been a better choice. He would have happily published it. But he knew nothing about it. I suspect your brother convinced her to give it to you because you and your husband would make sure it was published in her preferred form. But you did nothing with it, as Charles knew you wouldn't. You betrayed her."

Helena stiffened. Another small crack in that aura of supreme self-confidence appeared.

"Why would I ever decline to publish something Emma had written?"

"Because your brother begged you not to, for fear of damaging his arrangement with Judge Hilton."

Helena's eyes narrowed with a flash of violent anger. Nellie knew she had hit the mark. Before Helena could reply, the young receptionist tapped on the half-open door and walked in carrying a tray with a teapot, two porcelain cups, a bowl of sugar, and a small pitcher of milk.

"Ah, Martha. Thank you." The young woman set the tray down on a table in front of Nellie. "Have Mr. Gilder come in please, would you?"

"Right away, Mrs. Gilder."

Martha walked out. Helena followed her with her eyes, the same way she had stared at Nellie. The interruption had allowed Helena to regain her psychological footing.

"I'm sorry, Miss Bly. I cannot produce a manuscript I never saw."

Helena braced for more questions about the manuscript, but Nellie changed the subject, like a field general opening a second front.

"You say Charles was devoted to Miss Lazarus. That he would have never harmed her."

"Yes."

"Did they speak of marriage?"

"No."

"Why not? They were companions for years, as I understand it."

"For one thing, Emma was not of the proper social class."

"But her family had all the respectability there is. Her father was an original member of the Union Club. They owned a mansion in Newport. Her close friend was Julia Ward Howe. What else could she possibly lack?"

"Emma was a Jew. Charles would never have married a Jew." She said it so emphatically, Nellie almost shuddered.

"Was she in love with him?"

"No." She seemed to smirk when she said it.

"And yet they remained together for ten years."

"They enjoyed each other's company. Charles admired Emma. She was a remarkable poet and provided a valuable entrée for him into the literary world. Have you changed your

193

mind about the tea?" asked Helena, pouring herself a cup.

"I will have some, yes. Thank you." Helena leaned forward and poured her some tea.

"And Miss Lazarus? What did she derive from the arrangement?"

"The mantle of respectability."

"Surely she had that without your brother."

"Among her literary peers, yes. But not among her social peers."

There was another tap at the door. A thin man in his midforties with a thick, graying walrus mustache and narrow eyes stood there, mildly impatient. His waistcoat and vest had a tailored flair that set him apart from the commercial world.

"You wanted to see me, Helena?"

"Yes. Richard, this is Miss Nellie Bly. My husband, Richard."

Richard frowned. "The Cuban woman who lost her memory. Good afternoon."

He nodded formally.

"Good afternoon."

"Miss Bly is not here to write a magazine piece, dear." Gilder relaxed.

"Richard has no use for newspaper writers. He feels we are putting out a *literary* magazine. Miss Bly is writing about Emma, Richard."

"Oh? What about Emma?" It was the perfectly natural thing to say, but Richard did not say it in a perfectly natural way.

"The manner of her death," said Nellie.

"Miss Bly seems to think that before she left for Europe, Emma submitted a manuscript involving the Montauk tribe. Do you know anything about that?"

"Not a thing," he said, without bothering to search his memory.

"Did she submit any manuscripts at all around that time?" asked Nellie.

"None that I saw. She was immersed in her political activities. We hadn't seen any submissions from her for months."

"And after she returned?"

"She was deathly ill. She devoted her dwindling energies to arranging her writings in a proper order."

"Before her sisters gained control of her work."

"Yes," he said sadly. "We met almost every day. But that was not enough."

Helena looked over at Nellie. "There you have it, Miss Bly," she said. "Is there anything else you would like to ask my husband?"

"Would you care to join us for tea?"

"Thank you, but I must decline. I have pressing work to complete."

"Richard is not one for tea. He prefers coffee. To him tea tastes like water."

"Good day, Miss Bly."

"Thank you, Mr. Gilder. Good day."

He walked out. Helena did not follow him with her eyes as she had Martha and Nellie. Instead she sipped her tea and glanced at Nellie's breasts. Helena enjoyed making people uncomfortable.

"You were saying that Emma sought a 'mantle of respectability,' I believe is the way you put it, from your brother," said Nellie. "Why, because she was a Jew?"

"She needed the appearance of male companions."

Nellie looked puzzled.

"In literary and artistic circles," Helena continued, "Emma's choice of companions would never raise a second thought. But in others ... well, let us say that as her world became more one of politics, appearances became increasingly important. Charles, at some considerable sacrifice to himself, agreed to provide Emma the necessary respectability for almost ten years. He received something from the arrangement, granted. But a man of his appetites was forced to make definite ... compromises."

"And once Emma had died, Charles could ask for Miss Coffey's hand in marriage."

"Yes. They had been meeting quietly for some time. He would call upon her at her home. She never knew about Emma."

Helena expected Nellie to be shocked, but Nellie had no

surprise to hide. All along Charles had seemed too shallow a person to hold Emma's interest for that length of time.

"Who was Miss Lazarus's companion?"

"I am not at liberty to say."

Helena sipped her tea. The topic, as far as she was concerned, was closed. But they both knew the answer to the question, and Nellie saw no reason to pretend otherwise.

"Did your husband know about the arrangement?" Helena stiffened at the impudence.

"Did he?" repeated Nellie.

"No. Charles went to great lengths to protect me."

"And repay his debt to you for getting him a position after his scandal."

"Possibly that as well."

She sipped her tea again.

"You are convinced your brother did not poison Miss Lazarus," pressed Nellie.

"Yes."

"Then who did?"

"She had many visitors her last three months. It could have been any of them."

"It would have to be someone she saw frequently. Someone she trusted enough to eat from a plate that person handed her. The poisoning was gradual, not immediate."

"I have no idea who that might be. I wouldn't even know where to begin to look."

Nellie set down the teacup. "Well, thank you for your time, Mrs. Gilder."

"You do believe me when I say it was not Charles?"

"I believe you are convinced of his innocence. Let us leave it at that." She stood up. "I can show myself out."

Nellie walked out of the office. She could feel Helena's eyes following her until she closed the door behind her. She walked through the reception area, where Martha was sitting at her desk. As Nellie reached the front door, she stopped.

"Martha, is it?"

"Yes."

"How did you enjoy Miss Lazarus's manuscript? The one about the Montauks?"

"Mrs. Gilder would not allow me to read it."

"A pity. I think it was her finest work." Nellie walked out the door.

CHAPTER TWENTY-TWO

AUSTIN CORBIN

As Nellie waited inconspicuously around the corner from the Lazarus home, coat pulled tight against the cool morning air, she thought about Emma's sexual proclivities. It had little to do with the murder. The most likely path still led to Henry Hilton. But Emma's lesbian activities unsettled her. It made her realize how little she really knew about Emma. From the time Emma was a young girl, men had been charmed by her intellect and wit, but Nellie had heard of no incidents of painters devoting their canvasses to her, or diplomats canceling trips abroad to be near her, as happened with Helena DeKay. Nellie had attributed this absence of such suitors to a fixation with Charles DeKay or an indifference to romantic affairs in general relative to far greater passions for poetry and social causes. But Emma obviously had appetites and longings like everyone else.

Nellie had known several women who were considered "spinsters" but who never lacked for female companionship. She herself had been approached by women on several occasions. But sex with another woman held no interest or curiosity for her. Then again, she had never been approached by the likes of Helena DeKay Gilder.

It must have been next to impossible for Emma to hide her sexual preferences. Constantly surrounded by family and admirers, she inhabited a world where gossip was currency. In her writings, Emma was formal and well-mannered, never delving into the private or the personal, and she conducted her life accordingly. Any liaisons on her part would have to be guardedly private to the extreme.

And yet she and Charles and Helena had kept up the charade for ten years. The visit to Dr. Barker for a contraceptive device had been a clever stroke to divert anyone from suspicion. Nevertheless, Nellie found it surprising that Helena would be Emma's lover for so long. Helena, like Charles, had seemed too promiscuous and calculating to carry on an intimate ten-year partnership with anyone as substantial as Emma. Then again, Helena's beauty was undeniable. She was breathtaking, and someone as appreciative of beauty as Emma may have found her simply irresistible.

Still, as Nellie reminded herself, this musing was pointless. It was Emma's murder she was investigating, not her private life, and though one often had something to do with the other, it was Emma's political activities and her generosity of spirit that had led to her demise. What was it that Hilton and Corbin were up to on Long Island? Emma had figured it out and wanted to make it known in the *Century* manuscript. Nellie was sure of it. Helena DeKay, supposedly Emma's closest friend, had lied to her and done nothing with the manuscript. Breathtakingly attractive as she was, Nellie did not like this woman and would not to hesitate to embarrass her if the opportunity arose.

"Paper, miss?" A newspaper boy held a shoulder bag of copies of the *Herald*.

"No, thank you," said Nellie.

"The election is only a few days away. Read about Mr. Cleveland getting cozy with the Brits."

"I'm not one for politics. Sorry."

The boy moved on. At that moment, the front door to the Lazarus home opened, and maidservant Sarah, bundled up in a dark ankle-length overcoat, descended the steps. It was a crisp autumn morning. Most of the trees had shed their leaves, and the bright October skies had given way to the gray of November. To Nellie's good fortune, Sarah turned and walked down Fifth Avenue in her direction. Had she turned the other way, Nellie would have had to hail a carriage and circled round the block in order not to pass by the Lazarus home, something she hoped would not be necessary.

As Sarah started to cross Fifty-Seventh Street, Nellie called out in a loud whisper.

"Sarah!"

Sarah looked up and saw her, anxiety passing over her face. Nellie beckoned her to come over, out of the view of anyone in the home. Sarah did so, clearly uncomfortable.

"Miss Bly. How long have you been waiting?"

"Not long. I hired a boy to keep watch and tell me when you left the house. He said you went to the postal office every morning about this time." She indicated the satchel in Sarah's hand.

"I shouldn't stay long," Sarah said nervously.

"I know. I wanted to tell you that the pillow covering you gave me was very helpful. Miss Emma was indeed murdered."

"I knew it." Sarah's lips pursed and eyes narrowed in anger.

"Sarah, I need to find out who did it. Can you make a list of all the people who visited Miss Lazarus during her illness, up until she died?" Although Nellie knew Hilton was behind the murder, she needed to know who'd actually given Emma the poison.

Based on what she had so far, the case against Charles was flimsy, and with such sensational accusations, the story could leave no room for unanswered questions.

"I'm not sure I can remember them all. There were so many."

"Think hard. The killer was someone who visited her during that period. I will be here tomorrow morning at the same time. Give it to me then."

Sarah nodded. She started to walk away.

"Sarah, did Miss Emma have any companions?"

"What kind of companions?"

"Private ones. Whom no one would know about."

Sarah stiffened. "I wouldn't know. And I wouldn't say so if I did."

"I'm sorry. I didn't mean to pry. I thought it would be helpful. Thank you for your help, Sarah."

Sarah, once again the image of an implacable maidservant, purposefully crossed the street.

On a whim, Nellie walked over to Madison Avenue and down eight blocks to Forty-Ninth Street. On the corner, behind a tall iron fence and two uniformed guards stationed on the street, was the mansion of Jay Gould. She approached one of the guards.

"Stay right there, please," said one gruffly.

"I'm wondering if I might see Mr. Gould."

"Do you have an appointment?"

"No—"

"Then you can't see him."

"Please tell him I'm here. My name is Nellie Bly."

The guard opened a small iron door in the stone pillar to reveal a telephone, a wire running from the pillar to inside the house. The guard cranked the phone.

"Could you tell Mr. Gould that a Miss Bly is here to see him?"

The guard waited a moment. Unlike the sentries outside the newspaper offices, these guards didn't flirt or make conversation. They were focused entirely on the task at hand, guarding the household. Gould could afford to have the best protection possible, and given the number of threats he faced on a daily basis, he demanded nothing less.

"Yes," said the guard into the phone. "I'll tell her." He hung up the phone.

"Mr. Gould is leaving for his office. He would like you to ride with him."

"Thank you."

The guard returned to his post while she waited by the gate. Neither guard cast so much as a glance in her direction or a word of conversation with the other. They devoted all their attention to surveying the street for any threats or unwelcome activities. Jay Gould was a serious man indeed.

A few minutes later, a carriage emerged from inside the

gate. It was black, larger than most, but otherwise resembled a thousand other carriages on the streets of New York, with one exception: two guards sat on either side of the driver, carrying rifles. The carriage stopped by her. One of the guards had quietly moved into place as the gate opened. Gould, with those coal-black, penetrating eyes, opened the carriage door.

"Miss Bly. I am riding to the office. You can join me if you like."

"I would like that. Thank you."

The driver tossed down a small step. The guard caught it, placed it by the door, and helped her into the carriage. The inside was comfortable but not posh. The seats were a cloth weave, not leather. Gould tapped his cane against the roof. The carriage proceeded down Fifth Avenue.

"You should have alerted me you would be calling," said Gould. "Another five minutes and you would have missed me."

"I assume you know my whereabouts at all times."

Gould forced a mild smile. "My purpose before was simply to warn you, Miss Bly. And refute lies about Miss Lazarus. I have no need for further spying."

"I was nearby and thought I would pay a visit. I need help."

Gould wasn't one for chit-chat. "Go on."

"I am convinced that Miss Lazarus was murdered and that Judge Hilton was behind it, as you said. But I'm not sure *why* she was murdered."

"Assigning her blame for all his financial shortcomings was not enough?"

"That explains why he would welcome her death, but not why he could not wait a few months for the cancer to take her life. Something pressing forced his hand."

"You have a theory?"

"Right before she left for Europe, Miss Lazarus befriended a woman from the Montauk Indian tribe."

That got his attention. "Maria Pharaoh?"

"That's right," said Nellie, surprised.

"Well. That would explain just about everything." He said it to himself as much as to Nellie. "They mean to go ahead with it."

Gould was way ahead of her. Even though she had more information, she struggled to catch up. "I know that Hilton and Corbin had cheated the Montauks out of their land—"

"Not only the Montauks," interrupted Gould, "but *all* the Indians on Long Island. The Shinnecock, the Mattuck, the Quogue. Miss Pharaoh was making one final attempt to regain her land through the courts. No one gave her much of a chance, but they still had to go through certain steps. Miss Lazarus, on the other hand, could pose a serious problem to their plans. She must have offered to do all she could, even though she was bound for Europe."

Nellie was dazzled that Gould knew so much about the situation.

"She wrote a story for the *Century* about it," she said, "but it was never published. And they won't let me see the manuscript."

"Do you know what was in it?"

"No. But whatever it was accelerated her death."

"Of course it did. Miss Lazarus was smart enough to deduce their plans," he said admiringly. "Hilton and Corbin could brook no interference, even from someone as well-established as Miss Lazarus."

"Interference with what? Their plan is obvious, isn't it? New York is crowded. People will begin moving out of the city, and Hilton and Corbin bought up all the land. Eventually it will be extremely valuable."

"But that will be years from now. You need to think bigger, Miss Bly. They could have purchased land anywhere on Long Island and created a residential area. It was *Montauk Point* they were after."

"I don't understand."

He struggled to contain his impatience that he had to spell it out to her as if she were a child. "Corbin has a monopoly on all train travel on Long Island."

"Yes—"

"His trains go all the way to Brooklyn and Queens. He owns the ferries to take passengers to Manhattan. And I suspect before long, he will get the city to finance a bridge so his trains can go all the way *into* Manhattan as well. In effect, he will have a monopoly on all rail traffic from the north and east into New York."

"That's worth a fortune."

"No, Miss Bly. That is worth merely a great deal of money. What they have in mind is a real fortune. All ships arriving from Europe now dock at Battery Park and unload around the wharf at the East River. Everyone and everything coming from Europe arrives there. More passengers and cargo go through that area than all the other harbors in the country combined."

"Yes. I know that—"

"Hilton and Corbin want to have all ships from Europe land one hundred miles farther east, at Montauk Point. The passengers and cargo would then disembark and go aboard their trains, race across Long Island, and arrive in Manhattan a day or so earlier than they do currently. Or they might connect with the Pennsylvania or the Southern Railway or the Central Railroad of New Jersey, which they also own, without having to go into Manhattan at all. Europe and England are our major suppliers of goods and our major outlet for everything this country produces. Their plan would transform the nation's commerce and spell the end of New York City as a major landing point."

"A million passengers a year arrive here!"

"Two million. Not to mention the tonnage of cargo. Plus rents from merchants and ship owners, plus the ability to set monopoly prices and control workers' wages. That is an enormous amount of revenue, by anyone's standards."

Nellie struggled to grasp the full, astonishing extent of their plan.

"It would be costly to build a harbor," Gould went on, "and I wasn't sure if they were prepared to spend all that capital, but now we know the answer. For the plan to work, they had to secure Montauk Point. That is the integral piece. Anything farther west would lessen their time advantage and pose a navigational hazard."

"Maria Pharaoh could have made a mess of things."

"By herself, no. No court would have taken her seriously.

But with Emma Lazarus, that would be a different story. Hilton must have learned about the manuscript and managed to suppress it, through the work of Charles DeKay, I suspect—"

It was remarkable how much he deduced.

"—and once she returned from Europe, he could not have her interfering in the trial."

"When was the trial?"

"December of last year. One month after she died."

Absolute control of the major arrival point from Europe. A monopoly on all rail traffic, for both passengers and cargo, to points north, west, and south of New York City. And total ownership of the surrounding land. The scope of the enterprise was almost beyond comprehension.

"Can they be stopped?" she asked in trepidation.

"I don't see how."

"What about the railroad commission?" The previous year, amid great fanfare, Congress had enacted the Interstate Commerce Act, to put an end to monopolies in the railroad industry.

Gould scoffed.

"The president appoints the commission members. Thanks to this nonsense with the Murchison letter, that will be Harrison. He will choose exactly whom Hilton says. And if any commission members should exercise independence, Congress will be sure to rein them in. No, Miss Bly, I'm afraid no one is going to stop them."

"What about you?" she asked desperately.

"Me? I'm an old man. My wife is not well, and my children make my life difficult. The truth is, if Hilton and Corbin approach me to buy the Manhattan Elevated, I would be inclined to sell it to them."

"But you can't! You carry three million passengers a year!"

"At present. But once they begin diverting commerce through Long Island, the Manhattan Elevated will not be worth very much. I might as well take what I can get for it now."

"But to let Judge Hilton get the best of you—"

"This is business, Miss Bly. There is no room for emotions."

"Let me write the story first, Mr. Gould. Please. Mr. Pulitzer will publish it. Maybe that can stop them."

"As you wish, Miss Bly. But I assure you it will make no difference."

CHAPTER TWENTY-THREE

MAYOR HUGH J. GRANT

The article set off a firestorm.

Pulitzer, of course, was only too glad to put Henry Hilton in a bad light. With the *Sun*, the *Herald*, and the other Republican newspapers making the Murchison letter the lead story in the run-up to the election, the *World* had the story of the two craven monopolists all to itself. "Railway Barons Out to Destroy NYC," screamed one headline. "Port of New York Faces Shutdown," proclaimed another. "Crime Pays: Profiting from Thievery" was the main editorial headline and recurrent theme.

Mayor Hugh J. Grant, at thirty-two the youngest mayor in the history of New York City, demanded that the state government put a halt to the monopolists' plans, but as a young Irish Catholic Democrat his power was limited, and no one outside New York City seemed to care. Richard Croker, the head of Tammany's patronage system—the city's 1,200 workers, entirely beholden to him, turned out for candidates or halted construction projects at his pleasure—implored the city's businessmen, from whom he demanded "one-stop shopping" bribes, to decry the project at Montauk Harbor, but their entreaties had no effect. Even J.P. Morgan, who saw the future value of his vast real estate holdings dropping considerably with the shift of business away from the port of New York, got nowhere with Hilton and Corbin. When Morgan invited the two barons to a private meeting at his home, they tersely declined.

The two magnates had anticipated a backlash once their plans were made public and employed considerable resources to elicit sympathetic statements of support. State Senator Philip A. Robinson from Syracuse, a failed businessman who had amassed a small fortune carrying water for Hilton at the state capital, said that "all of New York, and indeed all these United States, will benefit from the harbor at Montauk." Assembly Speaker Thomas R. Shill, a nativist from Rochester, played to the anti-New York City bias rampant throughout the rural parts of the state by claiming that "the only ones complaining about the new system are the micks and guineas in New York City." When Mayor Grant declared that "Hilton and Corbin not only set out to acquire a monopoly, but they accomplished it by stealing from the Indians," Senator Robinson responded, "that is exactly the point. Hilton and Corbin have done the state a great service by ridding Long Island of unwanted savages."

Hilton and Corbin had planned well. The business press immediately lined up in favor of the new Montauk harbor. "State government," proclaimed the *New York Herald*, the nation's largest paper outside the *World*, "has no business interfering in the wisdom of free enterprise." "We welcome the new Montauk harbor," declared the *Sun*, "as it will lessen the stranglehold of the unions on commerce."

At almost any other time, the Montauk Harbor story would have run for days and sparked a national debate, and the two robber barons would most likely have had to answer for the way they'd acquired the land and their plan to strangle Manhattan by siphoning off its life source upstream. But readers outside of New York City were focused on the presidential election, as the country itself was at a critical political juncture. President Cleveland had put in place a reformist agenda to shift power from the extremely rich (a census showed that 1 percent of the country's population owned 25 percent of the wealth) to the middle class. Harrison and the Republicans were pushing back hard, exploiting every fear at their disposal, especially resentment of immigrants. The battle of the 1888 election was for the helm of the ship of state. Who would control the future: the wealthy and the powerful or the middle class and the powerless?

In New York City, though, panic was setting in. Thousands of workers made their living on the docks unloading cargo or assisting passengers at this major port, busier than all the other ports in the country combined. Immigrants may have been forced to live in cramped, even squalid conditions, but there was almost always work, and they knew if they saved enough, they could improve their lot in life. If the main harbor shifted to Long Island, many of the wharf and ancillary jobs—the street vendors, the shopkeepers, the apartment owners—would disappear or go with them. The political power in the state would shift as well. For twenty years, Tammany Hall had controlled New York City and much of Albany. All of that would change when the state's point of entry shifted one hundred miles east, and of course Hilton and Corbin would handpick the representatives from those new districts.

Rather than allaying the public's fears, Hilton and Corbin sought to exploit them. With great fanfare that included bands, performers, reporters, and photographers, they brought in tenant farmers from the Deep South to build the harbor and proudly showed off the makeshift housing where their families would stay (provided that the husbands agreed to work at subsistence wages indefinitely). They loudly promised not to hire any Irish, Italian, or Jewish workers to build the harbor, announcing that ethnics were most definitely not welcome on their property—or in America itself, for that matter. Most brazenly, and as Gould had predicted, they made an offer for his Manhattan Elevated, which would give them a monopoly on all elevated train transportation in New York's five boroughs (all trains in the boroughs were elevated above the street), to match their near monopoly on all train transportation in and out of the city. They wanted to demonstrate that even Mephistopheles himself could not stand in their way, and to everyone's amazement and heightened paranoia, they succeeded. The offer was just under $20 million—about half of what the elevated was worth. Gould asked for some of the payment to be in the form of stock in their company, but they refused. Hilton did not want Jay Gould riding the coattails of their success. As a fallback, Gould insisted on a cash transaction. Eager to wrap things up quickly and increase their momentum, Hilton and Corbin agreed on the spot, and Gould took their offer without further bargaining. The business press ridiculed the sale as total surrender on Gould's part, with Hilton giving long, caustic interviews trumpeting his victory. At long last, someone had gotten the better of Jay Gould.

Their power and superiority were only confirmed a few days later when Harrison defeated Cleveland in the presidential election. The two barons had poured a fortune into the Harrison campaign, and it had paid off. Although Cleveland won the popular vote, Harrison prevailed in the Electoral College 233–168, only the third time in U.S. history when the candidate receiving the most popular votes did not win the election. The Electoral College race, however, was far closer than the 233–168 margin indicated.

Cleveland lost his home state of New York—the same New York that was about to be assaulted economically by Corbin and Hilton—by less than 1 percent of the total vote. Had he won New York's twenty-nine electoral votes, Cleveland would have carried the Electoral College by 204–197. The Murchison letter that Hilton had shown Nellie did indeed determine the election, with the Irish of New York voting against their own economic interest out of a deep-seated hatred of the English. But Hilton and Corbin, leaving nothing to chance, did not rely entirely on the Murchison letter to secure a Harrison victory. In Indiana, voters were paid $15 if they voted Republican. In other states, they employed duplicate voting, voter intimidation, and nonresident balloting. The 1888 presidential election would go down as the most corrupt in the history of the United States.

Hilton and Corbin got the result they wanted. With Harrison in the White House, the Republican majorities in both branches of Congress and on the Supreme Court, the federal government was no threat whatsoever to slow them down. Given their attendant stranglehold on politicians in Albany, they would be operating without any authorized restraint. Nothing stood in their way to achieving total commercial dominance.

The re-election of Grover Cleveland, the former governor, had been the New York citizenry's last hope. The day after Harrison's victory, Mayor Grant in effect sued for peace and called for a meeting with the two barons, but they declined his overture, citing "prior obligations," and did not propose an alternate date. The young Irish mayor, insulted and embarrassed, vowed to make life difficult for the two barons the moment he got the chance, but with Hilton and Corbin holding all the cards, including new ownership of Gould's Manhattan Elevated, Grant's threat was not taken seriously even by city Democrats.

Hilton also used the opportunity to settle a personal score with Pulitzer. Two weeks after the election, one of his Congressmen-on-retainer, Senator H.W. Blair of New Hampshire, introduced the "Day of Rest Bill," which would ban selling or delivering newspapers on Sunday, the *World*'s most profitable day.

Nellie followed all these developments with dismay. She knew the kind of blackguards Hilton and Corbin were. The two of them were about to inflict a terrible blow to the city of New York and become phenomenally rich in the process.

She sat with Alan Dale in a restaurant off Newspaper Row, having tea and a scone and reading about the mayor's latest futile overtures to the two barons. The restaurant was limited to reporters, and Nellie was the only woman there. She drew cold stares from men at the bar and at nearby tables, but the hostility went no further; no one wanted to take on Dale's sharp tongue in a direct confrontation. Besides, Nellie had been the one to break the story about Montauk Harbor, and though the men in the room didn't like the idea of women reporters, she had earned some stripes with that one, they'd give her that.

"I can't believe they are actually getting away with this," she said with chagrin. "Fraud, theft, murder ..."

"No one can stop them. It's the way of the world, my dear." Dale, as a native Englishman, was used to the upper classes operating with impunity.

"We can stop them."

"You can't bring them to trial. Or throw them in jail."

"No. But this is still a democracy. No one can survive the public's deep anger."

Nellie knew she had a powerful tool at her disposal, a tool that was just coming into its own. Since the emergence of telegraphy, news stories could spread throughout the nation, even the world, in a matter of days if not hours. The public had an undeniable antipathy toward robber barons—the Interstate Commerce Act of 1887 had made it through a Congress with two Republican houses. Hilton and Corbin and the other railroad barons might run roughshod over the Act, but if there were enough outrageous stories of their corruption, enough infuriating examples brought before the public, the outrage would be so great that people simply would not stand for it anymore. She genuinely believed that. She had traveled enough and reported enough to know she wasn't being naïve. Only twenty-five years before, the country had fought a devastating Civil War—in which one out of every ten Americans had been in uniform, and 2 percent of the entire population had been killed—in order to preserve American institutions. If the people saw that those institutions had been taken over by greedy men whose wealth was already beyond imagination, they would rise up in a fury. She just knew it, she knew it in her bones. And she had the perfect vehicle for spreading that truth, the paper with the largest circulation in New York, the *New York World*.

"Well, you haven't much time," noted a skeptical Dale. "The inauguration is in March. Construction on the harbor will begin the next day, I would guess, when Cleveland's people can no longer make any mischief. After that, it will be too late."

"I agree. By that point, the two of them will be in a commanding position. We have three months." Actually it was less than that, she thought to herself. The story would need to pick up steam before any government officials would feel forced to act.

"How exactly do you plan to go about it?"

"I don't know."

That was the problem. She had no concrete way to connect Hilton to Emma's murder. She needed facts. Insinuation would not be enough, even for Pulitzer. He would have no hesitation publishing something scandalous about Hilton and making it the lead story in every paper he owned, but it would have to be irrefutable. Taking on two men who had stolen Indian lands and were threatening the economic well-being of New York City wasn't enough, that was already clear. She would have to show they engineered the murder of a famous poet, a woman of grace and charity and prominence. And she only had three months to do it.

"What are you ladies doing here?" said a gruff voice. "This place is for *men*."

Standing next to them was a man in his early thirties in a coat and tie, with red muttonchops with a thick mustache, holding a pint of beer. She recognized him as a reporter from the court she had fooled into sending her to Bellevue months earlier.

"No," spat out Nellie, "what are *you* doing here? This place is for *reporters*." The room grew quiet. They didn't expect her to stand up to the hazing.

"I'm a reporter," said the man defensively.

"No, you're not," said Nellie. "You write for the *Herald*. They don't have reporters, they have parrots. You're a parrot."

Some chuckles from the *Herald* haters. Dale smiled.

"Chirp, chirp, chirp, chirp," clucked Nellie.

"Watch yourself, lady—" snarled the man.

"You just write what the highest bidder tells you to write. You don't report anything. The city could be on fire and you would just look the other way if the arsonist paid you enough."

"You're done talking," he said menacingly.

"No, I'm just getting started. We are in trouble. Big trouble. And you just sit on your fat arse and drink beer and pick on people minding their own business instead of doing something that might make your wife and your kids proud. Or are they already ashamed of you, like the rest of us?"

His face turned red, and he clenched his fist. He may have started it, but now he was getting pummeled, and he didn't like it.

"Go ahead," she challenged. "Take a swing. That will help your reputation."

The man didn't know what to do next. Everything out of her mouth was making him look lower and lower in his colleagues' eyes. And Nellie wouldn't ease up on him.

"It's easier to take a swing at me than at Henry Hilton, isn't it? Let him ruin the city. What do you care? You're getting paid, at least for a while."

Impulsively the guy poured his beer on Nellie's head. He didn't know what else to do. She didn't move, just sat there and took it and smiled at him defiantly. The guy looked around for approval, but the crowd just averted their eyes, embarrassed for him. And Nellie was unbowed.

"You write about prostitutes all day. Why don't you just write about yourself? It's the same thing, and that way you wouldn't have to leave the office."

Utterly humiliated, the man slunk out, stripped of all dignity. The rest of the reporters looked at one another pathetically. But standing tall, even though she had beer on her head, was Nellie. She lifted her glass to the room.

"To the gentlemen of the press. May they someday come out of hiding."

Dale lifted his glass. "Hear, hear."

They clinked glasses and drank. She sat back and sipped her tea. She was due home and behind schedule, but she'd be damned to let them think she was running off. Better to get home late than give these fellows one moment of satisfaction.

CHAPTER TWENTY-FOUR

BENJAMIN HARRISON

Although Congress was normally in session less than half the year, and the new president would not be sworn in until March 4, the Fiftieth Congress, dominated in both houses by Republicans, convened on January 4, 1889, with one item on the agenda: legislation to provide federal funding for an immigration inspection facility at Montauk Point, New York. President Cleveland, in office for another two months, vowed to veto any such bill that came before him, so after whisking through the House, the legislation sat at the Senate desk, until President-elect Harrison would take the oath of office. At that point, the Senate would act quickly, and the bill would be the first presented to the new president after inauguration. The legislation, though dormant for the moment, signaled what was coming and added to the psychological assault on the city.

Nellie continued to look furiously for some irrefutable link between Henry Hilton, Charles DeKay and Emma's murder, but the going was slow, much too slow. The one ray of hope was the list from Sarah, Emma's maidservant, which set out all the people who had visited Emma from the time she returned from Europe until her death three months later. It was surprisingly comprehensive, with detailed notations beside each name. Sarah had taken the assignment seriously and searched her memory for anything that might lead to Emma's murderer.

There were thirty-five names on the list. Hopefully one of the visitors had noticed Charles DeKay give Emma the arsenic or even been an accomplice themselves. But which one?

And how would she go about asking? Nellie spent two afternoons painstakingly reviewing the list with the *World's* archivist, a retiring man in his late sixties who seemingly knew everyone whose name had appeared in the New York papers over the past forty years. Nellie eliminated Emma's immediate family—they were unlikely to cooperate—and anyone likely to protect Charles, such as Helena and Richard. That left about a dozen people. But one name in particular jumped out at her: Mary Hallock Foote.

Mary Hallock Foote was a well-known Western writer and illustrator and, according to the archivist, Helena Gilder's college friend and apartment-mate. She had moved to Colorado and Idaho shortly after Helena and Richard had married and rarely made it back to New York. Yet she'd visited Emma twice in the three months before she died, and according to Sarah's notes, "they engaged in a shouting match, and Mrs. Foote stormed out of the house." Nellie certainly wanted to know more about that but didn't know how to get in touch with Molly Foote, as she was known. Although Foote was published in the *Century*, it was unlikely Helena or Richard would cooperate, and she knew no one else in that world. Dale was in Boston for the holidays. He might have some ideas when he got back.

Other matters were occupying Nellie's attention as well. Her mother's senility was getting worse. At times Mary Jane didn't recognize her or know where she was. The disorientation also made her tired, and Mary Jane would nap for several hours every afternoon and retire for bed right after supper. Nonetheless, the move to Ingram's house had been a helpful tonic, and Nellie was grateful for that. Mary Jane was not as lonely during the day, with Ingram stopping in every so often to inquire about her health and taking walks on her own to the park in Washington Square, where she would enjoy the ducks and children for hours. Ingram arranged for a twelve-year-old boy, whose mother Ingram had cured of a nasty case of pneumonia, to keep an eye on her whenever she left the brownstone. In Harlem, the confinement had been almost unbearable and accelerated the senility: her days had been limited to sitting in the common room and staring out the window at the peddlers on the street below. And when she did venture out on her own, there was always the very real possibility she would not find her way home.

The three of them took meals together at morning and evening. Ingram, who employed a cook since he often worked late into the night, simply had her prepare for three rather than one. He was pleased to do it. This allowed him to see Nellie every day.

Mary Jane did not give much thought to her daughter's relationship with Ingram. Nellie had told her mother that she wanted to live closer to the paper—the trip from Harlem to Newspaper Row was nearly an hour each way—and she had seen a lovely place in a home owned by a doctor she had met through her work. Mary Jane had balked, assuming that all New York doctors were like the pervert who had given Nellie a breast exam, but Nellie assuaged her concerns by telling her that the new doctor had very unpleasant things to say about that first doctor they had seen. Mary Jane found Ingram perfectly agreeable and consented to the move, especially when he had two large men help them transport their belongings and look after them. She also liked that those same two men took turns each evening standing outside the front door and making sure no one bothered them with loud noises or unwanted interruptions.

The dinners themselves were pleasant affairs for each of them. Dining with Mary Jane alone night after night had become extremely tedious for Nellie, and she welcomed Ingram's conversation. Mary Jane had begun to find dinners with her daughter equally tedious, and she enjoyed conversing with a handsome young man who treated her with respect and interest. And Ingram was happy for some semblance of normal life in an eighty-hour workweek seeing patients, visiting the asylum, and conducting research. The fatigue that had hounded him all his life seemed to vanish, and he would refer to his meals with the two women as his prescription tonic.

They enjoyed a lovely Christmas dinner together, the finest Nellie had had since she was a child. It was a feast: Ingram's cook prepared a roast, Nellie and Mary Jane made pudding and pies, and Ingram supplied three different kinds of wine. Mary Jane had held on to a lovely tablecloth ever since her husband died, and she brought it out for the occasion. They also exchanged gifts. Nellie presented Ingram with a leather-bound ledger for his research. He presented her with a virtually identical leather-bound journal for her notes. Both had to smile at the similarity of their thoughts. Maybe it was that, or it could have been the wine, but the curtain of formality seemed to drop, and they were suddenly back to their old ease and familiarity. Almost on cue, Mary Jane announced that she was tired and got up from the table. After Nellie put her mother to bed and returned for tea, she and Ingram sat in silence. The sexual desire was still there, more than ever, and it would be the easiest thing to slip into a bedroom and engage in prodigious lovemaking. Both of them thought often about that every time they were together. One glimpse of a hand or the nape of a neck would conjure up images of wonderful pleasures. But uncertainty about the future always hung over them, and both held back. It was at the Christmas dinner, over tea and dessert, with Mary Jane gone to sleep, when they finally broached the subject of their future once again.

"Have you heard from your colleague in Vienna?" asked Nellie.

"Yes. Regularly. We still correspond."

"Was he upset with you for staying here?"

"He understood."

"You no longer mention spending time in his clinic."

"Other matters occupy me here." The brevity of his answers only compelled her to learn more. She looked at him intently.

"You have to go, Ingram. You are exploring a new field with great discoveries to be made. You need to be with scientists doing similar research. I feel horribly remiss that you are not there already."

"I would have worried myself sick had I left you here."

"I understand. But when my story is completed, you must go. I insist."

"And what of us?" he asked.

She hesitated.

"Do you still wish me to come with you?' she asked.

"I would marry you in an instant. You know that. But the decision is not mine alone. And I suspect the possibility will soon be out of the question."

"Why so?"

"I see your excitement with your work. I also see the quality of your work. Mr. Pulitzer will dare not let you go abroad for a year. And you wouldn't ask."

"If I fail in this story, I fear Mr. Pulitzer will have nothing to do with me."

"Mr. Pulitzer will hold on to you no matter what."

"Not if I were married." She blurted it out. She surprised herself. She hadn't realized how much she had been thinking about this.

"He would find a way," he said. "But marriage is not the issue. You need to be here. Your heart is with your work. It captures your imagination, and I will not deprive you of that. This is where you belong, not in Europe with me."

The quickness of his breathing seemed to punctuate the finality of his conclusion.

"Then what do we do?" she asked.

"I don't know."

Tears came to his eyes. She saw how much he loved her, and she was humbled.

Tears came to her eyes as well, that someone she loved and genuinely admired could love her so much and treat her so kindly.

He stared at her, saying nothing but his eyes pleading with her to come over to him. But she dared not do it. She knew what she would be giving up, as did he.

She stood up.

"Thank you for dinner."

She hurried to her room while she still had the power to think straight, before she was overcome by passion and sadness.

CHAPTER TWENTY-FIVE

HENRY HILTON

As it turned out, Alan Dale had also been looking for Nellie.

When she arrived at work the day after Christmas, there was a note on her desk.

"Please join me for a play tonight. I suspect you will find it of significant interest. Dale."

She searched the office for him to learn more, but he was nowhere to be found. She sent a message to Mary Jane that she would not be home that night and to Ingram asking him to check in on her mother from time to time. Dale did not return until late in the day. He had been out all afternoon reviewing a matinee in Chelsea.

"You received my note?" he asked.

"Yes. What is this play that is of such great interest?"

"*Held By the Enemy*, in Brooklyn. Tomorrow is the official opening, but tonight is for critics and honored guests."

"I know nothing about it."

"Nor do I—except that two names on its list of financial backers are Mr. Charles DeKay and Judge Henry Hilton. They will be at tonight's premiere."

Nellie had to smile. He handed her a flyer.

"The play is described as 'a sympathetic view of the Confederacy'—Richard Gilder's main cause these days, and of course Charles DeKay's as well, now that he has taken up with the granddaughter of Robert E. Lee."

"I have some other questions for you—"

"We will have plenty of time, Miss Bly. More than you'd like, I'm afraid—the theater is a long ride away. I have to write my review of the god-awful matinee I just saw, and then we will have dinner, courtesy of Mr. Pulitzer."

The elevated train to Battery Park, then the ferry ride to Brooklyn, and finally the elevated train to the Brooklyn theater district in Sheepshead Bay took ninety minutes. Nellie mused that all three legs of the journey were now owned by Hilton and Corbin, which meant the prices were about to rise dramatically and the quality of service about to drop equally so. Dale, as a nonpolitical person, normally didn't much care about travelers suffering since most of his time was spent in Manhattan between Newspaper Row and the theater district, but he, too, became agitated that "a man of such low sensibilities" as Hilton could have such an impact on so many people.

They had time for a brief dinner at a local restaurant—Dale complained the whole time and vowed never to eat there again, determined to warn his readers to stay away as well. Nellie had guessed right: Dale knew a great deal about Mary Hallock Foote. He had many friends in both the art world and the lesbian world, and nearly all of them had a strong opinion about Molly Foote. She was an enormous personality, one of the genuine artists of her time, but as difficult and unrestrained as she was talented. Dale delivered a wealth of varied anecdotes about her. Molly Foote did not seem the kind to protect Charles DeKay no matter what. Yet, despite all of Dale's insights, it was hard for Nellie to keep her attention on Molly Foote now that she was about to see Charles DeKay and Henry Hilton, the men responsible for Emma's death, together for the first time.

She sat behind Dale in his balcony box overlooking the orchestra. For some in the crowd, it was another white-tie affair, though because of the Brooklyn location and the nature of the subject matter, most of the balcony seats and much of the orchestra were filled with people in more conventional dress: men with suits and waistcoats, women with long dresses and modest jewelry. This made those with white tie and tails and opulent gowns and jewels stand out all the more, though they seemed to prefer it that way.

Charles DeKay sat in the middle of the fifth row with his new wife, Lucy Coffey. Next to Lucy was Judge Hilton, apparently there by himself. Hilton was transfixed by Lucy's charms, and the younger couple hung on the older man's every word. Nellie made sure to stay in the background. She wanted to observe the two men interacting naturally, with no awareness that a journalist was watching them. But she needn't have worried.

DeKay was not looking around for others who could help him make his way up the social ladder; his primary benefactor was already sitting just two seats to his right. On Charles' other side, sitting quietly with her husband, was Helena DeKay Gilder. The two of them stared straight ahead, totally disengaged, as if their attendance were required, until finally Richard checked his pocket watch, walked to the aisle, and climbed the few stairs onto the stage. The audience quieted as Richard stopped and waited at stage center. He had a surprisingly commanding presence.

"Good evening. My name is Richard Gilder, and I would like to thank all of you for coming tonight."

Polite applause. Gilder was among friends and admirers.

"I am the editor of the *Century* magazine, and as many of you know, for the past three years, we have published a series on the Civil War, including memoirs by officers and soldiers on both the Union and Confederate side. These memoirs, I am pleased to say, have sparked a great deal of interest on the part of the public, so much so that we now distribute over two hundred thousand copies a month."

The audience reacted accordingly, with genuine applause.

"Our magazine is located in New York City, the largest city in the Union, and yet there is extraordinary interest in the Confederacy, some twenty years after the war's end. One explanation, of course, is the exemplary way the southern soldier conducted himself. I saw that with my own eyes, as a member of the Pennsylvania Regiment."

That's not how my father described it, thought Nellie. *And he also served in the Pennsylvania Regiment, as a cavalryman. He saw friends die at the Rebels' hands and said they were animals. He swore he would never forgive them. I wonder if Gilder was even there—or if he just made it up.*

"They were fine men, honorable men, and if the southern politicians had been up to the caliber of their soldiers, the years following the war would have been very different indeed. I wrote a poem about these men I saw, these brave, devoted Americans, and with your indulgence, I would like to recite it now."

He straightened his back, like an actor reciting lines:

> *Better than honor and glory*
> *And History's iron pen*
> *Was the thought of duty done*
> *And the love of his fellow men.*

Thunderous applause. Nellie felt marooned in some bizarre world and wanted to scream. *The South had nearly destroyed the Union! And Gilder was calling them heroes. Didn't these people lose loved ones in the war? Or did they just buy their way out, like so many New Yorkers she'd read about in the Pittsburg papers?*

"We owe so much to our southern brethren. Speaking as a publisher, how much more national, in the best sense, our periodicals have become because of the presence of southern writers. It is well indeed for the North, well for the nation, to hear in poem and in story all that the South has to tell of her romance, her landscapes, her heroes, and yes, of her cause."

More applause, sustained and louder. *Her cause?! What, slavery? Destroying the Union? Do people really want to hear more of their cause?*

"There is another explanation I would put forth of the great interest in the Confederacy these days, and that is the way of life in the Old South itself. It had its appeal, beyond question. A serenity, a simplicity, compared with our way of life now. I heard something interesting yesterday, at one of the previews we were holding for the play. We invited audience members from the local neighborhood, and I sat behind a young boy and his mother. The boy asked the mother, 'What did the Yankees fight for?' Now, at that moment the orchestra was striking up 'Marching Through Georgia,' and the mother said, 'The Yankees fought for the Union.' Then the young boy asked, 'And what did the Confederates fight for?' Before the mother could answer, the music changed to 'Home Sweet Home.' "

The orchestra in the theater began playing the song. The audience, stirred at the sound of the southern ballad, cheered. The melody filled the theater with pathos.

"The mother leaned toward her son," continued Gilder, "and said, 'Do you hear this song? *That* is what they were fighting for.' "

" 'You mean they fought for their *homes*?' asked the boy."

" 'Yes,' said the mother. 'They fought for their homes.' "

"And the young boy looked at his mother and said with a voice of absolute determination, 'Oh, Mother. Then I will be a Confederate.' "

Huge applause, now even louder and more enthusiastic than before. Nellie was disgusted. She also realized, for the first time, how dangerous Gilder was.

"We are honored to present this play. Several people made it possible, and I would like to introduce a few of them now. First is my sister-in-law, our guiding light and the granddaughter of the great General Robert E. Lee, Mrs. Lucy Coffey DeKay."

Lucy stood up and took a bow, to heartfelt applause. Nellie was appalled that the granddaughter of Robert E. Lee, a man her father despised for prolonging the war at least three years, would receive such a reception in the North's largest city. Watching Lucy wave gently and nod to the crowd as if they were beloved servants, Nellie recalled a story her father often told that brought a smile to his face. Before the war, Lincoln had asked Lee, the federal government's most outstanding military leader at the time (he had led the capture of John Brown at the federal arsenal at Harper's Ferry), whether he would remain loyal to the Union if the South seceded. Lee said yes, or at least Lincoln understood that he said yes. After the Confederate attack at Fort Sumter, when Lee resigned his commission to lead the forces of Northern Virginia, Lincoln was furious. Three years later, when the idea came up for a national cemetery to honor the Union dead, Secretary of War Stanton proposed using the Lee family estate at Arlington, which the Union Army had overrun. Lincoln approved the idea immediately and signed the proclamation that very day. As she watched Lucy Coffey, it pleased Nellie, as it must have pleased Lincoln, to think that for all time the major cemetery for Union soldiers was on land that once belonged to the family of Robert E. Lee.

"The other person I wish to acknowledge is esteemed Judge Henry Hilton, who has worked tirelessly to honor veterans on both sides of the Mason-Dixon line, sponsoring joint parades and dinners in New York City and in Richmond and generously financing plays such as this that give greater understanding and well-deserved respect for our southern brethren. Judge Hilton, would you grace us with a few words?"

All of those in the orchestra section—that is, those in white tie and tails and long gowns and diamond necklaces—applauded with exuberance. Hilton was reluctant to stand, though Nellie knew it would take very little coaxing.

"Please," insisted Gilder, leading the applause and beckoning at the same time.

Finally, gesturing as if he was simply giving the audience what they wanted, Hilton stood and made his way to the aisle and up onto the stage. He and Gilder shook hands warmly, and then Gilder stepped to one side so that Hilton had the stage all to himself. Nellie felt her stomach knot with revulsion.

"Thank you, Richard." Hilton spoke in that extra-loud voice that still rang all too often in Nellie's brain. "And thank you all for being here tonight. I am so pleased with the reconciliation finally taking place among us northerners and southerners. I am particularly happy this is occurring now because I don't like what is happening in these United States, and we need to return to what we are, who we are. Foreigners enter our shores by the hundreds of thousands. Workers and farmers engage in anarchy. Our women no longer remain in the home. Looking back, I think it is fair to say that the Confederacy, not the Union, may have been the real America, and that is why so many of us long for it now."

A burst of applause. He'd struck a deeply resonant chord with this audience. "So stand shoulder to shoulder with me, my friends, against these corrosive elements. Do what you can to stop the destruction, the mongrelization of our nation. Urge your friends to see this play. And make those immigrants and anarchists ruining this country wish they had never set foot here."

More applause, louder and more sustained. Hilton headed back to his seat, pleased with himself, receiving handshakes and approving nods along the way. Nellie looked over at Dale, who was every bit as appalled as she was. No doubt Hilton's comments would find their way into Dale's review, but his was a minority view. Most people in the audience, and in America, felt exactly as Hilton did.

Looking at this spectacle of bile, Nellie felt like she was suffocating. She grabbed her purse and stood up.

"I need some fresh air," she whispered to Dale and hurried outside.

She raced down the stairs and out to the street. She sucked in the air as if she had been held underwater. The theater entrance was on a side street. Standing there, gasping for air, Nellie realized beyond question that Hilton had it in him to murder Emma, that he could impose his will on almost anyone he deemed necessary to carrying it out. His resources and his hatred gave him that power. Just as he and his ilk had taken over the government, he would take over the justice system as it suited him. Colonel Jackson back in Kittanning was minor compared with Hilton. Hilton could get away with murder. The matter would never even make it to a jury, though no doubt Hilton would win there, too. At first she'd thought the real scoundrel in Emma's death had been Charles, currying the doddering older man's favor, but now she realized that many people were more than willing to carry out Hilton's wishes; they would be lined up to volunteer because the rewards and opportunities he could provide them were so great.

Suddenly she heard a male voice. "You're the reporter woman."

She looked up. A man had emerged out of the shadows. It was the burly man who had picked her up when she'd gone to Hilton's house in Saratoga Springs.

"What are you doing here?" he asked roughly.

"I came to see the play." Her answer was defiant, but it sounded hollow. No one else was around, and he was twice as big as she was.

"Then why aren't you inside?"

"I wasn't feeling well. I wanted some fresh air."

He grunted. She didn't like the way he looked at her. "And how are you feeling now?"

"Better, thank you."

She started back inside, but he blocked her way.

"The play is about to begin," she said.

"Then you don't want to interrupt it."

He looked her over with an unmistakable hunger. She knew how vulnerable she was. Hilton and his thug would have no hesitation about killing her. And even if she somehow survived, Hilton would make sure no one was punished for it.

"You know who I am. You know I work for the largest newspaper in New York."

"Judge Hilton thinks you served your purpose."

"What does that mean?"

"It means he won't care if you go missing."

"Yes, but other people will."

"They don't matter."

She looked around for help, but they were completely alone. He grabbed her wrist. His hands were huge. She cried out. He squeezed tighter and twisted. He was breaking her wrist.

"I want to go inside," she said through the pain.

"I'm sure you do."

He pulled her into an alley. It was totally dark. She started to scream, but he punched her in the stomach, and all the wind went out of her. She couldn't breathe, she couldn't cry out. He grabbed her other wrist and pinned her against the wall of the theater. She could feel his erection pressing against her. She moved her leg to knee him in the groin, but he hauled off and smacked her again across the temple, even harder. He ripped open her bodice and cupped her breasts. His hands were cold and calloused, and she winced in pain, which only seemed to arouse him more. He put a hand under her skirt and ripped at her undergarments, but there were too many layers. He couldn't get to her flesh. She tried to turn away from him. He smacked her again across the temple, almost knocking her out, then dug a shoulder into her chest, pinning her, and slipped both hands under her skirt and tore away the underskirts as if they were paper. His hand felt around and grabbed against the hair of her pubis. He sighed with pleasure. She could feel the other hand reaching to unbutton his pants. All his weight was pressing against her. There was nothing she could do. She was blacking out, could barely breathe, and he was twice her weight. She tried to scream yet again but nothing came out.

THWACK!

She heard what sounded like wood hitting a wall. The rapist seemed to freeze.

THWACK!

He grimaced in pain. His weight fell away from her. His hand dropped from her genitals, and suddenly he was on his knees.

THWACK!

Dale's cane smashed across the man's face, with all of Dale's strength behind it.

The rapist went face down on the ground in a daze.

THWACK!

The cane smashed him on the back, snapping his shoulder blade. He cried out in pain.

THWACK!

Dale swung the cane into the man's ribs. THWACK! THWACK! THWACK!

Again and again and again he smashed the man's side and chest. The rapist howled in pain, but Dale swung the cane against his head, his shoulders, his neck, bringing whimpers and then silence. The man clawed to move, but Dale raised his arm yet again, and this time came down on the head, full force.

THWACK!

The man lay there lifeless. He might be dead or seriously hurt, Nellie didn't know which and didn't care. She looked at Dale, who was breathing heavily from the effort.

"Thank you," was all she could say.

"Are you all right?"

She nodded. She looked down at herself. Her blouse was torn open, her skirt ripped, her underskirts strewn on the ground.

"Let's get you home."

Dale took the coat off the unconscious man and slipped it around her. It covered her completely. He gathered up her clothes and purse.

"I have some theater friends not far from here," he said. "They'll take care of us."

"Where did you—?" She was amazed he had been able to so thoroughly dispatch the thug.

"Years of experience, Miss Bly."

He led her out of the alley. She was shaking and in shock. She took a look back at the rapist, lying on the ground, a bloody pulp.

"I guess they won't be getting a favorable review."

"No, I don't think so."

CHAPTER TWENTY-SIX

MARY HALLOCK FOOTE

The next day, Nellie went to the fourth floor of the Tenth Street Studio Building, the most famous studio in New York. Her head and chest ached from the assault in Brooklyn, and every breath made her wince. Ingram and Dale had urged her to rest for a few days, but the attack and the speeches before the play only motivated her to go after Hilton with even greater vigor. Time was getting short. Hilton might never be held legally responsible for Emma's death, but Nellie would settle for destroying his reputation. All she needed were a few facts. Hilton might be able to control a prosecutor or a jury, but he would never be able to control Joseph Pulitzer.

The Tenth Street Studio housed a dozen artists at any one time, including William Merritt Chase, Winslow Homer, and, when she was in New York, Mary Hallock Foote. Despite her romantic portrayals of the American West, Dale pointed out snidely, Foote found the Idaho winters too harsh and quietly spent those months in New York. As a first-rate illustrator and storyteller of the exotic West, as well as an inveterate charmer, she was always assured of space at the Tenth Street Studio.

Inside the large warehouse building, makeshift partitions separated the work areas and artists conversed freely. At the far end of the corridor, Nellie saw a striking, vivacious woman in her early forties holding court, surrounded by a bevy of male artists. By her uninhibited affect, denim western skirt, and siren-like effect on the male admirers, Nellie knew it was Molly Foote.

Even from afar, Nellie had never beheld anyone quite so vibrant in her entire life. Helena DeKay was beautiful and witty, but within the confines of a conventional, eastern, blueblood mold. Mary Hallock Foote's allure was one of the spirit, of total independence and freedom, a true artist in both her manner and her work. Foote had forged her way into obscure towns in Colorado and Idaho, towns with scarcely any other women within hundreds of miles, and had written compelling stories and drawn vivid illustrations of the life there. Like so many others, Nellie was drawn to that spirit and looked forward to meeting Foote for herself.

But Nellie was also ill at ease. She had heard from Dale, and it was borne out in the writings, that Mary Hallock Foote could be extremely difficult. Her courage and talent were undeniable, but her writings conveyed an insufferably arrogant easterner. She portrayed people in the West as crude and uneducated, and while the territory itself was rugged and magnificent, its people, as presented by Foote, most decidedly were not.

Foote had made a strong point in her magazine pieces of sending her son back East for school at the nation's oldest prep school, St. Paul's in Massachusetts, and then on to M.I.T. to study engineering. Nellie, on the other hand, identified much more with the western settlers than the upper-crust easterners—Pittsburg was considered the Gateway to the West—and Molly's caustic remarks rankled her. It bothered Nellie that on some level she still wanted the acceptance of these people, given all she had seen of them since moving to New York.

Nevertheless, she was there on a critical mission, and natural reporter that she was, she willed herself to put aside personal antipathies and insecurities as she approached Molly's work area. She was struck by Molly's latest painting, portraying a mother in her thirties carrying a baby down to a creek in a lovely mountain setting. It was done on a large canvas and somehow captured the ruggedness and beauty of both the setting and the woman. Rather than join the crowd of Molly's would-be suitors, Nellie stayed back and admired the painting.

"What do you think?"

Mary Hallock Foote approached Nellie, her eyes locked on hers, demanding an answer like an impatient schoolmarm. She had a wildness about her, an excitement that was incredibly seductive, enhanced by shimmering blue eyes, auburn hair, and a nearly perfect mouth. Few men or women, Nellie saw instantly, could resist the charms of Mary Hallock Foote. Then again, Nellie had considerable charms in her own right.

"I think it is marvelous," said Nellie. "You must love the West."

"I love my West when I am in the East," she said, drawing a chuckle from Nellie. Molly was pleased for both the laugh and the anticipation of continuing the conversation in a more intimate setting. "Are you a painter?"

"No. Only a reporter, I'm afraid."

"Even better." She perked up. "Then I am entirely at your disposal."

"I'm not a reporter for the arts. I want to ask you about something else."

"Ah." Molly did not hide her disappointment. "Miss Bly, I presume."

"I take it Mrs. Gilder spoke to you."

"She sent a note, actually. That is our preferred way of communicating these days." Molly Foote was the kind who placed a value judgment with every statement. That she and Helena communicated only through letters was mentioned with the irritation of a spoiled child who must follow silly rules.

"Why is that?" asked Nellie, all innocence. "You are in the same city."

Nellie, of course, knew perfectly well the answer to the question. Alan Dale had told her the story of Helena DeKay and Mary Hallock Foote. The two had met at Cooper Union College and become intimate friends—most probably very intimate, according to Dale. Following college, they had moved to a studio apartment together in New York, where they lived for eight years until Richard Gilder came in and swept Helena off her feet. Molly had taken it hard when Helena accepted

Richard's proposal of marriage. Shattered, Molly married Arthur Foote, an engineer, weeks later and moved west with him. Helena and Molly corresponded frequently, and the *Century* regularly published Molly's illustrations and writings—a good thing, too, noted Dale, because Arthur Foote was a fine engineer but his income was not dependable. Molly rarely saw Helena or Richard on her trips to New York, even though they were her editors and publisher; it was simply too painful for her to see Helena with someone else. Nellie, however, acted oblivious when asking Molly about Helena. The subject was obviously a sore one. Molly's countenance changed immediately.

"How can I help you, Miss Bly?" she asked with a chill, ignoring the question.

"I understand you visited Miss Lazarus before her death."

"That's right."

"On two occasions, I'm told."

"Yes."

"And the first one ended with you shouting at her."

"And in the second one I apologized for my behavior."

"What was it that made you scream at a dying woman?"

"Jealousy." Unlike Helena, Molly spoke impulsively, uncensored. "I learned that Miss Lazarus had taken my place as Helena's … confidante. After she returned from England, I visited her and behaved badly. Years of frustration came out, I'm sorry to say."

"You had no idea Helena and Emma were intimate?"

"Helena had lied to me. She said that Charles had taken up with a Jewess and that of course it would lead nowhere. I believed her until Richard mentioned in passing that Emma had taken my place."

Molly winced as she heard herself utter those words.

"Why did it bother you so? You had moved away and started a family, made a life for yourself in the West."

"Helena and I had vowed that our souls would remain as one forever." She said it with pride and defiance.

"And what made you apologize to Miss Lazarus?"

"Helena convinced me that nothing had changed. Emma

was simply keeping my seat warm. I paid Emma another visit, to offer an apology, and she graciously accepted."

The callousness of these women was appalling. Helena and Molly deserved each other. But Nellie remained focused on the task at hand.

"I need to know who poisoned Emma, Mrs. Foote. I know it was not you."

"Why is that? Do I strike you as too genteel?"

"No. I'm sure you would have considered it if you'd had the chance. But whoever poisoned her did it over the course of several weeks. You were there only twice."

"I am relieved to be out from under your suspicions," she said caustically.

"Did you see anyone put unusual items in her food or drink? Some powder? Or liquids? Anything that might have been out of the ordinary?"

"No one. And certainly not Charles. He did not poison Emma."

"I take it Mr. and Mrs. Gilder urged you to tell me that."

"Not at all."

"But then, you would not tell me if they had," Nellie said, not intimidated by the eastern artist. "They are your publishers and your primary source of income, now that your husband's engineering firm is struggling. No doubt that is another reason you communicate with Mrs. Gilder in writing rather than in person: Mr. Gilder must have no reason to end your publishing relationship."

Molly blanched. She wasn't used to being spoken to this way by someone of inferior stock. Nellie could tell the words hit home. Molly Foote prided herself on saying or doing whatever she pleased, but she was beholden to Richard Gilder, the man who had taken the love of her life, and it made her chafe inside.

"If you knew I would heed Mr. and Mrs. Gilder," Molly said, containing her ire, "then why are you here?"

"You apologized to Miss Lazarus. That means you respected her."

"Yes. I did. As a woman and as a writer."

"Then I assume you want to see her murderer brought to justice."

"Possibly. But the murderer was not Charles."

"He had every opportunity for it. Miss Lazarus always took tea in the afternoon, a habit she developed in England. I'm told he visited then and often prepared her tea."

"So did several other people. Her sisters. Her maidservant. Other friends."

"But none of them had reason to kill Miss Lazarus. I assume Helena told you about his arrangement with Judge Hilton."

"Helena has always confided in me and always will, until the day she dies. Whatever his arrangement with Judge Hilton, Charles is not a murderer. He lacks the stomach. I learned that living in the West. Some men are sickened at the sight of blood; others see it as a fact of life. Charles was seventeen when the war ended and never had to serve. He was extremely relieved. He would have paid whatever it took to stay out."

"He is a champion fencer. He founded the New York Fencers Club."

"There is a big difference between a college fencer and a swordsman. Charles is a critic, not a player." It was true, Nellie realized. She had suspected all along but had resisted facing it. She remembered Charles when he begged her not to publish the first article. He was lying that day, but she saw that he lacked the ruthlessness of Hilton, or of Carnegie or Frick or Gould, men who would vanquish anything in their path if necessary. Molly Foote was right: Charles DeKay had never killed another person, and he never committed murder for one, either.

"Then who poisoned Miss Lazarus?"

"What difference does it make?" shrugged Molly. "Emma is dead and buried."

"She was a great woman. I would like to know how she died."

"The public does not care. No one cares, not even her family. Most of the public do not know Emma Lazarus or appreciate her."

"But *I* know her. And *I* appreciate her. And apparently so did Mrs. DeKay."

Molly went flush. The old jealousy was not completely put to rest, even after a year. "I cannot help you, Miss Bly. If you'll excuse me, I have business to tend to."

She headed off to a group of male artists who were delighted to receive her.

Nellie was short of breath and sick to her stomach. Her entire theory of the case—that Charles had poisoned Emma at Henry Hilton's bidding—had just exploded in her face. It caused her to question everything about the story. She wondered if Hilton was even behind it and how it had been done. She even wondered if Ingram was wrong and Emma had not been poisoned at all but instead had died of cancer, as Barker had insisted.

She decided to clear her head and walk back to the *World* along Tenth Avenue instead of taking a streetcar. It was a cool January day, much like when she'd entered the asylum a year before. That had been an incredibly exhilarating moment, filled as it was with opportunity. This was the opposite, a sinking feeling, the air leaving a balloon. She had been so close, and now everything was falling apart. It had happened so many times in her life. The jury finding in her favor against that thief Jackson and then the judge stealing it. The front-page stories in the Pittsburg papers that riveted the public but then the publisher assigning her to garden stories and fashion. The beautiful house she lived in as a little girl that was suddenly taken from her, consigning her to live in tenements and scrub floors as a ten-year-old. That was the pattern, she reflected bitterly; that would always be the pattern.

She forced away the panic and tried to think rationally. Emma had been murdered. That was a fact. Ingram *had* found arsenic on both the pillowcase and the letters to Julia. Whoever had administered the poison had been part of her inner circle. That was another fact. They may have had their own reasons, which she could not fathom as yet, but they were almost certainly acting at the behest of Henry Hilton, who had more than enough reason to want Emma Lazarus dead: revenge for the boycott that damaged his fortune and reputation, plus the threat she posed to the new port at Montauk.

She went over the list in her mind of everyone who had been with Emma during those final months, and one by one eliminated each one as a suspect. Helena was in love with Emma and too haughty to do Hilton's bidding. Richard was editing Emma's papers and would want to keep his literary star alive as long as possible. Charles, as Molly had pointed out, lacked the backbone to kill anyone, especially someone whose murder would require repeated acts of chilling betrayal. Sarah was the only servant Emma allowed near her, and by her actions and demeanor, it was obvious Sarah was not the murderer.

Then who could it be?

Without realizing it, Nellie had arrived at Battery Park. She looked around at the chaos surrounding the arriving immigrants at Castle Garden, the poverty-stricken families carrying little more than the clothes on their backs, descended on by hustlers preying on their innocence and dreams. Relatives who had gone ahead to America fought through the hordes to locate loved ones. Over by the docks, two tall sailing ships were joined by a giant steamship that dwarfed the older ships. An endless stream of passengers disembarked from the ships. Nellie could swear the hustlers' eyes got wider and wider.

By the entrance to the Garden a play was going on in Yiddish. The audience, children and adults waiting for their next step in the New World, was enthralled. Nellie had to smile. Emma would have liked this.

She surveyed the bay, crowded with ferries shuttling passengers from New Jersey and Long Island to Manhattan. In the distance she saw the Statue of Liberty, shiny and gleaming in its copper patina. Not far from the statue, dozens of workers removed sand from a giant barge and shoveled landfill on to tiny Ellis Island, the home of the new federal immigration center. Two huge barges loaded with sand headed toward the island, and Nellie followed the line back to the dock at Battery Park, where twenty or so horse-drawn carriages piled high with sand were lined up one after the other, and workmen transferred the sand to another huge barge waiting on the dock.

Nellie walked over to the carriages. An officious man in his early forties, with a bushy mustache and suit and tie, made notes and kept a tally on a tablet.

"What's going on?" she asked.

"We are doubling the size of Ellis Island, miss," he said proudly.

"The island is not big enough as it is?"

"No, miss. The new center will accommodate twice as many people as pass through Castle Gardens every day."

"*Twice* as many?" she said. "Are there that many ships coming over?"

"Same number of ships, miss. But these new steel hulls can carry three times the number of people. Eleven hundred passengers, eight hundred crew. We can't keep them waiting on the ships for a week."

"But if you add to the size of the island, won't they run aground?"

"A good question, miss. The new land has to go straight down rather than gradual. We have divers making sure of that. If it sets like a continental shelf, that's right, the ships can't land."

Something went off in her brain.

"How deep is the harbor here?" she asked.

"Twenty-four feet here at Castle Garden. Ellis Island is farther out, about thirty feet."

"Is thirty feet enough to accommodate the new ships?"

"Barely. It used to be seventeen feet here. It took years and years to get it to twenty-four. But we're blessed that this is an island rather than part of the shelf. It's easier to dig near an island."

"And if this were part of the shelf and not an island?"

"Then the federal government would have to look elsewhere for its new immigration depot."

Once again she could scarcely breathe, only this time it was from excitement. It didn't make complete sense quite yet, but she knew she was on to something.

"Thank you, sir," she said effusively. "You have been most helpful."

"Not at all, miss."

CHAPTER TWENTY-SEVEN

PATCHOGUE, LONG ISLAND RAILROAD STATION

Over Nellie's objections, Ingram had opted to forego his research for the afternoon and ride the train with her out to Montauk. He had grown increasingly worried about her safety. After the near-rape in Brooklyn and her other mysterious near-accidents on the streets, he had retained a detective agency to provide full-time protection, and a guard accompanied the two of them and Mary Jane on the trip. Nellie had protested all the security as unnecessary, but Ingram wouldn't hear of it. He was determined to be cautious.

Ingram said almost nothing the entire ride, and it was not simply that the sea air aggravated his respiratory problems. The night before, they had broached the subject of marriage once again, and the discussion again left them both in tears. He wanted to build a life with her, but they both knew she would never be happy living with him in Europe. She had too much drive, too much ambition. Some newspapers assigned reporters to work in foreign countries, but they were almost always in London or Paris. Ingram's work would take him to Vienna and Leipzig and Moscow. That was where the advances in psychology were taking place. The only way they could become husband and wife was if he gave up his interest in psychology and practiced medicine as a conventional doctor.

He offered to take that path, but he could not hide his dismay at the prospect. It was not that conventional medicine bored him. He was a natural healer, and as a scientist everything about the human body fascinated him. But he was convinced that so much of the physical pain and mental anguish humans encountered in life was due to forces beyond their control, as if they were afflicted with an emotional virus. He wanted to understand these viruses and find ways to treat and even cure them. There was so much work to be done in that area, and his research at Bellevue and with private patients had made him one of the three or four most forward-thinking physicians in the world in that regard. He could not give all of that up, any more than Nellie could give up her reporting. Try as they might, they could not see a way out.

He glanced over at her and saw her staring at the sand dunes getting swept about by the bitter cold January wind. She smiled at him and resumed looking out the window. It tormented them both to be so near and yet have no future together. If she was right about this harbor, Nellie thought to herself, her story would be finished soon, and she would move on to other things. There would be no need to protect her any longer. He would go to Germany, and she would remain here in New York.

"I think Mrs. Foote is right about Charles DeKay," he blurted out unexpectedly. "I don't think he poisoned Miss Lazarus."

It was a bold statement for him. Usually he confined his responses as a scientist, or a sounding board.

"Why do you say that?"

"DeKay is very comfortable with women. Women have always saved him. His mother, his sister, Emma. He is grateful to them. And he needs them. I don't think he could bring himself to harm a woman."

"That is speaking as a scientist?"

"As a psychologist, yes. That is what my training tells me. I take it from your skepticism you are now even less likely to join me abroad after this case?"

"Don't joke about that, Ingram. Please."

He nodded and resumed his silence. But personal feelings aside, she was impressed. She had reached the same conclusion after speaking to DeKay, Helena, and Mary Foote. His science had led him to the same result, and he had spent no more than five minutes with Charles DeKay. She wasn't skeptical of his new field, she was admiring. But she dare not tell him that or they would be embroiled in a difficult discussion all over again.

They arrived at Montauk, on the tip of Long Island that looked out to the Atlantic Ocean and Long Island Sound. To the east was a gray ocean with pounding waves as far as the eye could see. To the northwest they could see Block Island and, in the distance, Newport. Bundled up against the cold, they made their way through the small whaling town to a large clapboard house located among some fishing boats and a few luxury yachts moored for the winter and bearing the sign MONTAUK YACHT CLUB. By the dock a crusty man with deep, weather-beaten lines in his face sat in a mildewed shack with an open window despite the freezing temperature. Ingram and Nellie stepped forward as Mary Jane and the guard lingered behind.

"Mr. Blake?" said Ingram.

"That's me."

"I'm Dr. Ingram. And this is my wife. I sent you a telegram."

"Yes. Good afternoon, doctor. Mrs. Ingram."

She had to smile. It did have a nice ring to it. "Good afternoon, Captain Blake."

Blake's chest puffed out at being addressed as Captain.

"I would like to inquire about joining the yacht club," said Ingram.

"Are you familiar with the area, doctor?"

"Somewhat. I work in Manhattan and recently profited from some fortunate investments. I decided the best use of my profits was to take advantage of your marvelous setting."

"A wise decision, doctor. May I ask the size of your yacht?"

"I have my eye on a sixty-foot schooner."

"A hundred and twenty feet," piped up Nellie.

"A hundred and twenty feet," conceded Ingram, the good husband going along.

Blake frowned. "How deep is the hull?"

"Twelve feet. Maybe fifteen."

"I'm sorry, doctor. The deepest we can accommodate is ten feet."

"We will be glad to pay extra," said Nellie.

"It's not a matter of payment, ma'am. Our harbor cannot take in anything larger than ten feet."

"Are you sure of that?" said Nellie. "We so want to dock our boat here."

"I am sure, Mrs. Ingram. I would like nothing more than to make you and your husband a member of our club. But the laws of nature are governing us, not the laws of men."

"What about these plans to make Montauk Harbor the new landing point from Europe?" asked Nellie. "I've been reading about that in the paper."

"As long as the ships go no deeper than ten feet, they should have no problem."

"But most of the ships will have hulls that sit twenty feet or so," she said. "There must be plans to make the harbor deeper."

"None that I've heard. And for good reason."

"Oh? Why is that?"

"Because it can't be done. The floor is bedrock. We can't even build a bridge here, and believe me, we've tried. It would take years to make the harbor twenty feet deep. No, this harbor is staying as it is for some time."

Nellie glanced at Ingram. She had heard enough. "Well. Thank you for your time," said Ingram to Blake.

"This is a lovely spot," said Nellie. "Perhaps we can find something smaller."

She put her arm through Ingram's and they walked away, like any other young married couple.

"I hope so, ma'am," called Blake. "You won't regret it."

Nellie squeezed his arm. She was excited. "Well done, Ingram. Extremely well done."

"Thank you, Mrs. Ingram." The appellation made her smile, but he wished it had been for real.

She didn't bother to stop and wait to be announced. She just barged right in.

Maybe it was the fact that she was a woman, or maybe it was because she had been there before, but the guards and secretaries outside Gould's office expected her to stop and ask to see the Great Man, as everyone else did. But Gould could have told them she was not like everyone else.

Neither, of course, was he, so when she sailed straight into his office and strode up to his desk, he seemed as if he had been waiting for her for the past half hour.

"You knew all along, didn't you?" she demanded.

Gould looked directly at her, understanding in an instant exactly what she knew.

One of the guards grabbed her by the arm. "You have to leave, miss—"

"Not until I'm finished."

"Sorry, Mr. Gould—" The guard started to pull her away.

"Let me go!" She clenched a fist and threatened to punch him. "Now!"

"It's all right, Mike. She can stay."

The guard released her arm. He did not take kindly to being shown up in front of his employer. "Sorry for the intrusion, Mr. Gould. I thought she was more of a lady."

"Oh, she is a lady, Mike. She's simply more insistent than the rest of them." The guard left the room.

"So," said Gould. "What can I do for you, Miss Bly?"

"Hilton's plan for a harbor at Montauk. It's not going to work."

"No."

"How long have you known?"

"Since they began buying up the land from the Indians. I hired divers to measure the depth. At low tide, it is four feet a half mile offshore. There is no machinery currently in existence that could create a harbor for a modern ship out of those conditions."

He leaned back in his chair and waited for her next question.

"How could Hilton and Corbin not realize that the ships won't be able to dock there?"

"They have been too busy congratulating themselves. You see, they are railroad men, and there is no railroad problem engineers cannot solve. Mountains, deserts, valleys, rivers—

engineers have figured out ways around all of them. The same is not true for ships. If anything, the problems have become more challenging as the ships have gotten larger and larger. The weather has been too cold to begin construction. I suspect by March or April Hilton will realize that fortune has not smiled on him."

"Why did you not say anything? Why let them be the fools?"

"I was looking to sell the Manhattan Elevated. Certain changes are about to occur that will dramatically reduce its value, and I needed an eager buyer."

"What kinds of changes?"

"You'll find out soon enough. So will they. There are very few buyers who could afford such a purchase on short notice, and with cash. Essentially only two people: Hilton and Corbin. Fortunately, it only took two."

"But they would never do business with you," she said, starting to put it together, "unless they thought they were getting the best of you."

"Precisely."

"And that's where I came in. You brought me in to get under Hilton's skin, to rile him up so he wouldn't think straight and would jump at the chance to hurt you."

Gould nodded.

"So you used me."

"We used each other. Your publisher sold quite a few newspapers thanks to this story."

"Not $20 million worth. What else did you lie about? Did you even know Miss Lazarus?"

"In passing. We met at Seligman's funeral. When I learned of her involvement with the Montauks, I became more interested and learned what I could about her."

"So when I told you about Maria Pharaoh going to Emma, you already knew all about that, even though you acted like you were hearing it for the first time. You just wanted me to print a story that would let Hilton and Corbin feel so full of themselves, they would make an offer on your railroad."

"It was you who insisted on writing the story, Miss Bly. I

actually recommended against it, if you recall."

"Knowing that it would only make me want to write it all the more."

Gould said nothing. He didn't have to. Nellie knew she was right. She felt completely manipulated, like a child's puppet.

"When you first brought me to your office, how did you know I would believe you?"

"I didn't, but I had to try something. I had an asset worth $20 million that was soon going to be worth nothing. Hilton and Corbin were two of only a handful of possible buyers. Hilton has obvious character weaknesses. I needed someone who could prey on his irrationality about defeating me, and from what I could tell, that would come easily to you. Knowing your history, in fact, you would relish it. Now, don't look so put upon. Before we met, you were about to give up on the case and tell Pulitzer that Miss Lazarus died of natural causes. If not for me, you would not even have a story at this point."

"Possibly. But thanks to me, you are $20 million wealthier."

"Yes. And I am most grateful."

His brazen indifference to truth stunned and disgusted her.

"I'm going to write all this in a story, let people see what a liar and scoundrel you really are."

"They already know, Miss Bly. It makes no difference to me. Now that Hilton and Corbin's cash sits safely within my bank, you can write whatever you like."

CHAPTER TWENTY-EIGHT

JAY GOULD

With the help of Ingram's strong coffee, she stayed up much of the night writing the Montauk Harbor story. She had never really drunk coffee before and was surprised how alert her mind felt, though her body was aching for sleep. It felt as if little factory workers were coursing through her veins. Ingram was used to keeping long hours on little sleep, and he kept a fresh pot of coffee brewing throughout the night for her. She even did something she never did with anyone: she showed him her story before she turned it in. She trusted Ingram. Somewhere along the line, she realized, she had fallen hopelessly in love with him. It may have been when he'd invited her and her mother to live with him, or when he dropped everything to ride out to Long Island. Or it may have even been when they first met and he saw through her disguise but went along for the sake of the patients. But she knew he had captured her heart, and she never wanted to leave him.

Maybe she would move to Europe with him after all, or maybe he would decide to stay in New York. But she could not bear the thought of living apart from him.

"Stop daydreaming and write," he said. "Or we'll never get to sleep."

She never did get to sleep. She stayed up all night fussing with the story, getting every detail precisely correct, going over every word, making sure everything was exactly right. But sleep turned out to be unnecessary since the story generated so much excitement that it would have woken Nellie from the dead. She took a horsecar from Ingram's house to the *World* and was waiting for Cockerill when he arrived at 7 a.m.

Cockerill immediately recognized its import and raced to show it to Pulitzer, who did what no one at the *World* could ever remember him doing: he came down to the newsroom and began editing the story himself. He said it would be the biggest story since the election, and he intended to play it up as such. The three of them worked together, with Pulitzer and Cockerill verifying facts and incidents and pressing her for more because they wanted the story out for the afternoon papers. With his genius for the public's taste, Pulitzer knew exactly what he had on his hands. They printed twice the normal number of afternoon papers and still sold every single one.

NEW YORK HARBOR TO REMAIN NATION'S LARGEST

Montauk Point Fails to Hold Water

By Nellie Bly

New Yorkers can breathe a sigh of relief, as the commercial wharf at Battery Park will remain the nation's largest for the indefinite future.

The wharf, and the city, had been threatened by the announced plans of Henry Hilton and Austin Corbin to open a competing wharf at Montauk Point on Long Island. The two railroad magnates had touted that their wharf would be a faster and less expensive embarkation point for travelers and cargo from Europe. Indeed, Congress had allocated funds for a new immigration center at the new wharf. However, according to knowledgeable engineers, divers, and ship captains questioned by the World, the water around Montauk Point is no more than ten feet at its deepest point. This is below the twelve-foot hulls in standard use for immigrant ships today, and well below the twenty-foot depth of the ships expected to be in operation next year. This means that Montauk Point can be a viable harbor for nothing larger than small sailing yachts or fishing trawlers.

 Hilton and Corbin have expended enormous sums of money on Montauk Point, including a right-of-way through the entire length of Long Island and a twenty-square-mile area of land around the Point itself. When asked what they planned to do with the land instead of a wharf, the two magnates offered a surly "No comment" to the World.

Hilton and Corbin had completely rattled the city with their plan to ruin New York Harbor, and people were overwhelmed with relief that the biggest economic component of the city's well-being, bigger even than Wall Street, would remain intact. Strangers stopped and hugged and congratulated one another as if a war had ended.

But the relief and joy were soon followed by a deep anger. How dare these two men jeopardize the city of New York! Millions of people had been genuinely frightened for themselves and their families, and they wanted these robber barons punished. Mayor Grant, like any good politician, knew when the public wanted its pound of flesh, and he began to extract it the very next morning, almost as if he had been lying in wait for it. He summoned the press to City Hall—Cockerill directed Nellie to go, along with a more senior reporter named Wiley, who ordinarily covered that beat—and announced that "It is time for all trains in this city to run underground. The blizzard of last winter brought us to a halt, and the ongoing pollution we suffer every day makes it difficult for many of us to get around and even to breathe. If the trains run underground, and the city takes over the new system, we can practically eliminate all of these problems. This afternoon I am sending to the Council a referendum for a subway system to be built with city funds, to begin as soon as possible upon voter approval. London has had a subway system for twenty-five years. It is time for New York City to have the same and even go them one better."

There was thunderous applause. The subway would cost a fortune, and no one had any idea where the city would get the money to pay for it, but everyone in that room, every New

Yorker who read about it, was thrilled to have the city build one and remove themselves from the clutches of Henry Hilton and Austin Corbin.

"What about the elevated railroads?" asked a reporter from the *Tribune*.

"The ones owned by Hilton and Corbin?"

"Yes."

"What about them?" shot back the mayor.

"Will they continue to run?"

"Under my proposal, within five years all trains in the city will have to depend on electricity and run underground. So, we won't be seeing much more of their trains."

The room was abuzz. This announcement would terminate a huge business. "Is that legal, Mr. Mayor? Aren't you destroying their business?"

"My lawyers tell me the plan is legal. Anyone who wishes to challenge it in court is of course perfectly free to do so. But we'll take our chances. As for destroying their business, I have the same compassion for them as they had for the people of New York."

More cheers.

"What will they do with their trains?"

"I haven't spoken to them. Maybe they can ship them out to Montauk. I understand there's plenty of room," said the mayor to much laughter.

The questions, all to his liking, continued. Grant was in political heaven, an elected official taking action with the public completely behind him.

Nellie tugged at the sleeve of the *World*'s old pro Wiley, who thought he'd seen it all.

"Why did he wait until now to announce a subway system?" she asked. "Why didn't he do it after the blizzard?"

"Because Jay Gould owned the Manhattan Elevated, and Gould controls the judges. He could have tied it up in court for years. But now Gould is out of it."

"Why didn't he do it the day after Gould sold?"

"I suspect Gould knew what was coming and told him to wait for the right time. And he did. Now the mayor is in his debt."

As Nellie surveyed the fawning press and cheering supporters, she had to shake her head in admiration. Hilton and Corbin's $20 million investment in the Manhattan Elevated had collapsed. Their investment on Montauk Point and Long Island would not pay off for decades, if then. And the mayor, along with Jay Gould, held all the cards.

She stayed late to work with Wiley on the story. A thirty-year veteran of City Hall politics, he didn't like having to share a story with anyone—male or female, young or old—and made that known to Cockerill.

"Just remember," Cockerill said. "Without her, there wouldn't be a story."

"I understand that," said Wiley. "But I can take it from here."

"So can she. And if you can't see your way clear to work with her, she'll do it herself."

"Is that coming from Pulitzer or from you?"

"Both." The newsroom had heard all about Pulitzer's favoritism toward Nellie. But if Wiley was trying to drive a wedge between editor and publisher, it wasn't working. Muttering not all that quietly, he walked over to Nellie. She was seated at her desk.

"So how do you want to go about this?" Wiley asked gruffly.

"I thought you would write the story, and I'd check your spelling." He looked at her to see if she was kidding.

"Cockerill said we're to work on it together," he said.

"I've read your stories, Mr. Wiley. When I worked at the *Pittsburg Dispatch*, one of the older reporters pulled me aside and said I could do worse than to pattern myself after you."

He wasn't sure if she was trying to flatter him or telling the truth. He hated flatterers. "And what older reporter was that?"

"Erasmus Wilson."

He brightened. "You know Erasmus Wilson?"

"He was my best friend at the paper. He said I should say hello for him."

"Why didn't you tell me that earlier?"

"I didn't want any special favors."

He shook his head. "You would have saved yourself a lot of trouble in this newsroom, Miss Bly."

"Is that so?"

"I would have pummeled any newsman who gave you a bad time."

"And now?"

"You don't need my help."

It was a begrudging compliment that she didn't take lightly.

"I meant what I said about you writing the story," she said. "Is there anything I can do to help? Anything to write or to check?"

"Can you make coffee?"

"I'm afraid not."

"Do you at least drink coffee?"

"Yes. But only recently."

"All right. Make yourself busy. I'll have something for you in an hour or so."

Wiley filled a kettle with some water and put it over the fire. Then he went to his desk and started writing. Nellie watched him. She was relieved he didn't resent her. She would have fought him had it been necessary, the way she'd had to fight almost everyone else, but what she could really use was an ally in the newsroom. The truth was, she had admired his writing ever since she started as a reporter, and she knew she could learn from him.

She still had work to do on the Emma story. She had thought she was done, once Hilton had been brought to a kind of justice, but Cockerill, after checking with Pulitzer, had said no. Hilton may have been responsible for Emma's death, but as Pulitzer pointed out, Emma's name was not even mentioned in Nellie's story. The assignment had been to get to the bottom of Emma Lazarus's death, and she hadn't done that. She had chafed when Cockerill delivered the news, but she knew he was right. She still wasn't sure who'd poisoned Emma, or how. In point of fact she had no idea.

She turned to the stack of Emma's writings on her desk. She had read everything Emma had ever written, searching for some clue of her murderer. The poems were remarkable. But future generations would never see most of them, like "The New Colossus" or "1492." It was a crime. Emma was in effect dying a second time, at the hands of her sisters. Her work was about to be buried forever. She had spent her last days with Richard Gilder, arranging the poems for her legacy, but the sisters were undoing all of that. And no one could stop them.

She reached for the poem Julia had given her, the last Emma had written, looking back on her life. The title was "Assurance." Nellie couldn't get it out of her mind:

> *Last night I slept, and when I woke her kiss*
> *Still floated on my lips. For we had strayed*
> *Together in my dreams, through some dim glade,*
> *Where the shy moonbeams scarce dared light our bliss.*
> *The air was dank with dew, between the trees*
> *The hidden glow-worms kindled and were spent.*
> *Cheek pressed to cheek, the cool, the hot night-breeze*
> *Mingled our hair, our breath, and came and went,*
> *As sporting with our passion, Low and deep*
> *Spake in mine ear her voice: "And didst thou dream,*
> *This could be buried? This could be asleep?*
> *And love be thrall to death? Nay, whatso seem,*
> *Have faith, dear heart; this is the thing that is!"*
> *Thereon I woke, and on my lips her kiss.*

At first it seemed an ode to a lesbian lover, no doubt Helena, but Nellie knew "her kiss" meant much more than that. The poem expressed a yearning for love that lay deep inside her and had remained there all her life. Now that she was dying it would stay buried forever. That the one who left the kiss on her lips and aroused the passion was female was beside the point. That was Emma the poet. Love and sexual fulfillment were female traits. Emma had such bravery, thought Nellie. Helena had used her, betrayed her, yet Emma still revered the fire of love.

The poem made her think about Ingram.

> *And didst thou dream,*
> *This could be buried? This could be asleep?*
> *And love be thrall to death? Nay, whatso seem,*
> *Have faith, dear heart; this is the thing that is!"*

Truly that was how she felt about him. Her love could not be buried or asleep. What better description for her love for him than "the thing that is!"

The kettle whistled with boiled water. Wiley grabbed two dark mugs and a can of coffee grounds.

"I hope you like it strong," he said. He set the mugs down on her desk. Nellie made a face of distaste.

"I don't mind it strong, but I would like my mug clean." The mug was a sickening dark brown color, almost black.

"It *is* clean."

He spooned out some of the coffee grounds and put them directly into the mugs. Then he poured in the kettle water. "Sugar?"

"Please. Lots of it."

He put sugar into their mugs. The coffee had foamed at the surface. She stirred her mug. Thick coffee sediment had settled at the bottom.

"What color were these mugs before?" she asked.

"I think gray. Or maybe beige."

He stirred his coffee grounds and sipped. Nellie watched, and suddenly an idea hit her. Not a normal idea, but one that moved in and utterly seized her imagination. She leapt to her feet.

"You only drink coffee from these mugs?"

"That's right."

"What about porcelain cups?"

"They would be ruined in no time," he scoffed. "The coffee eats away at these clay mugs as it is."

"Mr. Wiley, would you mind if I left you? I need to check on something."

"What about our story? Cockerill wants it for the morning edition."

"It will be fine in your hands. We both know that. You can remove my name if you like."

She grabbed her purse and hurried out, her skirts becoming soiled from the tobacco juice on the floor. But she didn't give that another thought.

CHAPTER TWENTY-NINE

RICHARD GILDER

It was impossible to overstate the stench that constantly pervaded New York City. That was what Nellie hated most about the city. Everyone, including those in the brownstones along Fifth Avenue, dumped their garbage into the streets or back alleys. Stoops in brownstones were elevated not for design purposes but so that people could stand above the dung and dead animals. Many a street urchin made his living with a broom sweeping away filth to clear a path for passersby.

Although some government money was set aside for the collection of garbage, the bulk of those funds always found their way into the pockets of Tammany "middlemen," and so garbage collection became mostly a private undertaking. One of the entrepreneurial opportunities for immigrants, in fact, was to remove the garbage from large wooden boxes outside residences and dump them in sewer drains or directly into the East River. When Nellie realized she needed to speak with Sarah immediately, she went straight to the Lazarus family garbage collector as the conduit.

The Lazarus family, like many along Fifth Avenue, had their garbage picked up every night. It was a relatively inexpensive way of keeping the stench to a minimum. In trying to contact Sarah weeks before, Nellie had taken note of the comings and goings of the Lazarus household. Every night, the hired help would eat in the kitchen, at the rear of the house, while the family members took dessert. When the staff finished their dinner, the cook would set the garbage outside in large wooden crates. The garbage man would then transfer the contents into burlap sacks and haul them down the back steps and onto a horse-drawn wagon waiting in the alley.

The garbage man was a Russian immigrant in his mid-thirties who spoke very little English, but Nellie managed to communicate her request. A gold dollar coin no doubt helped him catch on. When the man knocked on the kitchen door to check on the last of the garbage, he handed the note to the cook and pointed to the name on the envelope. (The hired help frequently got notes from suitors or family members, so no one took notice when the garbage man handed a note to the cook with Sarah's name on the envelope.) The cook nodded, pointed to more mess for him to take out, then handed the envelope to Sarah. Hidden in the darkness below near the basement, Nellie watched Sarah read the note and suddenly turn serious. Sarah muttered something to the cook and headed down the back stairs.

She was extremely agitated as Nellie emerged from the shadows. "I shouldn't be seen with you."

"I need you to get something for me."

"Please, Miss Bly. I've done enough."

"Just one more item, Sarah. I promise. It's very important. It will help me expose the person who killed Miss Emma."

Sarah struggled to calm down.

"You said nothing has changed from Miss Emma's room?" said Nellie. "Nothing at all?"

"That's right," said Sarah. "It's the same way it was the day she died."

"I need you to bring me something from the room."

"Tomorrow morning?"

"No. I need it now."

Sarah became nervous all over again.

"It may take some time. The sisters are having tea in the parlor."

"That's all right. I'll wait all night for it if I have to. Take as long as you need."

＊　＊　＊

Martha, admiring the way her magenta skirt picked up the cranberry pinstripes in her cream-colored blouse, was behind the desk at the *Century* magazine reception area when Nellie walked in the next morning.

"Mrs. Gilder is not in," preempted Martha coolly before Nellie could even extend a greeting or state her business.

Helena must keep this girl around to look at when she has nothing better to do, thought Nellie. *There could be no other reason.*

"I am not here to see Mrs. Gilder. I am here to see Mr. Gilder."

"Is he expecting you?"

"No. Please tell him I'm here."

"Mr. Gilder is extremely busy."

"Please tell him I'm here!" she snapped. Nellie had put up with this girl long enough. Martha bristled, but something in Nellie's tone told her not to fight it. Without a word Martha glided down the corridor to one of the back rooms. Nellie's heart was racing. She ordered herself to calm down. She touched the coffee mug in her purse as a talisman.

"Miss Bly."

It was Richard himself, looking very put-upon. "What can I do for you?"

"I would like a private word with you."

"I'm sorry, our magazine is due at the printer this afternoon."

"I think it is very much in your interest to see me."

He caught the edge in her voice.

"All right," he allowed with an impatient sigh. "Come with me."

He led her down a hallway to his office, the living room of the house. It was a spacious room, with a Persian rug, oak floor, and high ceiling. Several of Molly Foote's illustrations decorated the walls, along with a photograph of a young Richard Gilder in a Civil War uniform, musket erect by his side. The bookshelves were lined with back issues of *Scribner's* and *Century*. The couch and desk were covered with manuscripts. He cleared a chair by his desk for her to sit down.

"Would you like some coffee?" he said.

"Actually, I would. Thank you."

He walked over to a table by the fireplace and spooned out some coffee from a can into a mug. He started to put a spoonful into another.

"I brought my own mug," she said.

She produced a dark mug from her purse. His eyes fixed on it.

"Look familiar?" she asked.

"Vaguely."

"It was the mug Miss Lazarus used when you were cataloguing her poems right before her death."

"Ah. So it is."

She handed him the mug. He put in a spoonful of coffee, then poured in some hot water from a kettle over the fire.

"I assume it's been washed?" he asked.

"Yes. Several times. I even washed it myself."

He handed the filled mug back to her.

"But that still didn't remove the arsenic," she said.

"Arsenic? What are you talking about?"

He sat down behind his desk and stirred his coffee, focusing intently on the dark brew.

"It was very clever of you," said Nellie. "Emma insisted on the two of you working alone. She was racing to arrange her poems in a proper order with her editor before she died. That presented you with an irresistible opportunity. There was no one else in the room to see you poison her. And with the dark mug, there would be no stains, so no one would ever notice."

"Miss Bly, I realize you are in the business of selling newspapers, but that would be far-fetched even for the *New York World*. I would never harm Emma. She was a monumental talent—and a genuine asset to this magazine. She had been a close family friend for years, and tragically she was going to die in a few months as it was. Why would I possibly want to accelerate her death?"

"You thought your wife was in love with her."

Gilder scoffed. "Helena had no romantic longings for

Emma. And vice versa. It was her brother whom Emma loved—though the feelings were not requited."

"That was the public arrangement, yes. And for years you believed it. When you found out the truth, you must have been furious. You thought you were done with Helena straying. Oh, she might have an occasional tryst with a friend or secretary but nothing of real concern. She had been in love with Molly Foote, of course, and promised to put all of that behind her when you married, but then she couldn't. She kept up a correspondence, and the two of them would disappear for days at a time when Molly was in town. You finally put a stop to it by using Molly's ambition against her. You wrote to her and said you would publish anything she wrote or drew, but she had to stop seeing Helena. And Molly accepted the offer because she lived thousands of miles away and knew she wouldn't be published elsewhere. You were her lifeline to legitimacy as an artist and a member of New York society. But you had no such hold over Emma."

She sipped her coffee.

"Once Molly moved west," she went on, "you thought you would finally have Helena all to yourself, but she didn't love you. She wanted nothing to do with you. She was lonely and needed companionship, and she sought out her friend Emma. They grew close and managed to hide it from you for years, but you saw the real truth after Emma returned from Europe. Emma was upset with her and scolded her for not publishing the manuscript. That's when you realized the depth of their intimacy. You must have searched Emma's room while she was sleeping and come across letters Helena had written, which confirmed your suspicions."

Gilder didn't bother to deny it. He sipped his coffee in silence.

"Three months at the most is what the doctors said," said Nellie in disgust. "Three months to live. And you couldn't even wait that long to abide your jealousy."

"Helena is the mother of my children. The hostess of our home. The betrothed of our marital vows. She is my *wife!*"

"And anyone who transgresses with her must be punished."

"Absolutely!" He was unabashed in his indignation.

Nellie had the confession she had come for. But she could not leave just yet. This man, who killed Emma Lazarus solely because his wife did not love him, revolted her.

"When you compiled Emma's poems as an anthology, I noticed that you left out 'Assurance,' her last poem. *'Thereon I woke, and on my lips her kiss.'* Those words must have enraged you."

"They did. And happily I was able to put a stop to their ever being published. More coffee?" He was remarkably unflappable. He took her mug and walked over to the table with the coffee can and kettle.

"Sadly, Miss Bly, there is nothing for you to write about. Any story you put forth would be dismissed as wild conjecture." He poured hot water into the mug.

"Oh, but there is a story, Mr. Gilder. One that will run for days and days. You used the arsenic in a dark coffee mug so it would not be detected as it would with a white porcelain cup. But the same arsenic that stains the cup remains with the cup."

"The mugs were washed every night."

"Yes. But arsenic does not dissolve in water. That is why the stains are so hard to remove. Traces of arsenic were found on the mug this morning."

For the first time, his composure cracked. "That's impossible."

"Emma's sisters kept the room exactly as it was the day she died. Nothing has been moved or added. The mug is exactly as it was a year ago."

"How do you know someone else didn't put arsenic in it?"

"With everyone else she drank tea. The only time Emma used the coffee mug was when she went over her writings with you. Her family, her maids, her visitors will all attest to that."

His hand tightened around the mug. A dark look came over his face. He glanced at the fireplace. Nellie read his mind.

"Don't bother, Mr. Gilder. That is the mug *you* drank from. The one you used to poison Emma is in a safe place."

He saw that he was boxed in.

"If you knew all this, why are you here? Why not simply

write your story?"

"I needed to understand what kind of man could not wait for a woman with cancer to die on her own. Why you would make her last weeks on Earth ones of unbearable suffering. Someone who trusted you and who had done so much for your success."

"Have you ever loved someone, Miss Bly?"

She thought of Ingram. "Yes."

"It is difficult to watch them deceive you and give their love to another. I could not bear witness to that for another day."

She was suddenly tired. She stood up. "Thank you for the coffee."

"Are you going to the police?"

"I don't trust the police. Not when you are so close with Judge Hilton. The story will be justice enough."

She walked to the door, eager to be out of his presence. But then she stopped.

"You misunderstood the poem, you know. Helena and Emma did not love one another."

Richard looked confused, uncertain. "They were lovers," he said insistently.

"Maybe. At one point."

"Then why go to the trouble of having Charles pose as her suitor for ten years?"

"Your wife was lonely. She needed someone with whom she could share her thoughts. That was not you; you could provide none of what she needed. You had forbidden her to see Molly, so she turned to Emma, who was no doubt infatuated for a while but must have realized your wife's limitations. That was the point of the poem. She simply chose to be a good friend all those years, to someone who didn't deserve it, while her own longings went unmet."

She opened the door.

"You see, theirs was a friendship borne not of love but of loneliness."

She walked out.

CHAPTER THIRTY

BELLEVUE HOSPITAL AMBULANCE

She had been thinking about the story for days, ever since the pieces began coming together, and finally decided to write it in as straightforward a way as possible. The facts of the story were sensational enough. She didn't need to embellish them with the writing.

EMMA LAZARUS MURDERED, EVIDENCE SHOWS

Death Attributed to Cancer Was Due to Poison

By Nellie Bly

The World has learned that the death of Emma Lazarus, the revered poet and social reformer, was caused by arsenic poisoning rather than a cancer, as originally believed, and that the person who administered the poison was Miss

Lazarus's editor at the Century Magazine, Richard Gilder.

A highly respected physician and chemist utilized by the World has examined samples of Miss Lazarus's clothing and handwritten letters, which have revealed the presence of fatal levels of arsenic in her system in the weeks immediately prior to her death. Although arsenic can be useful in the early stages of cancer, all of the doctors providing care for Miss Lazarus had ordered arsenic treatments stopped six months before her death. Yet according to our physician's tests, the arsenic levels in Miss Lazarus continued to rise until her demise.

Further investigation by the World revealed that arsenic was given to Miss Lazarus almost daily and without her knowledge by Mr. Gilder, her longtime editor at Scribner's and the Century. The two met every afternoon during the last three months of her life to catalogue her writings before her death. It was during those meetings that Mr. Gilder administered the poison to Miss Lazarus through a coffee cup. The World has obtained the mug in question and turned it over to the New York City Police Department.

When questioned by a World reporter, Mr. Gilder acknowledged making coffee for Miss Lazarus daily and providing the cup to her that contained the arsenic. According to the staff at the Lazarus home, no one besides Miss Lazarus ever drank from the cup, and no one besides Mr. Gilder ever poured coffee into it.

The apparent motive for the murder, revealed in a conversation with a World reporter, was Mr. Gilder's jealousy over the infatuation of his wife, Helena, with Miss Lazarus. As Miss Lazarus's medical condition became graver, Mrs. Gilder became increasingly pronounced in her feelings for Miss Lazarus, and Mr. Gilder became determined to put a stop to it.

Miss Lazarus was expected to survive no more than six months following her diagnosis of cancer. The poison, according to the physician, shortened that already limited time by three months.

Nellie chose to steer clear of any mention of Hilton and the land theft of Montauk Point. It would simply confuse matters, and in the end had nothing to do with Emma's poisoning. Of course, Hilton would learn that he had lavished Charles DeKay with undue rewards, and Charles would suffer as a result. But that was fine with Nellie. After all his duplicity, it was richly deserved.

As she read over the story before handing it to Cockerill, Nellie did not feel the satisfaction of a reporter finally completing a story after months of digging for the truth. All she felt was a profound sadness for Emma. Her closest friends had betrayed her, one had even killed her. Emma had died without knowing real love. It was such a pity, a woman who had given so much to others. No doubt she had tried for love, with Helena and possibly with Charles, but they were unworthy of her and violated her trust at every turn. But Emma was not alone. In the confined arrangements of the day, a spirit as free and strong as hers could almost never find fulfillment. She obviously yearned for it—that was the message of her last poem—but it was denied her to the end. For all Emma had done, for all the people she had helped and wrongs she had attempted to set right, the one thing her heart craved most would never be hers.

Unlike Emma, Nellie had found a love, but she had failed to embrace it. She lacked Emma's courage. Nellie had been too frightened, too hardened, to accept love. She had rebuffed Ingram at every turn, yet he had shown a patience with her she found nothing short of remarkable. Had he treated her the same way, she would have left him long ago.

All her life she had closed herself to love. There had been so many shattering moments that she had lost the capacity to trust anyone, male or female, friend or lover. She was fond of Ingram and she enjoyed their lovemaking, but there was a part of her that always held back, though one could never ask for a better, more devoted companion. What Emma would have given for an Ingram in her life!

She suddenly was ashamed of herself and felt the urge to hurry to his house, run into his arms, and declare that she'd been a fool. She would ask for his forgiveness and tell him she'd been so hurt that she could no longer trust her heart. More than that, she hadn't allowed any room in her heart. The daily struggle to find work and support herself and her mother and her sisters had overwhelmed her. Between the bad memories of her childhood and her solitary struggle to survive every day, she had given up on love. But Emma had convinced her to open her heart, to realize at last that nothing was more important than love. That was the message of the last poem. And Emma was right. She saw that now. She walked over to Cockerill's desk without bothering to read over the story, handed it to him, and said she was going home.

Nellie's excitement only grew on the streetcar ride to Ingram's house. She spent the entire time planning her life together with him. Ingram's work would take him to Prague and Vienna for a year or two. Nellie would use the asylum story and the Emma story to convince Pulitzer to let her report stories from Europe. No other paper had a reporter based abroad, and many New Yorkers, especially *World* readers, were interested in news from their former country. As an American, Nellie would be the eyes and ears of the reader. It was an excellent idea, she decided, one Pulitzer could not resist. She would have to figure out what to do with her mother, but if Pulitzer agreed, Nellie would have enough money so that her sister would no longer need to work and could look after her.

All the plans left her as giddy as a schoolgirl. She hadn't felt this way since before her father died. That was why she was so unprepared for what awaited her when she stepped off the streetcar.

The first thing she noticed was the ambulance. Ingram kept it in the rear of the house for emergencies. It was essentially a large wooden box with a white canvas on top and a five-foot-high door and painted red cross on the side, set on the axles of a horse-drawn carriage. A crowd of gawkers had gathered around it, and two policemen were trying to clear them away. Mrs. Fairley, standing by the ambulance, had a large red welt on her forehead and was sobbing uncontrollably. Nellie's first thought was for Mary Jane, but she saw her mother wandering on the outside of the crowd, looking disoriented. Near the front entrance the security guard Ingram had hired sat against the brownstones, holding a blood-soaked bandage to his head. Suddenly two other policemen emerged from the front door and hurriedly carried a man on a plank toward the ambulance. Nellie peered closely to make sure because she didn't believe her eyes. The man lying unconscious on the plank was Ingram.

She raced toward Mrs. Fairley and pushed her way through the crowd. "Mrs. Fairley. What happened?"

The older woman tried to hold back the tears but was overcome with emotion.

"Please. Mrs. Fairley. Tell me what happened."

Mrs. Fairley nodded and forced herself to speak. "Some men started rummaging through the house, asking about a cup. The doctor tried to stop them and suddenly he grabbed his chest and collapsed. They got scared and ran off. I ran outside and screamed for help—"

She looked over at Ingram on the plank and started sobbing again.

"Is he breathing?" pressed Nellie.

"I don't know. The policeman told someone to get an ambulance, and I said the doctor had one here. They're taking him to St. Mark's hospital."

The rubella, she thought to herself. Ingram always said it would kill him. But she never believed him.

Over the policeman's protests, Nellie insisted on climbing into the ambulance and making the twenty-minute ride to the hospital with them. She clutched Ingram's hand and whispered to him, in between shouting at the ambulance driver to hurry.

"I'm here, Ingram. I'm here. I love you. Please know that. I love you ... *Hurry! He's barely breathing!!*" she shouted to the driver.

Nellie wanted Ingram to get to the hospital as fast as possible. But the fastest route was over cobblestone roads, with multiple turns that shifted the ambulance carriage from side to side and nearly turned it over. The jostling, she knew, was killing Ingram. Racing through Chelsea, she could feel the life slipping out of him.

"Ingram. Don't leave me! Please don't leave me! We have so much to do together. We have so many plans to make—"

His breathing was becoming so weak, she could hardly hear it.

"Ingram! I will go to Europe with you. I will go anywhere with you. Breathe, Ingram. Please. Breathe—"

But his breathing had stopped. And she knew, as they were tossed back and forth in the ambulance bouncing over the cobblestones, that it would never resume. She kissed his hand and began to cry, as helpless as she had ever felt in her life.

CHAPTER THIRTY-ONE

She lay in bed for a week, barely moving. Her mother brought her meals, but Nellie couldn't touch them. She knew she had to eat, that it was harmful to starve herself, but she was too depressed to ingest food. And guilty. It was bad enough to lose the love of her life, but he had died defending her, and she felt totally responsible.

Ingram's family took his body back to their home in Albany for burial. Nellie did not go along. She had said her good-byes in the ambulance and was too shattered to contemplate leaving the house, let alone the city.

Mary Jane stepped in as caretaker and quietly stayed nearby

without bothering her. Nellie appreciated it. Her mother had always been fiercely loyal and was proving so again. But mother and daughter needed money. Pulitzer had sent flowers and words of condolence and told her to take as long as she needed before returning to work, but no mention was made of money, and Nellie and Mary Jane had no savings. They had used up what little they had when they moved to New York. It was well and good to know a job would be waiting for her, but she had nothing to live on in the meantime. Adding to her financial woes, Ingram's family would soon be selling the house.

And so, after five days of little sleep, no food, and terrible heartache, Nellie dragged herself out of bed and took the streetcar to Newspaper Row. She had sent Mary Jane out every day for a copy of the paper, to try and occupy her mind and to see the reaction to the Emma Lazarus story, but it hadn't yet appeared in the paper. Nellie assumed Pulitzer or Cockerill had some questions for her—it was, after all, accusing one of New York City's leading literary editors of murder—and were waiting until she returned, out of a sense of decency. Still, she had to admit to a certain surprise, even annoyance, that the story had not run, and wished her first dealings with the newspaper after her return did not arouse her impatience.

She walked past hulking security guard Flaherty, who had heard what happened with Ingram. Seeing that the stuffing had been taken out of her, he merely nodded. She entered the building and walked to the newsroom but without the thrill she felt every other time she'd smelled the newsprint and heard the clatter of reporters and machinery. She headed toward her desk and lifted her skirts above the tobacco juice on the newsroom floor without her usual resentment or disgust. Those reactions seemed so minor now, so beside the point.

Cockerill was sitting at his desk, editing a story, as she approached him. "Hello, Mr. Cockerill."

He looked up with surprise. "Miss Bly." Cockerill was a hard man, but there was pain on his face when he saw what Ingram's death had done to her. "I am so sorry."

"Thank you." Mixed in with his sympathy, she could see,

was also a puzzlement. Why exactly was she here?

"I'm here for my next assignment." Her request unsettled him.

"You need to see Mr. Pulitzer."

"Is something wrong?"

"No. But he wanted to see you when you returned."

"Well, I have returned. Shall we go see him?"

"He said it was to be alone."

"Then I suppose I should go to his office."

"Yes."

She took the elevator to the eighth floor. She wondered what Pulitzer wanted with her. Maybe he just wanted to thank her for her work on the Emma story. Or perhaps it was to tie up some loose ends. She was eager to get the story out. Gilder had murdered Emma and arranged for the thugs to search for the coffee cup, which had led directly to Ingram's death. The world needed to see Richard Gilder for what he was.

Outside Pulitzer's office the same two male secretaries who had treated her so coldly now sat up stiffly when she approached.

"Please tell Mr. Pulitzer I'm here," she said.

It was a directive—not quite an order, but also not a request. The two men did not like taking directives from a woman but sensed that now was not the time to assert their authority. One got up without a word, tapped on Pulitzer's door, and walked inside.

Nellie stood there quietly, making no attempt at conversation with the other secretary. "Mr. Pulitzer will see you," said the secretary as he emerged from the office. He held the door open for Nellie as she walked inside.

The room was darkened, as before. It took her a moment to adjust to the light. Pulitzer walked around from behind his large desk to greet her.

"Miss Bly," he said, grabbing her hand with both of his and looking at her earnestly. "We are so sorry for your loss."

"Thank you, Mr. Pulitzer. And thank you for the flowers." He dismissed it with the wave of his hand.

"Please. It was nothing. You are back to work now?"

"Yes."

"Well, then. Let us talk about your next story." He indicated for her to sit down.

"I want to talk about my current story first. Is there a problem?"

"Problem? No, not at all. You did exactly as I asked. Excellent, beyond what I expected." He sat down at his desk, immensely pleased.

"Do you have any questions about it?" said Nellie.

"Questions? No. None."

"Then when will it appear in the paper?"

"It is not going to appear in the paper," he said with finality.

She sat there dumbfounded, at a complete loss. This was a sensational story. Why would he not publish it?

"I don't understand."

"Your assignment was to find out who killed Miss Lazarus. And you did."

"You asked me to write a story about it."

"Yes. But I had no intention of publishing it. You see, Miss Lazarus wrote a marvelous poem that everyone who comes to this country, everyone who *lives* in this country, should know about. That poem belongs on Lady Liberty, on the base where thousands of people can read it every day. But her sisters were determined to keep it to themselves."

Nellie nodded. She wasn't sure where he was going with this. "They plan to withhold it. They were very emphatic about that."

"I tried everything to obtain their permission to use it. I offered them money. I offered to show them the design and the placement of the poem. I offered to publish Emma's poetry myself. I offered to publish their *own* poetry myself, even though it is wretched. But they denied me at every turn. They said that Emma had caused the family enough embarrassment. They did not want their family remembered that way."

Nellie recalled her encounter with the two sisters, when they were putting together the anthology of Emma's poems. Some of Emma's finest work was lying discarded on the parlor room floor, never to be published again.

"I had to find a way to pry 'The New Colossus' from their hands," Pulitzer went on. "If what they feared most was the family embroiled in scandal, then I would give them scandal, one they would do anything to avoid. I went to the sisters and showed them what you had written. The thought of their sister depicted publicly in a lengthy intimacy with a woman, a married woman, especially one as contemptuous of them as Mrs. Gilder, was wholly unacceptable. And so, I am pleased to say, they agreed to let me use the poem."

"In exchange for not publishing the story."

"Yes."

"But Gilder *murdered* her. When she was already dying and only had three months to live. That man needs to be brought to justice and punished."

"I agree, Miss Bly. But how would you go about doing that? Let us say that we publish the story and Mr. Gilder is tried for murder. A jury might convict him, but I doubt it. You have seen the law at work. With Hilton's money at his disposal I would not wager on a conviction."

"But the world will know he is guilty."

"Perhaps. But Miss Lazarus's poems would not be published and might even be lost to us forever, while a guilty man walks free with a bad reputation. Such an outcome would be tragic."

"The man is a murderer, Mr. Pulitzer. He is also responsible for the death of the man I loved."

"I know that. And I can only imagine the anguish that causes you. But ten years from now no one will remember Dr. Ingram or Mr. Gilder—"

"*I* will remember!"

"Yes. And a handful of others. But the entire world will know the poetry of Emma Lazarus."

She could say nothing. With great reluctance she saw his point. "He is getting away with murder," she declared.

"Yes. He is. And someday he will have to account for that with his maker, if such a being exists. But millions and millions of people will derive inspiration from Miss Lazarus's poems. Her voice will not be silenced. That is the choice, Miss Bly. Bringing a murderer to justice—perhaps—and losing an inspiring voice forever, or leaving things as they are and capturing that inspiring voice for the ages."

Nellie thought about all the time she had put in on this story, all the danger, the worry.

"You tricked me."

"I was not totally forthcoming, that is true. But would you have worked as hard if you had known it would not be published?"

The answer, of course, was no. But she still did not like being manipulated. "What is to prevent me from taking the story elsewhere?"

Pulitzer frowned. "I understand your desire to bring Mr. Gilder to justice, Miss Bly, and to see your story in print, but that would be foolish. No one except this paper would ever publish such a story. Mr. Gilder and Judge Hilton would see to that. I would also be disappointed in you and have to cancel our plans to see if Mr. Jules Verne is correct in his assertion that someone can travel around the world in eighty days. "

She knew it was a bribe, delivered at the most opportune moment. And yet, to her embarrassment, it tempted her.

"Cockerill and I will help plan your journey," he went on, "and you can wire us your stories. But you must decide soon. Another reporter is planning to undertake the same story tomorrow for a magazine."

He had thought of everything, it seemed, even the notion of a competitor to spur her on. Nevertheless he sensed her misgivings about the Lazarus story.

"It is not easy to live with a grave injustice, Miss Bly. I understand that. But I ask you: is the world not better off this way?"

He was not simply asking her to make a choice; he was asking her to change her entire way of thinking, her view of the world. All her life, the choices had been between black and white, good versus evil. For a young girl thrown out of her home, and for a young woman going out on her own, that was how the world worked. Pulitzer was not simply asking her to see the world as gray; he was asking her to live with the existence of evil, something she had sworn to fight forever. He was asking her to look the other way for a greater good—for not only Emma Lazarus and her poems but for the chance to work in a man's world, to pave the way for others, to do things as no one had ever done them before. Remaining a soldier in the war against evil might be more truthful, but it meant seeing all of those other things melt away, perhaps forever.

"Here is your ticket."

He placed a steamship ticket for Southampton on the desk. Southampton was the first stop she had planned herself. She stared at the ticket. The decision was not sitting well.

"What will happen to Gilder?"

"For now, nothing. I will look for an opportunity to ruin him, I promise you that. But it will have to be with something other than the matter of Emma Lazarus."

He leaned back in his chair and waited for her answer. They both knew what she would do. She had come too far, struggled too hard, to turn her back on an opportunity like this.

"I need to make arrangements for my mother."

"I will hire someone to be her companion until you return. It is the least I can do." The course was clear, but she felt sullied. She had lost her moral chastity, something she had clung to all her life. She had always prided herself on her integrity, but now she was crossing a threshold from which there was no return.

"You say someone else is leaving tomorrow?"

"Yes. In the afternoon."

She reached for the ticket.

"Well, then, we don't have much time."

EPILOGUE

NELLIE BLY made it around the world in seventy-two days, finishing on January 25, 1890, two weeks ahead of her competitor from the New York *Cosmopolitan*. In 1895, she married a millionaire industrialist forty years her senior, Robert Seaman, and retired from journalism. When he died in 1904, she went on to become one of the leading industrialists of her time. (The company she took over from her husband owned the patent and manufacturing rights to the fifty-five-gallon steel barrel.) She became active in improving the social organizations of the day, especially orphanages, and returned to journalism only to cover the Eastern Front during World War I. She died on February 17, 1922, at the age of fifty-seven.

RICHARD GILDER continued as editor of *Century* magazine until his death in 1909. The magazine published nearly all the great American writers of the time, though Gilder did have a falling-out with Edith Wharton. He remained active in the cause of Confederate Civil War veterans. His 1903 portrait by Cecelia Beaux currently hangs in the National Portrait Gallery in Washington, D.C.

CHARLES DEKAY was appointed Ambassador to Germany in 1894 by President Grover Cleveland. He served as arts critics of the *Times* for eighteen years and published minor literary works, most notably "The Love Poems of Louis Barnaval," before his death in 1935. He co-founded the National Arts Club in 1898, and the New York Fencers Club a year later. In 2008, he was elected to the U.S. Fencing Hall of Fame.

HELENA DEKAY GILDER remained editor of the *Century* until her death in 1916. Her close friend MARY HALLOCK FOOTE continued to write and illustrate from the West. Their relationship formed the basis of Wallace Stegner's book *Angle of Repose*.

HENRY HILTON died on August 29, 1899. By 1896, the A.T. Stewart fortune that Hilton had inherited, estimated to be worth $50 million, had vanished under Hilton's stewardship. As the *Times* put it in his obituary, "Stewart's fortunes and the great commercial business he had founded had disappeared." Nearly all the newspaper space at the time of his death was devoted to his business failings and his hatred of Jews.

JAY GOULD died on December 2, 1892, of tuberculosis. At the time, his fortune was estimated to be $72 million; he is ranked the ninth richest American in history. Once he sold the Manhattan Elevated, he retired. He is generally considered the greatest scoundrel in the history of American business. During the Great Southwestern Railroad Strike of 1888, he hired strikebreakers and was quoted as saying, "I can hire one half of the working class to kill the other half."

JOSEPH PULITZER continued to be a successful newspaper publisher and founded both the Missouri School of Journalism and the Columbia Graduate School of Journalism before his death in 1911. His legacy also includes a bequest for the Pulitzer Prizes, among the most prestigious in American letters. His favorite reporter was Nellie Bly, and he worked doggedly to return her to the fold when she left the paper. His failure to bring her back, he always said, was his greatest disappointment.

THE NEW YORK WORLD continued to dominate newspaper publishing throughout the remainder of the nineteenth century and the first part of the twentieth. Its battles with William Randolph Hearst's *New York Sun* ushered in the era of yellow journalism. Following Pulitzer's death in 1911, the *World* remained innovative, with the first crossword puzzle, regular columns by Heywood Hale Broun and James M. Cain, and a twenty-part expose of the Ku Klux Klan. In 1931, Pulitzer's heirs went to court to sell the *World*, and the court decided in their favor. The final issue of the *World* was printed on February 27, 1931. On May 16, 2011, the Columbia University Graduate School of Journalism announced that it was launching an online publication named *The New York World*, in honor of the original *New York World* published by Pulitzer, the founder of the school.

"THE NEW COLOSSUS" was memorialized in 1903 when a bronze plaque bearing the entire poem was placed on the inner wall of the pedestal at the Statue of Liberty. It is by far the most viewed poem in the world. Approximately four million people visit Lady Liberty, and read the poem, every year.

HISTORICAL NOTES

Because the narrator in *The New Colossus* shared the same time and place as Nellie Bly, the reader was denied some interesting pieces of information. For instance, the city of "Pittsburg" was not misspelled. The "h" was not added until 1911—twenty-three years after the events in the story—in a community stab at respectability. A more omniscient narrator might have passed along the following:

CHAPTER ONE

Bellevue Hospital is the oldest hospital in the United States. George Washington was four years old when it was founded in 1736. Originally it was an alms house for the poor, and that remained its essential identity ever since, to the present day.

Nellie Bly's investigative stories spawned the muckrakers of the early twentieth century and generations of investigative reporters thereafter. Upton Sinclair, Frank Norris, I.F. Stone, Seymour Hersh, Bob Woodward, Carl Bernstein and dozens of others can all trace their roots directly to Nellie Bly and the scandal at the Bellevue Women's Asylum.

Nellie Bly was born Elizabeth Cochran, the favorite daughter of a well-to-do miller, Judge Michael Cochran, in Armstrong County, Pennsylvania, just outside of Pittsburg. Cochran's first wife produced ten children but died shortly before the Civil War, and one year later he married a widow from nearby Kittanning, Mary Jane Hogan, and started a second family. That second family became the joy of his life and he pampered them to no end. He built the largest house ever seen in Apollo ten miles away, moved Mary Jane and their three young children there, and provided them with servants, a governess, and a cook. But Michael Cochran was a judge in name only, and his ignorance of the law proved calamitous to his second family when he died suddenly of heart failure, just after Elizabeth turned seven. Cochran left no will, and under the rules of intestacy at the time, none of a man's property went to his widow—his entire estate was to be divided among his children. (The law in its infinite wisdom assumed that a man's children would take care of his widow.) The children from Cochran's first wife, however, were well into adulthood and insisted upon selling the Apollo home even though their father had clearly wanted his new family to live there. The proceeds of the sale were divided among the sixteen children, and little Elizabeth, her mother, and three young siblings were forced to move into a tenement in town with Mary Jane's drunken sister, Lucy. The young children's inheritance might have buffeted the transition, but the court placed it in trust with a local banker, Colonel Thaddeus Jackson, who embezzled the money and eventually filed for bankruptcy. The inheritance money meant for Elizabeth and her siblings was gone. Mary Jane and the children became penniless.

At the *Dispatch,* Nellie produced exposés on a half dozen Pittsburg factories, most notably a Squirt bottling plant where women and children worked on icy cement floors for fourteen hours at a stretch and wrapped rags around their feet to keep their toes from freezing. Her stories generated outrage from *Dispatch* readers and she developed a strong following— too strong, as it turned out, when the companies threatened to pull all advertising from the paper. The *Dispatch* editor-in-chief, so glad to have her initially, reassigned her to gardening and fashion stories, and refused to let her work on any more investigative pieces. At that point, she quit her job and moved with her mother to New York.

The Bellevue Asylum story was not the first story Nellie wrote in New York. After four months of getting nowhere on the job front, she hit upon an idea. She informed her *Dispatch* readers that she had received a letter from an "ambitious young woman who wanted to be a journalist and wanted to know if New York was the best place to start." She decided "to put the question to the newspaper gods of Gotham" and, as a reporter doing a reverential story for an out-of-town paper, was able to get around the guards and interview the powers that be in the New York newspaper world. She delivered a piece that pulled no punches. The publishing lords of New York were portrayed as arrogant and disdainful—"I cannot imagine a gentleman in all delicacy asking a woman to have anything to do with the normal class of news," averred James Gordon Bennett, Jr., the *Herald's* publisher. The story was such a compelling read— and New York and its financial and cultural power so thoroughly resented across the nation—that the piece was reprinted in newspapers and periodicals in Philadelphia, Boston, Chicago, St. Louis, and elsewhere around the country. Excerpts of her interviews were even reprinted in *The New York Mail and Express*, where Nellie was hailed with customary condescension as "a bright and talented young woman who has done a great deal for the nation's newspapers."

But public embarrassment failed to move the publishers. Still no offers or even inquiries came her way. A less determined person would have slunk back to Pittsburg and spent twenty years writing gardening stories at subsistence wages. Instead Nellie Bly went to every sentry along Newspaper Row, showed him the *Mail and Express* article, pointed to where his boss was quoted by name and demanded to see the editor. Only Colonel John Cockerill, managing editor of the *World*, would see her.

CHAPTER THREE

No doctor was a true cancer specialist in 1887. The scientific means of investigating the disease, aside from the invention of the microscope in the 1830s, simply weren't available. Theories on cancer ranged from transmission through the bloodstream to the dominant explanation for all disease in the nineteenth-century—*miasma*, dirty particles that carried disease through the atmosphere. Nevertheless many who feared a diagnosis of cancer sought out the physicians at New York Cancer Hospital. Those doctors may not have known much about the disease, but most patients didn't realize that.

Meeting a doctor at a hospital or an office was unusual in the 1880s. Doctors ordinarily visited patients at their homes. In fact, the notion of "doctor" itself was far different in the 1880s from a century later. State licensing of the medical profession, for instance, did not begin until the early twentieth century. Anyone so inclined could call himself or herself a doctor, beholden to no one other than the marketplace.

"Barker listened intently with only his ear, using no stethoscope." Though the stethoscope had been invented decades earlier, it did not gain wide use until the early twentieth century.

CHAPTER FOUR

Out-of-wedlock trysts do not fit the image of Victorian morals, yet they were much more commonplace than people realized even at the time. Part of the explanation, of course, is massive self-deception. The prevailing view in academic circles, for instance, was that women had no interest in sex. "The majority of women (happily for them)," wrote the revered Dr. William Acton in the mid-1860s, "are not very much troubled with sexual feelings of any kind … No nervous or feeble young man need, therefore, be deterred from marriage by an exaggerated notion of the duties required of him." Women's aversion to sex was thought to be so fundamental that the law in England guaranteed a man access to his wife's body whether she desired it or not.

In fact, however, free love societies were very much a part of women's intellectual landscape in the 1880s. Although modern history books tend to focus on suffrage, for many women the more pressing issue was the disparate treatment with sexual behavior. Susan B. Anthony, the legendary founder of the women's suffrage movement, argued that for the sake of a healthy society, men should be forced to adhere to the same moral standards as women. Victoria Woodhull, who with her sister published the *Woodhull and Claflin Weekly* with the masthead "PROGRESS! FREE THOUGHT! UNTRAMMELED LIVES!", took it a step further, proclaiming that women should "live with the complete sexual freedom that men enjoy." The subject of numerous liaisons in the New York papers, Woodhull pronounced that it was her "inalienable right" to have as many lovers as she pleased, and she did her level best to meet to that standard. Though some, including the conservative Mrs. Anthony, were horrified at such a display of lax morals, it struck a chord with many younger women, especially those who, like Nellie, ventured out on their own into the working world.

Alan Dale, as the critic James Huneker once observed, founded "the school of literary criticism based on the flippant remark." Critics around the country and in succeeding generations sought to match him, but none ever could. Dorothy Parker came the closest, offering such Dale-like *bon mots* as, "*The House Beautiful* is the play lousy." In 1895, William Randolph Hearst hired Dale away from the *World* to the *New York American* and made him the leading critic in America for the next nineteen years, until Dale resigned because he "did not want to be part of an era of commercialism in journalism," after Hearst agreed to a writer's request for a different *American* critic to review his play.

When people think of immigrants from Europe arriving in America, they usually think of Ellis Island, and well they should. Before it closed in 1954, twelve million immigrants had entered America through the federal processing center at Ellis Island, adjacent to the Statue of Liberty. But Ellis Island did not come into existence until 1892. Before then the main port of entry for European immigrants coming to America was Castle Garden, in Battery Park.

Originally erected as Fort Clinton to protect the harbor back in the 1600s when New York was New Amsterdam, and then serving as the largest theater in New York in the 1830s and 1840s, Castle Garden became the arrival point for eight million immigrants from 1855 to 1890—about the same yearly influx as Ellis Island. But unlike Ellis Island, all the immigrants who arrived at Castle Garden were free to walk off the boat and into the New World without permission from any immigration officers.

The scale of the Jewish exodus from Russia exceeded the Hebrews leaving Egypt in Moses' time and matched European Jews fleeing the Nazis fifty years later. Three million Jews lived in Russia and Poland in 1880, and one million of them took flight to the West following Alexander II's death.

CHAPTER SIX

There is actually more to the story of Mrs. Astor and the Metropolitan Opera House. With her sycophantic ferret from Savannah, Ward McAllister, she developed "Mrs. Astor's 400," a list of the families blessed enough to be invited to her annual ball at her mansion at Thirty-Fourth and Fifth Avenue, and whose own invitations she might descend from her lofty perch to accept. Mrs. Astor and her 400, as mentioned, had no use for the *nouveau riche* of nineteenth century New York, lowlifes such as the Vanderbilts, the Morgans, the Rockefellers, and anyone else who made their fortunes through the world of business.

But after the Met opened to great success, Mrs. Vanderbilt was still not satisfied. She wanted more than victory, she wanted surrender: an invitation to Mrs. Astor's yearly ball, the true acknowledgement of one's rightful place in New York society. It was Mrs. Astor's last line of good taste, one she vowed to defend to the death. Alas, she underestimated Mrs. Vanderbilt's resourcefulness. Three months after the opening of the Metropolitan Opera House, Mrs. Vanderbilt planned a $3 million masquerade ball to celebrate her newly constructed French chateau on Fifth Avenue, but she failed to extend an invitation to Mrs. Astor's daughter Caroline. Young Caroline was terribly hurt and demanded to know (through an intermediary, of course) why she had not been invited.

Mrs. Vanderbilt responded, "Why, I don't know her mother."

Caroline begged her mother to go calling on Mrs. Vanderbilt; it would be dreadful, unacceptable, to miss the Vanderbilt ball. Mrs. Astor, good mother that she was, swallowed hard and called on Mrs. Vanderbilt with an invitation to her annual January ball. Mrs. Vanderbilt graciously accepted, and invited both mother and daughter to her masquerade ball. A precedent was shattered, the *nouveau riche* flooded New York society, and Mrs. Astor's role as *doyeness* faded away into history.

CHAPTER SEVEN

Laboratories as we know them today did not even come into existence until the early twentieth century. The lab Nellie and Ingram saw was state of the art for the time: Bunsen Burners (invented thirty years before), thick glass beakers and flasks made of blown glass (pyrex would not be invented for another thirty years), electric lights, and copper piping (the Anaconda copper mine had begun producing at an incredible rate only eight years before).

CHAPTER EIGHT

The law of defamation in 1888 was far different from what it would become. From the mid-twentieth century forward, America has prized freedom of speech above all else. The era was defined by *New York Times v. Sullivan*, where the Supreme Court held that a newspaper was free to write whatever it wanted about a public figure, no matter how damaging, as long as it wasn't a deliberate lie. Eventually that principle was expanded to *any* matter of public interest—write whatever you please, as long as you believe it is the truth. But Colonial and nineteenth century America were less concerned with speech and much more concerned with reputation. A man's most valuable commodity was his reputation, and besmirching him was tantamount to ruining him. (A woman's reputation, while also important, was a less complicated matter: question a woman's chastity and you went to jail, paid financial damages, or lost your life in a duel.) In a land based on opportunity and second chances, an attack on a man's reputation was an attack on America itself. In fact, in the early-1800s a person could be thrown into jail for harming a man's reputation *even if the statements made were entirely truthful.* Gradually, though, freedom of speech became more valued by American society, newspapers became more powerful politically, and by 1850 truth had become a valid defense in criminal defamation cases—you could no longer be thrown in jail for telling the truth. But Cockerill was rightly concerned with the *World's* legal exposure: in 1888 no court was yet willing to say that a newspaper publishing a hard-hitting but accurate story would be protected from libel damages in court. That would not come for another thirty years.

The men Nellie was impugning, Barker and DeKay, were from the strata of society that defamation laws were meant to protect: powerful men, professional men, respectable men.

CHAPTER NINE

Suicide was very much a mystery in the nineteenth century. Most people didn't live long enough to take their own lives. For the upper classes, the life expectancy was fifty for the landed gentry, forty-five in manufacturing areas. For everyone else, no matter where they lived, it was under thirty. Like deficit spending or the makeup of prison populations in more modern times, everyone had strongly held theories on the causes of suicide but remarkably little evidence to support them. In the 1880s there was no real understanding or even acknowledgement of mental illness. Suicide was simply the sign of a troubled soul.

Although Gould's building at Eighth and Twenty-Third was garish, his own offices were modest, almost stately. The building had been chosen by Gould's more flamboyant partner, James Fisk, in order to be closer to his mistress, the actress and singer Josie Mansfield. Fisk's affair with Mansfield would eventually lead to his murder by one of Mansfield's many lovers, Edward S. Stokes, who schemed with Mansfield to extort money from Fisk by threatening to make public Fisk's affair with her.

CHAPTER TEN

A hundred years later, the outcome of Nellie's lawsuit would be clear-cut. The bank would have to pay Nellie and her sisters all the money lost through its employee's malfeasance, plus interest, plus punitive damages. The embezzler would have gone to jail for at least seven years. Mary Jane would have been entitled to 50 percent of Judge Cochran's entire estate, no matter what the children of his first wife said or did. And Mary Jane and her children would have been represented by an attorney well-versed in the laws of wills and estates, who would have won a substantial verdict, large enough for all of them to live comfortably for a long, long time.

In 1888, however, the outcome was far less certain. Mary Jane, as a widow, would have no legal claim, and Nellie, unable to afford a lawyer, would have to represent herself and her sisters in court, which would pose quite a challenge since women were not allowed to serve as lawyers or jurors. The case would be before a judge who was a part-time lawyer and frequently employed by the First Pennsylvania Bank. The judge would undoubtedly know Colonel Jackson and want to protect his reputation. (Colonel Jackson was a leading citizen of Apollo and had commanded the Eleventh Pennsylvania Reserves in the Civil War.) And even though he was its president at the time, the bank would deny all financial responsibility for the actions of Colonel Jackson, and under state agency law they would have a strong case.

Originally the Constitution of 1789 had made no provision for a jury trial in civil *or* criminal cases, an omission that provoked outrage and threatened ratification. The right to a trial by jury in *criminal* cases had been part of English law since the Magna Carta in 1215, and a constitutional guarantee to that right was quickly made part of the first ten amendments, with little resistance. But the right to a jury trial in *civil* cases (that is, when the issue is money damages) had no such precedent. In order to maintain commerce with English merchants (the States' primary trading partners), the framers took pains to assure those merchants their contracts would be enforced in American courts. But local farmers and merchants, mistrustful of the plantation-owning framers and fearing that judges would become tools of wealthy creditors, insisted on a right to a jury before their peers in civil cases, and that led to the Seventh Amendment.

By no means was it clear that Nellie's case would even be heard by a jury. Although the Seventh Amendment explicitly guaranteed a litigant's right to a jury trial in civil cases, the Supreme Court in 1805 had drastically narrowed that right as to render it almost meaningless. Under a legal doctrine that continues into the twenty-first century, a litigant was entitled to the Seventh Amendment right to a civil jury trial *only if an analogous case in 1791 would have been tried by a jury*. Otherwise the case would remain with the judge, a part-time lawyer whose bias and interests would almost always be with the wealthier party.

CHAPTER TWELVE

Hilton's house outside of Saratoga Springs would eventually become the campus for Skidmore College.

CHAPTER FOURTEEN

Nellie asked herself who visited Emma frequently those last three months. The most natural step for future generations, of course (pre-Google), would be to pore over the obituary tributes to Emma in a large library and see who was at her bedside. But although New York City had passed Paris in population and was second only to London as the world's largest city, it had no libraries in 1888 other than the private collections of Henry Clay Frick and J.P. Morgan. The New York Public Library would not open for another twenty-three years. (The first public library in the United States had opened in Boston forty years before, in 1848.) Information that would be at one's fingertips in later times was essentially inaccessible to Nellie. Her only hope was the *World's* archives.

CHAPTER SEVENTEEN

The full correspondence between Moses Seixas (Emma Lazarus's great-great-uncle and the founder of the first synagogue in America) and George Washington is set out here:

The letter from Moses Seixas to President George Washington

To the President of the United States of America. Sir:

Permit the children of the stock of Abraham to approach you with the most cordial affection and esteem for your person and merits — and to join with our fellow citizens in welcoming you to NewPort.

With pleasure we reflect on those days — those days of difficulty, and danger, when the God of Israel, who delivered David from the peril of the sword, — shielded Your head in the day of battle: — and we rejoice to think, that the same Spirit, who rested in the Bosom of the greatly beloved Daniel enabling him to preside over the Provinces of the Babylonish Empire, rests and ever will rest, upon you, enabling you to discharge the arduous duties of Chief Magistrate in these States.

Deprived as we heretofore have been of the invaluable rights of free Citizens, we now with a deep sense of gratitude to the Almighty disposer of all events behold a Government, erected by the Majesty of the People — a Government, which to bigotry gives no sanction, to persecution no assistance — but generously affording to all Liberty of conscience, and immunities of Citizenship: — deeming every one, of whatever Nation, tongue, or language equal parts of the great governmental Machine: — This so ample and extensive Federal Union whose basis is Philanthropy, Mutual confidence and Public Virtue, we cannot but acknowledge to be the work of the Great God, who ruleth in the Armies of Heaven, and among the Inhabitants of the Earth, doing whatever seemeth him good.

For all these Blessings of civil and religious liberty which we enjoy under an equal benign administration, we desire to send up our thanks to the Ancient of Days, the great preserver of Men — beseeching him, that the Angel who conducted our forefathers through the wilderness into the promised Land, may graciously conduct you through all the difficulties and dangers of this mortal life: — And, when, like Joshua full of days and full of honour, you are gathered to your Fathers, may you be admitted into the Heavenly Paradise to partake of the water of life, and the tree of immortality.

Done and Signed by order of the Hebrew Congregation in NewPort, Rhode Island August 17th 1790.

Moses Seixas, Warden

The letter from George Washington in response to Moses Seixas

To the Hebrew Congregation in Newport Rhode Island. Gentlemen,

While I receive, with much satisfaction, your Address replete with expressions of affection and esteem; I rejoice in the opportunity of assuring you, that I shall always retain a grateful remembrance of the cordial welcome I experienced in my visit to Newport, from all classes of Citizens.

The reflection on the days of difficulty and danger which are past is rendered the more sweet, from a consciousness that they are succeeded by days of uncommon prosperity and security. If we have wisdom to make the best use of the advantages with which we are now favored, we cannot fail, under the just administration of a good Government, to become a great and happy people.

The Citizens of the United States of America have a right to applaud themselves for having given to mankind examples of an enlarged and liberal policy: a policy worthy of imitation. All possess alike liberty of conscience and immunities of citizenship. It is now no more that toleration is spoken of, as if it was by the indulgence of one class of people, that another enjoyed the exercise of their inherent national gifts. For happily the Government of the United States, which gives to bigotry no sanction, to persecution no assistance requires only that they who live under its protection should demean themselves as good citizens, in giving it on all occasions their effectual support.

It would be inconsistent with the frankness of my character not to avow that I am pleased with your favorable opinion of my Administration, and fervent wishes for my felicity.

May the children of the Stock of Abraham, who dwell in this land, continue to merit and enjoy the good will of the other Inhabitants; while every one shall sit in safety under his own vine and figtree, and there shall be none to make him afraid. May the father of all mercies scatter light and not darkness in our paths, and make us all in our several vocations useful here, and in his own due time and way everlastingly happy.

G. Washington

CHAPTER EIGHTEEN

On a map Long Island looks like a pitchfork with two prongs facing east. The northernmost prong, stretching out to Orient Point, has more rugged terrain, rockier shorelines, and fewer people. The southern prong, with Sag Harbor and the beaches of the Hamptons, is more inviting and was settled more quickly. But in the 1880s, except for a few fishermen here and there, most of the population of Long Island lived in the western part, a spillover from the contiguous Brooklyn and Queens. Or rather, most of the *white* population lived there. Native Americans had settled throughout the territory.

CHAPTER TWENTY-TWO

Lesbian relations were simply not the first explanation one thought of regarding an unmarried, wealthy, brilliant, charismatic thirty-eight-year-old woman in nineteenth-century America. Female homosexuality was unimaginable for most of the nineteenth century, as women, according to prevailing thought, had no sexual impulses. In fact, after British moralists sought to make lesbian activity a crime in the 1870s, Queen Victoria declined to go along with such a condemnation because she refused to believe that female homosexuality even existed. But it did exist, of course, and nineteenth-century American and British society were at a loss to explain its presence. At first it was dismissed as a practice limited to prostitutes, but with the increasing presence of lesbian couples on city streets, that explanation was obviously insufficient. Instead, in an era uncomfortable with the notion of a female sex drive, lesbians were deemed to be "no longer women, but usurpers of masculine roles who have become desexualized." Unfortunately, the empirical reality meant that an inordinate number of males, far too many, were being usurped in their masculine roles. Consequently, many reactionary males sought to outlaw lesbian activity altogether, making it a crime for a woman even to dress as a man. That helped normalize the streets and put men at ease, but financially-able women simply went behind closed doors and lived together in what was called a "Boston Marriage." (The term originated with the wife of Jay Gould's philandering business partner, James Fisk. While Fisk chased women all over New York City, his wife lived for twenty years with a female companion in Boston.) Finally, with the criminal sanction unable to rid society of the moral pestilence, society began labeling lesbian activity a "mental illness." Anyone who felt "abnormal" emotions, that is, an attraction for the same sex, was deemed "sick," and in the 1880s the term "homosexual," to describe a poor soul thus abnormally afflicted, came into being.

CHAPTER TWENTY-THREE

During the 1888 election, voters in Indiana were paid $15 if they voted Republican. That would be equivalent to $366 in 2014 dollars.

CHAPTER TWENTY-SIX

Prior to the Civil War an artist's personal studio was essentially the great outdoors, but by the 1880s many artists, especially in New York City, had moved their day-to-day work inside. The studio became both a space to produce the art and a gathering place to display it.

CHAPTER TWENTY-NINE

Regarding the stench and garbage in New York City, it was not until 1898 that the Metropolitan Board of Health issued a proclamation forbidding "the throwing of dead animals, garbage or ashes into the streets." At the time, cholera and diphtheria epidemics were commonplace. Five thousand people died from a cholera epidemic in 1881 alone. When word arrived of an epidemic in New York, the rich would clear out of the city until the danger had passed, while the poor remained and hoped for the best.

CHAPTER THIRTY

Since the 1950s heart disease has become the number one killer in the United States, due mostly to a more sedentary lifestyle and richer diet. But in the 1880s the leading causes of death were from communicable diseases like pneumonia, tuberculosis, and diarrhea.

Heart disease was ranked only number four. But some heart disease occurs no matter what the era, and that was the case with Ingram. A case of rubella during his mother's first trimester had narrowed the valves in his heart and impeded the blood flow. Twenty years later, he might have had an electrocardiograph that would have alerted him to the condition; thirty years later it could have been treated with medication; and fifty years later cardiologists would have made it as good as new. But in the 1880s, doctors had no idea how to detect or prevent a heart attack. Ingram was entirely at the mercy of his defective heart.

A hundred years later, the steps for helping a heart attack victim were well-known: put them in a comfortable position. Place aspirin or nitroglycerin under their tongue. Get help immediately—time is absolutely of the essence. Position them in as stable position as possible on the ride to the hospital. Give them oxygen. Administer CPR if their heart fails. Nellie, of course, knew none of those things, nor did anyone else at the time. She just wanted Ingram to get to the hospital as fast as possible. But the fastest route to the hospital was over cobblestone roads, with multiple turns that shifted the ambulance carriage from side to side and almost turned it over. That alone would have killed most heart attack victims.

ACKNOWLEDGMENTS

So much happens between an idea and a finished book. Research. Writing. Selling. Assembling. Fortunately I had skilled and caring help all along the way.

I wanted to learn as much as I could about my characters. George Goodwin and the Rhode Island Jewish Historical Society enlightened me on Jewish life in Colonial New England, and Rabbi Mordechai Eskovitz, and my dear friend Jim Tobak, gave me a lengthy tour of the storied Touro Synagogue. The Apollo Area Historical Society directed me to Nellie Bly's childhood home and offered a treasure trove of her time in western Pennsylvania. The Carnegie Library of Pittsburgh was kind enough to share some of Nellie's original letters; there is nothing quite like spending years with a character and then reading something penned with her own hand. My daughter Kate, with an eye far sharper than mine, spent several afternoons with me wandering New York City in the exact spots I would later write about. Castle Garden, Battery Park and the old Newspaper Row made particularly strong impressions.

Not all research can be done first-hand, of course, and several historians made life considerably easier for me. I read dozens and dozens of books and articles on Nellie, Emma, Pulitzer, Jay Gould, Henry Hilton, Helena DeKay, Mary Hallock Foote, Richard Gilder and Charles DeKay. I won't list them all here, but Esther Schor's biography *Emma Lazarus* was especially helpful and prompted my first fan letter to a Princeton professor.

Some writers can crank out a polished draft without ever needing to change a word, but I am not one of them. Kate Zentall, Marc Green, Ed Stampler, Pat LoBrutto and Elizabeth Cobbs Hoffman all provided excellent editorial suggestions that improved the book and made it much more readable. David Dornbusch, Helen Dornbusch and Ilene Block always let me know when I go off track, and received the book well early on. Their enthusiasm was worth hours of line edits. Finally it is my good fortune to have two voracious readers under my roof, my wife Anne and daughter Rachel. Each has remarkable strengths as manuscript readers, and together they cover a large waterfront. They also keep me humble.

I'm sure there are harder things than selling a first-time novel in today's fiction market, but I can't think of one right now. When I had trouble landing an agent, I asked my friend Joan Harrison for help. She introduced me to Joe Veltre, who read the manuscript and wanted to handle it. Without Joan, I'm not sure you would be reading this right now. Joe was unwavering in shopping the book and found a warm home for it at Diversion Books. The people at Diversion plunged right in, especially Sarah Masterson Hally. With all the pictures and newspaper articles and clearance issues, the book was not easy to lay out, but Sarah doggedly pushed to make the final product look as good as possible. We also had a crack copyright expert in Rachel Goldberg, who obtained all the necessary clearances.

So far I have mentioned only functional support, but three years of writing a novel, and two years waiting until it reaches a general audience, requires emotional support as well, and in that regard I am blessed. My wife and daughters are my biggest fans, with my extended family and friends a close second. I am profoundly grateful. Dedicating the book to them all is my attempt to say thank you.

ABOUT THE AUTHOR

 Marshall Goldberg has had a varied career as both a lawyer and writer.

An honors graduate of Harvard College and Stanford Law School, Goldberg was lead counsel on the extension of the Voting Rights Act of 1965 and later served as legislative liaison for the Civil Rights Division at the Justice Department.

In 1979 he moved to Los Angeles and spent the next 24 years writing for such shows as "Diff'rent Strokes," "The Jeffersons," "Paper Chase," "Newhart," "L.A. Law," "It's Garry Shandling's Show," and "Life Goes On," along with eight television movies, three screenplays and an animated feature. He has been a Humanitas Prize and Writers Guild Award finalist, and taught screenwriting at USC Film School.

From 2003-2005 Goldberg put aside his writing career to serve as General Counsel to the Writers Guild of America, west. In late 2005 he left the WGA and began writing novels.

He is currently an adjunct professor at both Stanford and Michigan Law School.

CPSIA information can be obtained at www.ICGtesting.com
Printed in the USA
BVOW05s1745200516

448848BV00004B/8/P